TABLE OF CONTENTS

Chapter One.

Chapter Two.

Chapter Three.

Chapter Four.

Chapter Five.

Chapter Six.

Chapter Seven.

Chapter Eight.

Chapter Nine.

Chapter Ten.

Chapter Eleven.

Chapter Twelve.

Chapter Thirteen.

Chapter Fourteen.

Chapter Fifteen.

Chapter Sixteen.

Chapter Seventeen.

Chapter Eighteen.

Chapter Nineteen.

Chapter Twenty.

3

Chapter Twenty-One.

Chapter Twenty-Two.

Chapter Twenty-Three.

Chapter Twenty-Four.

Chapter Twenty-Five.

Chapter Twenty-Six.

Chapter Twenty-Seven.

Chapter Twenty-Eight.

Chapter Twenty-Nine.

Chapter Thirty.

Chapter Thirty-One.

Chapter Thirty-Two.

Chapter Thirty-Three.

Chapter Thirty-Four.

Chapter Thirty-Five.

Chapter Thirty-Six.

Chapter Thirty-Seven.

Chapter Thirty-Eight.

Chapter Thirty-Nine.

Chapter Forty.

Chapter Forty-One.

Chapter Forty-Two.

Chapter Forty-Three.

Chapter Forty-Four.

4

Chapter Forty-Five.

Chapter Forty-Six.

Chapter Forty-Seven.

Chapter Forty-Eight.

Chapter Forty-Nine.

Chapter Fifty.

Chapter Fifty-One.

Chapter Fifty-Two.

Chapter Fifty-Three.

Chapter Fifty-Four.

Chapter Fifty-Five.

Chapter Fifty-Six.

Epilogue.

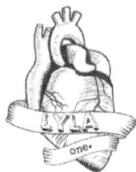

Brushing the hair behind my ears, I groan as I check the stack of papers still sitting next to me on the desk — quizzes from today's lesson that still need to be graded underneath the quizzes from the last class. Professor Moxley had been on a rampage today once a group involving multiple students began a conversation amongst themselves during his lecture. He had sputtered a few insults under his breath, bitching quietly about the lack of respect these days, before slamming them with a pop quiz. Though tyranny is the general mood of his classroom, I've found myself holding out with hope that his attitude might thaw during the semester. We're halfway through October and while the changing autumn leaves and decimating hot weather has relaxed most of the professors at the University of Houston, Professor Tyson Moxley remains apathetic. He's yet to show any personal emotion, outside of the passion he feels in teaching, that would make him appear as a thoughtful, personable human being.

"That stack doesn't seem to be dwindling this evening."

Professor Moxley nods towards the stack on my desk as he walks past my desk, having gone out for a breath of fresh air after the lone student had stopped in, hoping for an attempt to sway their grade above passing.

"Trust me, I'm well aware," I mutter, just loud enough that he's sure to hear. Through the brain fog, I can almost believe I hear him chuckle before closing the door to his inner office.

I rub my eyes, pressing down on my temples, as I work to prevent the oncoming migraine. I've been at this for over an hour, glancing between his answer key and the student quizzes in front of me while deciphering some of their ridiculous answers. *Of course, dumping your expired prescriptions into a lake is bad.* My phone buzzes on the table next to me and my body stiffens, inhaling a sharp breath and turning my head just enough to make sure Professor Moxley can't see me through the windows of his inner office before I reach for it.

> **PARKER:** Are you finished yet?
> **ME:** Nope. *eye roll*

Judging by the time, I should be almost done but I'd rather finish up this work, and perhaps—just maybe— that would be enough to make tomorrow slightly more pleasant.

> **PARKER:** We're supposed to go out with Lucy, Brian, and Marion in like 45 minutes, babe. There has to be a rule stating that he can't actually keep you here this long.

I sigh, this has been an ongoing battle with Parker since the beginning of the year. Professors were allowed to set their office hours and given the extensive workload he gives, Professor Moxley has always had extended hours— which is why none of his assistants ever made it through the first few weeks.

Until me, the one person that seems to be capable of putting up with his bad attitude day after day.

> **ME:** Just meet me here and we'll leave as soon
> as I'm done with this stack.

I snap a quick picture of the papers in front of me and send it to him, putting my phone back down. With my elbows resting on the desk, I place my face inside my hands and shake it as I grumble to myself. Some days I wonder why I put up with this shit, giving up two hours a night to work in this office— but mostly I wonder how I could have forgotten to put alternates into my paperwork when selecting a TA position over the summer. I'm in no way qualified to be a TA for an Environmental Law professor, it's not a course I have ever taken— or will ever need to take—for my career in paleontology.

Christ, Parker. Just leave it alone and come meet me— I think as my phone buzzes again. Annoyance ripples through my skin, knowing that I'll never finish up if he keeps checking up on me. A sigh of relief rushes over me as I see it's Lucy this time, the screen lighting up again after being ignored.

I giggle, stuffing my fist into my mouth to stifle the sound in the large, empty room as I wonder where Lucy learned such a word. I had pegged Lucy as an art major from her overall shorts and her blonde hair in a wild bun on top of her head within minutes of meeting her. I can only assume she'll be showing up tonight with paint smudges somewhere on her body. Starting as dorm mates our first year, it still surprises me how quickly we developed such a close bond. Where my quiet reserve gives off the homebody vibe, Lucy is the outgoing partier that ultimately brought our group together.

ME: Someone pissed in his breakfast this
morning. Pop quizzes.
LUCY: Damn, girl. The only good thing about
that man is his spectacular ass..
ME: LUCY! Watch yourself.

I blush, knowing she's not entirely wrong, but gasp as I peek back over my shoulder at the sound of footsteps. I throw my phone down, again, ensuring that I'm working when he comes out of his office. I glance through the quiz sitting out— *another failing grade.* Moxley's footsteps grow louder behind me as I scribble the score on the top of the test, shaking my head as I place it into my finished pile.

9

"Has anyone passed yet?" his deep voice asks, sending a shudder running down my spine.

As my heart rate increases, the breaths tighten in my chest. Long gone are the days that I tremble at him nearby, instead, my body ignites in defense— knowing that I'm competent enough to handle grading some papers correctly. The first few weeks he had hovered around, ensuring that I was capable of checking one answer against his key and knowing what variants of the answers were acceptable.

"So far, three of the-" I pause, counting the papers in the stack beside me, "nineteen, have passed." He clicks his tongue on his teeth, the sound causing the migraine to thrum against my skull. I twist my head towards him, narrowing my eyes as I look deep into his cerulean blue ones, gripping my pen tighter between my fingers. His hand is grasping the nape of his neck, fisting his blonde hair as he sucks in his cheeks. I tilt my head to the side, forcing a sly smile across my lips as I lean back in my chair. "Would you like to check over my work, Professor?"

His expression grows cold, glaring at me as if I've offended him with my sticky-sweet voice. Inside of me, laughter bubbles as I hold my smile and his eyes in mine. The hoods of his eyes push down, narrowing his eyes back at me that gives off a "keep testing me" vibe. *And testing you, pushing you until you show some kind of personality besides a straight-up asshole is exactly what I will do.* As if ready to test me himself, the corner of his mouth tugs up as he leans against my desk.

"Are you unsure of your abilities to match answers between two papers, Miss Fischer?" he asks.

My free hand clenches into a fist in my lap as I scrape my tongue along the inside of my teeth. We've been having these minuscule battles out for weeks and it's growing weary, fighting with him at every turn. Sure, I had begun instigating the arguments because at least it became a way to pass the time instead of the usual silence in the room— but he was guilty as well for baiting such arguments himself.

"I believe my competency is not up for debate, sir," I snap.

He chuckles, pushing himself off my desk and heading back into his corner— behind the walls and windows, he's secluded himself almost every night this semester. I let out a long sigh, returning to my work as I peer at the newest message on my lit-up phone.

> **PARKER:** Heading your way, hope you're finished up soon and we don't miss all the fun.

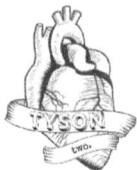

Watching Miss Fischer working diligently through our office hours tonight shines light on the fact that in the last decade of being a professor, she is the first TA that has stuck around after the first six weeks. I don't find that I'm any harder on my TA's than I am my students, but it wouldn't be breaking, headlining news that I'm generally disliked throughout the student body. I'm not here to be anyone's friend. I'm here to mold the minds of the students that will go on to make a difference in the world.

Leaning back in my chair as I push my hands through my hair, I pick up the most recent picture of my daughter sitting on my desk and take a deep breath, tapping the side of the frame twice with the top of my finger.

"Professor Moxley?"

Miss Fischer's timid voice breaks my train of thought and I place the picture frame back on the corner of my desk.

"What can I do for you, Ms. Fischer?" I reply, returning my attention to the stack of essays that need to be graded.

"I've finished with the quizzes," she states.

I glance up at her through my eyelashes. Sure enough, there's a large stack of papers in her hands that she's fixing her gaze on instead of meeting my eyes. She's biting her lip as she shifts her weight from one foot to another, a sure sign of being distressed by the mere conversation she's striking up with me after trying to push my buttons

12

before. Beyond her, Mr.Bennett—a former student of mine— is sitting back in a chair in front of her desk tapping on his phone. I struggle to refrain from rolling my eyes, but she knows my policy on boyfriends in the office during hours. He's come around a few times this semester already, usually trying to usher her out before her work is finished or impatiently grunting while she works. He seems to have forgotten my low tolerance for people that are incapable of following simple rules.

"You can add them to this pile," I say, pointing my pen towards the basket on the edge of my desk.

She nods, taking a few quick steps forward and dumping them inside before turning on her heels. Her pace quickens as she moves towards the door of my office.

"Oh, and Miss Fischer," I say.

"Yes?" she whispers, coming to a stop at the threshold.

"Please remind Mr. Bennett of the rules pertaining to boyfriends hanging out during office hours."

She spins around, her long black hair whipping against the door frame as her brow furrows against her golden eyes. Her pink lips are pressed together in a thin line.

"I am very aware of the 'rules' pertaining to the office hours," she says sternly, using air quotations with her fingers when she says rules. "I'll also have you know, in case you haven't looked at a damn clock lately, that those office hours ended forty-five minutes ago and I stayed to finish the quizzes from all three of your classes instead of just the one you asked me to complete."

She turns back on her heels and stomps out of the office as her heels click against the tile floors.

"Miss Fischer!" I yell. She stops at the edge of her desk, her hands clenched in fists at her side. "I am a professor at this university and you can not speak to me like that."

She turns back towards me so fast her long, black hair swirls around her shoulders. Her cheeks are flushed as her lips are pressed into an even thinner line, now almost even with the rest of her face. She stomps through the door , smacking the edge of my desk with the palms of her hands.

"Are you kidding me?" she whispers angrily.

I can feel the rage coming off her body in waves as her knuckles turn white from her grip. Standing slowly, I match her stance so we are at eye level with each other. Each in an attempt to assert our dominance of the situation.

"Do I sound like I'm kidding?" I ask.

"No, you sound like an ungrateful child that can't even thank someone for doing extra work, going above and beyond!"

Does she still need her work ethic praised as a grad student?

"Watch your tone, Miss Fischer," I demand.

"I will watch my *tone* at the same time that you learn to appreciate the work I do for you and keep your snide remarks to your damn self," she hisses.

"This is my office and you are my assistant. You will do what I say."

Calm down, Tyson. Calm the fuck down before she gets your ass in trouble with the Dean.

I bite my tongue as her face flushes deeper red with anger. She sucks in a deep breath as her eyes narrow to slits, her face only inches from mine. If her anger could turn to liquid, it would seep out of every pore of her body, filling this room to the brim.

"I will happily do whatever you say while office hours are still in session, not after I've given up close to an hour of my own time to help you out."

Dammit, this woman is infuriating.

I can feel my skin tingling with anger as my breathing deepens in my chest. I haven't felt this kind of anger since fighting with my ex-wife and under no circumstance am I about to let it be a TA that gets me sent back to anger management.

"You can leave now," I say and she's back out the door quicker than before.

Instead of stopping to grab her belongings from her desk, she breezes right past it and Mr. Bennett quickly begins to collect her purse before running after her.

15

"Lyla, what the heck? Wait up!" he's yelling, fumbling as he attempts to handle her purse while chasing after her.

I check my watch as they disappear into the hallway.

8:15 p.m.

I pull the stack of papers out that she just dropped into the basket. All three classes are graded— just like she said.

"Shit!" I slam my fist down on my desk and grasp the back of my neck with the other hand as I fall backward into my chair. The pens rattle in the ceramic holder and a picture frame falls off the edge onto the floor— the sound of glass breaking against the tile floor fills the small room. I'd tried to calm myself down, but sometimes I just can't suppress my rage on a whim. She's always found a way to push me, try and rile me up— and every fucking time I let her.

No wonder I can't keep a TA with the way I treat them. I'll be lucky if she comes back at all after this.

Quickly, I open a new email and begin typing an apology.

```
To: Ms. Fischer
From: Professor Moxley
Subject: Office Hours

Ms. Fischer,
       I want to offer my sincere apology for
keeping you late this evening and my stern
reminder of the policies involving my office
hours. Thank you for continuing to strive to
```

16

do work that is above and beyond what I ask of
you. Please, as an extension of my gratitude,
take tomorrow evening off.

Again, my apologies.
Professor Moxley

I drum my fingers along the edge of the desk before removing
the last sentence from the email. Just because she deserves an apology
doesn't mean she should be excused from her responsibilities.

*When was the last time I felt compelled to apologize to a student about
my behavior?*

Never, that's when— but I hit send on the email anyways.

If there has ever been one deserving of an apology, it's Lyla Fischer.

I grasp the back of my neck with both hands and squeeze my
eyes shut, shaking my head.

*It's late and I'll never relax if I keep sitting in this office and thinking
of ways I should have stopped that argument before letting it go so far.*

Shutting off my computer, I grab my stack of midterms and
shove them into my briefcase with a groan. I can grade these at home
where Miss Fischer's perfume isn't lingering in the air and I'm able to
think straight.

17

"Who does he even think he is?" I ask, pouring another shot of tequila down my throat. "Sure, he's a brilliant professor but he's not the damn king of the universe, and how dare he treat me like a child after I did all that extra work."

I read the email again before tossing my phone onto the bar.

What kind of an apology is that shit? Is that even an apology?

Parker slides another shot glass into my hand as I slam my empty one on the bar. I attempt a half-hearted smile at him but I'm still writhing in rage from my heated burst with Professor Moxley and his feeble attempt at an apology.

God, even his name is pretentious. Professor Tyson Moxley. What were his parents thinking when they named him? Did they just want him to become a self-entitled jerk when he got older?

"I can't believe you talked to him like that," Parker says, running his hand along my thigh. "He would have ripped someone's head off in class when I had him. It was terrifyingly brave, yet sexy, to watch you lose your shit."

"Seriously, Lyla," Lucy chimes in. "I wasn't even there and I want to convince this entire bar to chant your name in appreciation!"

I throw my head back as a deep laugh erupts from my throat. The quick movement makes me dizzy even though I'm sitting down and I grasp the edge of the bar to collect myself. I take a deep breath as I reach for the shot glass and toss it back, feeling the burn of the liquid sliding down my throat as it makes its way into my chest.

Brian wraps his arm around Lucy, her leaning into his chest and gazing up at him with doe eyes.

When did they even decide to turn their fling into a full-fledged relationship?

"So, are you guys like officially official now?" I ask, my eyes looking between them. Brian smirks, lifting his glass to his lips as Lucy shrugs.

"I guess so," she says, waving her hand to dismiss the conversation.

"I thought you didn't do relationships, Luc?" I taunt, sticking my tongue out between my teeth.

"Guess I got lucky," Brian says, pressing his lips to Lucy's head as she crinkles her nose— clearly uncomfortable with the amount of physical attention she's getting in a crowded bar.

"I need another drink," she announces, pushing away from Brian and stalking down the bar to order; Brian follows closely behind like a lost puppy.

That's not going to last long.

I sigh, twisting my body back towards Parker. Propping my elbow on the bar, I let my head rest against my hand as I watch Parker take another sip of his beer. His pastel yellow dress shirt hugs against his biceps as he moves his arms lifting and placing the glass back down.

"Maybe it's the tequila talking but you're looking even sexier than usual today," I say, waiting until he looks at me to give him a flirty wink.

His smirk is just enough to bring out the dimple in his left cheek, crinkling the skin around his deep, chocolate brown eyes. He runs a hand through his short, auburn hair and I watch as his shirt tightens around him, knowing there's a chiseled chest underneath. I lift a hand to run down the side of his face and graze his stubble with my fingers. He bites his lip as he places a finger under my chin, tipping my face up just slightly before leaning in to press his lips softly against my own.

I groan as I wrap my hand around the back of his neck trying to deepen the kiss. He slides a hand up my exposed thigh and fidgets with the hem of my dress while lightly caressing my lower lip with his tongue. I suck in a deep breath through my nose and pull myself closer to the edge of my barstool wanting to be as close to him as possible. He chuckles behind the kiss before pulling away, resting his forehead against my own.

"I think you've had a bit too much to drink," he laughs and kisses the tip of my nose.

"Ugh," I groan. "I don't care. I just want you to kiss me some more."

"Seriously, could you two get a room or something?" Lucy grumbles, having reappeared beside us.

"Not all of us avoid PDA, Luc," Parker says, rolling his eyes.

"Well not everyone in this bar wants to watch as you two go through some abnormal foreplay," she retorts. Brian snorts into his drink as I glare at them.

"Guess that's our cue to go," I say, smiling back at Parker now.

Parker grips my waist as I attempt to slide out of my chair gracefully and holds me steady as my feet touch the ground. My heels wobble on the sticky bar floor as I take a few steps and feel Parker sliding out of his seat behind me before wrapping his arm around my waist.

"Come on, sweetheart," he mumbles, pressing his lips against my hair. "Let's get you back to your apartment."

"Could be our apartment, you know," I grumble.

"Come on, babe, let's not start this argument up again right now. Please?"

My eyes roll as Parker snakes us around the others carefully, avoiding any quick movements as my head spins from the quick intake of booze on an empty stomach.

"Fine. Whatever you want, Parker. Can we at least order a pizza on the way, too?" I ask.

"Absolutely, babe."

21

The cool, Texas autumn air hits my skin as we step onto the sidewalk and Parker tightens his hold on my waist. We make our way down the side alley towards the lone lot he parked his car in. If nothing else good comes from today, at least Parker was responsible tonight while I was throwing back shots and he merely took a few sips of his beer. He opens the door to his black BMW M4 and helps me slide into the soft leather of the passenger seat. As he gets into the driver's seat and turns on the car, he puts the top down so the breeze will cool down the flush of my face as we make our way through the bright lights of Houston to my apartment.

Maybe I am badgering him about moving in together too much. He'll bring it up when he's ready.

Leaning my head against the side of the window, I reach out blindly to find his hand and entangle my fingers in his as he shifts through the gears. I close my eyes and let the wind blow through my hair, taking deep breaths through my nose as my stomach settles and the spinning in my mind slows down.

"You feel okay?" he asks.

I nod my head as he stops the car and I realize we're already back at my apartment. He squeezes my hand as the top comes back over our heads.

"Let's get inside so you can rest while we wait on the pizza."

I fumble with the car door as he jogs around the front to meet me as I'm stepping out of the car. He reaches out, catching my arm as

22

it slips, and I stumble forward into his arms. He presses his lips against my forehead as I steady myself, wrapping my hands around his shoulders—basking in the warmth of his skin. With my eyes closed and his arm around my waist again, he leads me to the door as I fumble through my purse feeling for my keys.

"Here we are," he says, taking the keys from my hand and opening up the door.

The smell of freshly washed cotton floats in the air and tickles my nose as Parker leads me to the soft, velvet couch in my living room and helps me sit down. I hear the movement of objects as Parker digs on my coffee table for the television remote underneath the papers for my latest research essay I've left sprawled across it this week.

How am I ever going to get the paper done if I'm always in class or working for Professor Asshole?

I chuckle to myself, pleased with the new nickname my mind has formed for him.

Maybe even Professor Sexy Asshole if he keeps wearing those tight pants like he had on in class today.

Ugh, that's definitely the tequila and Lucy talking. In no world would I soberly find someone as terrible as Professor Moxley even the slightest bit appealing and desirable.

"Pizza is on its way, babe," Parker says as he sits down and wraps his arm around me, letting my head rest on his shoulder.

"Thank you," I mumble, pressing my lips to the side of his neck. "Sorry I kinda ruined date night."

"Just rest, you'll feel better soon."

Today's class covering the History of Federal Wetlands Regulation was taxing on everyone's mind— especially my own. Between the necessary and needed knowledge around the topic mixed with feeling Miss Fischer's eyes on me during class, I was unusually distracted and kept veering off-topic. Ever since she called me out a week ago, she has been quieter than usual during our office hours instead of her outgoing, bubbly self that I have found out I enjoyed more than I was aware of. She hasn't picked a fight once, not even when I've asked her to do something ludicrous—like go on a coffee run—which makes me question if she's given up on me, like everyone else in my life.

Tonight, I can hear her aimlessly tapping her pen against the edge of her desk as she hums a light tune while grading the pretest for the upcoming exams. Her black hair has been pulled into a ponytail exposing the soft skin of her bare neck and tanned shoulders from her loose, turquoise-colored sweater hanging lower on the left side of her arm. Our fight had left me rattled, even after my polite apology. I've pondered many times if there's something else that I could do to turn the spirit of these drawn-out hours back around. I watch as time ticks by on the antique gold clock hanging from the wall across from my desk instead of focusing on preparing for the final exam.

25

I can always just reuse a previous test if I lose the motivation to switch it up again this year. Will the kids really think to cheat off a test from four years ago?

The sound of heavy footsteps running through the corridor grabs my attention and I look up in time to watch Mr. Bennett stumbling into the office. Even this far from him, a whiff of the scent of whiskey burns my nostrils. Miss Fischer stands abruptly from her desk, peering back at me with her mouth agape. Her widened eyes give away her fear of what will come from the interruption this time.

"Hey, babe!" Mr. Bennett proceeds to yell as he stumbles through the room.

"Um, Parker," she begins to say, "what are you doing here? We talked about you not showing up during office hours, remember?"

Her voice is hushed as she glances between myself and Mr. Bennett as he closes in on her. I stand and walk around the desk, leaning against it while crossing my arms— concern written in my expression.

Even if he's here with good intentions, he's drunk and the best intentions can come out wrong. Something I know all too well.

"What do you mean what am I doing here?" He asks her, grabbing her arm and pulling her to him closely. "I missed you and you're always stuck working with this jerk."

He points a finger at me and I feel the heat of anger rising from the pit of my stomach. I clench my hands into fists as they are hidden

26

underneath my forearms. The sting of the nails driven into my palms is enough to keep my focus grounded and not lose my shit.

"Shut up, Parker!" She hisses, pulling him back towards the door.

"What? Are you saying he isn't a jerk?" he asks her.
I hear her gasp in the silence of the room. She shakes her head and playfully pushes his shoulder.

"I'm saying he's my boss and you can not be here during office hours!"

"Seriously? You're choosing your boss over me right now?" he makes a gesture towards himself, making a point to showcase his genital area while he gives her a wink.

"No, Parker," she sighs, "I'm saying I'll see you after work. Go wait for me outside."

I feel my stomach drop as she talks.

Why would she want to spend any amount of time with someone that drinks too much? Is this not an uncommon occurrence? Does she also drink like this outside of my class and office?

I've missed the end of their conversation as I zoned out thinking about why she would want to be with a man like him and now she's standing at the edge of my doorway with her head hung.

"Professor Moxley," she murmurs.

"Hmm?" I say, raising an eyebrow as she bites her lip and nervously fidgets with the edge of the sleeves of her sweater.

"I am really sorry about Parker bursting in here. It was unprofessional and inappropriate and I would like to say that it will never happen again but I can't control his actions so I just want to offer my sincerest apology," she says without taking a breath. "Also I swear I don't call you a jerk behind your back," she picks her chin up, her amber eyes leering at me. A smirk forms across her lips as she tilts her head to the side. "I would just call you one to your face if I truly thought you were one."

I can't help but chuckle as she rambles on with her apology.

"There is no doubt in my mind that you would call me names to my face."

She nods slowly, her fingers fidgeting with her sweater again.

"I just wanted to make sure you weren't going to have a meltdown of epic proportions like you did the last time he showed up," she says, sucking her bottom lip between her teeth, her eyes drifting down to the tile we stand on. "And let you know that his actions don't reflect my own when I am outside this office."

Suddenly, I feel a twinge in my heart as I realize she is taken aback by his behavior. I drop my arms and walk towards her, placing a hand on her shoulder as her eyes peek up through the hoods of her eyelids to meet mine. The rims of her eyes are red as she's forcefully blinking back tears.

Her body stiffens at my touch.

"Please, don't touch me," she whispers.

I drop my hand and take a step back.

"I- I'm sorry," I stutter, "Mr. Bennett's behavior tonight is not a reflection of you. It was untimely and obscene, but you are correct about not being able to control another person's actions."

Her eyes flash to my face as her brow furrows together— trying to understand when I became a softie just like I am.

"Um, thank you?" she says.

"However, with that being said," I say, "I will need to report him for Public Intoxication within an educational building on school property."

Her mouth drops for a few seconds before she presses her lips into a thin line.

"Maybe you are a jerk," she hisses. "Or maybe you just get off by flaunting your superiority to all of those beneath you."

"Is that how you feel I treat you, Miss Fischer?" I ask.

She takes a deep breath as she taps her finger against her bottom lip and looks around the room.

"I don't think you really want me to answer that question," she chuckles.

I take a step closer to her, close enough now that I am practically bathing in the scent of her grapefruit and jasmine perfume.

"No, really, I do want you to answer that question," I challenge her.

She takes a deep breath and closes her eyes before responding.

"You are infuriating, to be quite honest," she says. "You are hot and cold and sometimes you're great and perfectly nice and pleasant to be around."

She stares into my eyes with her nostrils flared.

"Then other times you might as well be a solid brick of never melting ice because you shout demands and thank no one for fulfilling anything or you don't even respond when someone asks a genuine question in class. You pride yourself on your passion for teaching but the rest of us just see you as someone that lost out on their dream career and settled for teaching because it was the only option left."

She's crossed her arms during her speech and her squinting eyes feel as though they are glaring into my soul. I can feel my own eyes twitch in anger as I listen to her.

"You don't know a goddamn thing about my career," I snarl.

"Then why don't you enlighten me, oh high and mighty one?" her daring tone like daggers through my skin.

She wants to set me off, she's pushing again.

Pleased that we are finally back to normal, I give her a quick half-smile in return as I run a hand through my hair.

"There are only a few minutes left of office hours and I don't foresee anyone showing up. Why don't you go ahead and take off?" I tell her.

Her head leans to one side as her brow furrows again.

I pick a stack of papers off my desk and begin leafing through them as she stands frozen in place.

"Did you need something else?" I ask with a smirk.

"Are you seriously not going to rip my head off for what I just said about you? I didn't even make you the slightest bit angry?"

"On the contrary, Miss Fischer," I tell her. "You are also infuriating but unlike you, I'm smart enough to know when to not respond and when to walk away from a bad situation."

She spins around, stomping out of my office, and slams the door shut behind her. A deep rumble bellows out of my throat as I lean my head back, tossing the papers back on the desk before slamming my fists against either side of me. Once again, I've pushed her to the point of acting childish. How many more times can I do this before she doesn't come back?

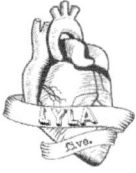

I take a deep breath before pulling open the staff door at the front of the lecture hall. It's been two days since I last saw Professor Moxley after telling him just some of the terrible things I think about him in his office. At least it had been a Friday when I chose to act out and wasn't forced back into a room with him right away. As I walk towards my desk at the front of the room, he's perched against the front of his desk, arms crossed with a smirk across his face, peering out as the students file into the room and take their seats. He doesn't acknowledge me as I sit down and open the laptop to prepare to take notes for the class today.

As the final student wanders towards their seat he claps his hands together with such force that it echoes throughout the room.

"Good afternoon, students," his deep, booming voice drawing everyone to attention. Every pair of eyes in the room is now on him — watching his every move, perplexed expressions on their faces. "It has been brought to my attention that I brush off questions during class time and today I think we will spend the day doing only that. You can ask me any of your questions and I will do my best to answer them for you."

He turns his head just enough to give me a quick wink and I realize my mouth is hanging open. It strikes my core, heating the skin on my cheeks as I realize he's taking something I said to him to heart.

32

Should I feel bad about everything else I said? Sure, I meant it, but he's still a great professor regardless.

I shake off my thoughts as the first student raises their hand and asks a question regarding the Clean Water Act and I quickly begin to type the notes. In a normal class, I spend the majority of the time bored and forcing myself to pay attention by making a game out of the students' reactions to his lectures. Today, I can't hang on to his every word close enough. He's answering every question with such knowledge and passion as he weaves through the room in a personable manner. His body language is mesmerizing, focusing on each student and taking the time to talk *to them* instead of just *at them*. Everything about his demeanor screams casual and relaxed today, even his attire; a pair of dark wash, form-fitting jeans, and a black button-up shirt with the top three buttons left undone. His shoulder-length blonde hair frames neatly around his face as he runs his hand through it every few minutes when he pauses, precisely working through the wording for his response before giving it. The scruff on his chiseled jawline looks as though he didn't shave all weekend — *maybe he was too busy mulling over the list of insults I hurled at him.*

The document I'm working on begins to fill quickly as students I've never noticed before are firing off questions and he responds with answers so competent you would think he knew what questions were going to be asked.

He didn't, right? He didn't plan out these questions just to make himself look good.

I shake my head discreetly, that's absurd to think about. There's no way he could have had the time to email each student a list of questions to ask. Questions that he would have prepared answers for. Some of the questions were even of the personal matters surrounding his time at the firm he left behind when he came to teach. I learn that he has a daughter, Ivy, with his ex-wife and he hasn't remarried since they divorced many years ago. I learn that his favorite color is dandelion yellow and his favorite car is his 1976 Camaro— that he owns in black. He lives in a generational family home in River Oaks and has no desire to leave Houston for any long period of time.

The clock in the corner of the screen indicates there are only five minutes left and I lift my hand to show him the number five— our signal for when he needs to wrap it up for the day. He gives a quick nod before jogging down the steps of the lecture room and perches himself back against the front of his desk.

"Alright class, that was a fun day, right?" he asks as the students erupt into a round of applause and cheering. He chuckles momentarily before putting his fingers into his mouth and blows out a shrieking whistle. Gasps fill the room, eyes widening back at us as everyone freezes in place. As the noise dies off, he crosses his arms before he speaks again.

"Sure we had fun today, I know I'm fascinating and love to hear myself talk… but that now means we are a day behind," he says. "So in that case, you will need to read the section covering the Wetlands Act in your books and write a two-page report on it before next class to show you comprehend the material." The class erupts in a series of groans as he begins to chuckle again. "Also, in case you were wondering, the person that brought my brash style of teaching to my attention and earned you this delightful homework assignment is—" *Oh my god, please don't tell them it was me.* I can feel my cheeks burning as I try to slide down in my chair. "None other than my TA, Miss Fischer! Let's give her a round of applause for a fun day!"

He claps his hands together, his amused smile beaming at me as the class begins to boo and point their thumbs down in unison. Heated tears begin to prick at the corners of my eyes as I bite my lip, my throat drying out as I choke them back. He dismisses the class and I quickly gather my bag before running out the back door into the hall. With the door swinging shut behind me, I bury my face in my arms against the wall as my body trembles in a failed attempt to hold back the tears.

What the fuck is his problem?

"Miss Fischer?" I hear his deep voice ask.

"Go away," I demand without looking up at him.

"Look at me," he says. I peek out from under my arm to see him leaning against the wall with a smirk on his face. Instantly, I feel

35

my body surge with white-hot rage and ball my fists. "Good, now why don't you tell me what exactly has you in tears in the hallway?"

I open my mouth as I try to find the right words to respond with.

Because you just embarrassed the shit out of me? Because you couldn't handle our private conversation in private? Because you are clearly abusing your power again?

A bitter laugh rumbles through my teeth as I stumble across the right words.

"Screw you, asshole," I say sternly, turning around and stalking away from him without looking back.

Once outside, I take off sprinting across campus. Students move out of my way as I pay no mind to my surroundings, the jumble of the crowds merely a blur behind my watering eyes. The words so angrily ripped their way out of my mouth, unable to hold them in with his antagonizing smirk and composed body language right next to me.

He's going to chew me up and spit me out, over and over again.

Not that I don't deserve the wrath I will face tonight.

Safely inside my apartment, I fill a glass to the brim with water and drink it down—quenching the burn of my parched throat. I yank my phone from the inside of my bag and find Lucy's name, my fingers shaking as I tell her what I've done.

> **ME:** Luc, I FUCKED UP.

LUCY: You just came from Professor Dickhead's class, didn't you? What happened?

ME: I made some cruel remarks towards him after Parker showed up, DRUNK! on Friday… which led to him calling me out in front of the entire class today.

ME: But, that isn't the worst part.

ME: Instead of just leaving it at that, he followed me into the hallway and asked me why I was so upset.

LUCY: I mean, that kinda seems like a nice thing to do since he's so heartless that he maybe didn't even realize he was being a dick in the first place.

ME: Sure, maybe. I think his smirk said he knew exactly what he had done though. Which is why I called him an asshole right there in front of the students.

LUCY: LYLA! Shit, girl. You can't just call a professor an asshole. Even if they are one! Fuck.

ME: How do I fix this, Luc? *cries*

LUCY: I mean, short of quitting or getting on your knees to beg for forgiveness, I'm not sure.

LUCY: I am fucking proud as hell of you, woman. Fuck him.

I could quit, sure, but then wouldn't that mean he wins?

Does it even matter if he wins? As long as I don't have to resort to begging for forgiveness— not to him.

How could she just walk away from me like that? Where the hell does she get off? My feet carry me swiftly, weaving through the crowds of students as I jog up the stairs to my office— still seething from my encounter with Miss Fischer in the hallway. She had been honest in my office Friday when she said she would always tell me the truth about how she felt but I did not expect that. Fuck, no one on this planet could have expected those words to spew from her delicate mouth; especially not in a hallway full of other students and peers. My cheeks are burning, teeth grinding together so hard my gums hurt, and the only thing I want to do is fire her snarky ass.

The only thing stopping me from doing that is the formal complaint she would file against me with Dean Marco, a room full of students to properly back her claim of harassment up.

I groan as I reach into the bottom drawer of my desk and grab the bottle of Scotch out and take a quick swig straight from the bottle. I don't usually condone drinking on campus, or during the day, but today is a shit show from hell and there are still office hours to get through tonight. If I'm lucky, she won't show up and save me the trouble of reprimanding her— if that's even what I decide to do.

I should have left it alone. I should have just fucking kept my comments to myself.

Leaning back in the plush chair, I clasp my hands on the back of my neck and close my eyes. The memory of seeing her tears

39

streaming down her cheeks as she called me an asshole is going to forever be ingrained in my mind.

I've been called a lot of names over the years but "asshole" has typically been reserved for Sloan. Never has a student had the balls to call me one to my face.

Maybe that's what makes Miss Fischer different from the other assistants I've had over the years. She has balls and brains instead of just the brains like most of the other students. Her feisty personality may clash with my authority but at least that assures me she will get somewhere in life. If she's able to stand her ground, putting me in my place when necessary, she could easily work her way to the top of a corporate company with that attitude and fire. Hell, she could be the fucking President with that demeanor.

Why do I even care?

This is becoming a common question these days.

Years and years of teaching have never left me with a desire to care about a single student and their future endeavors. Except for Miss Lyla Fischer.

The lights shining through the windows begin to fade as I glance at the clock on the wall— quarter after five. She'll be here soon enough if she chooses to show up.

I flip on the computer screen on my desk and force myself to work through the exam questions. After a decade, the endless amount of time spent preparing these short-sighted tests continues to baffle

40

me. A lawyer can never be judged by their work on paper in a timed setting. They'll be judged by their presentation, persuasion, tension, and ability to undermine their opponents. The seconds feel like minutes as I wait in the quiet room, hoping to hear the sound of footsteps coming from the hall.

Minutes pass, and pass, and pass.

At exactly five-thirty she rushes into the room and drops her bag at her desk before knocking on the doorframe to my office. I wave her inside as I barely peek at her from the corner of my eye over my screen.

"What can I do for you, Miss Fischer?" I ask, looking away and folding my hands on my desk in front of me. "Any other names you'd like to call me today?"

Dammit, why did I say that? Why do I need to egg her on?

I smile, unfaltering, but she refuses to look up from her arms crossed in front of her. I can see her biting her lower lip behind the waterfall of hair that is surrounding her face. She takes two steps closer to my desk and offers an envelope with my name on the front of it.

"I'd like to apologize for my behavior this afternoon," she answers sarcastically, "but I'm really not sorry."'

"Of course you're not," I respond. "I would be baffled if you were."

I force myself to hold in the chuckle rising in my throat as I take the envelope from her and she rushes back to her desk. As she pulls out a stack of papers and begins to go through them with a red pen, I hear her foot tapping anxiously against the tile floors. The envelope in my hand no longer feels like an apology letter— but something dreadful. I slowly tear it open, taking my time to be quiet and refrain from causing her any more anxiety over me reading whatever it is she has taken the time to write today. Taking a deep breath, I unfold the letter and place it on my desk to read.

Dear Professor Moxley,

      Firstly, I would like to thank you for allowing me to be your Teaching Assistant in the first semester of my final year at the University of Houston. You are an admirable and knowledgeable professor that the students are lucky to learn from.

This doesn't seem so bad....

I gaze out through the window in my office and catch her peeking over her shoulder before quickly turning away as my eyes meet hers. My brow furrows as I watch her lean into her hands propped up by her elbows on her desk and shake her head. A sudden twinge in my heart wants to console her, but I shove it down and go back to reading her letter.

With that being said, I am sorry to say that I will not be able to return as your Teaching Assistant in my final semester. I have opted to take an extra course to make up for the credit hours I will be out from resigning, but this arrangement is no longer serving my best interest. I understand how difficult it can be to start over with a new TA on such short notice which is the only reason I have chosen to stay through the end of the semester instead of withdrawing from my duties immediately.

I will be happy to leave a detailed list of instructions for the next person to fill this position so there will be no issues in transition for you and you will not need to take the time out of your busy schedule to train someone else.

I wish you the best of luck,
Miss Lyla Fischer

My chest tightens as my heart feels as though it is being ripped apart. I read the letter twice, carefully going through each word to ensure I'm reading it accurately. I went too far today, and I already knew that but reading this letter makes it that much worse; maybe there is still time to salvage the professional relationship we have.

She deserves an apology. An unhypocritical, wholehearted apology.

I leave her to work in peace, stealing glances through the window as she works quickly tonight. There are no interruptions from students, no sounds of a phone ringing or a buzzing of her texts coming in. The only sounds in the office are from my fingers hitting the keyboard and her pen tapping against her desk between writing. Usually, her humming fills the room and is a pleasant sound to work to, but not tonight. Tonight, there is only silence and thick tension between us.

Tension that I need to cut through and force to heal.

With twenty minutes left of office hours, I take a deep breath having decided on how to proceed. If I want to keep the best assistant I've ever had, I am going to have to try harder to stay calm when she begins to drive me crazy.

"Miss Fischer, can you come in here please?"

Her back straightens immediately at the sound of my voice. I watch as her shoulders rise and fall with a few deep breaths before she stands slowly and saunters through my doorway with an overbearing smile through her painted pink lips.

"What can I do for you, Professor Moxley?"

"Have a seat, please," I tell her, gesturing towards one of the smaller chairs in front of my desk.

She sucks in her lip, chewing on it as she takes another deep breath and walks towards the chair. She sits down slowly and tucks a piece of hair behind her ears so that her face is visible but she refuses to look at me. Her hands twist in her lap as she waits patiently for me to continue.

"Miss Fischer," I lean forward on my desk and run my hand down the front of my face, gripping my chin. "I owe you an apology."

Her eyes shoot up and pierce me with a bright, golden hue—sending a frenzy of quickened heartbeats through my chest. Had they

44

always been this bright and enticing? Her pink lips are pursed together as they appear fuller than usual and slightly wet from the glowing light in the room. Again, her perfume fills the room and causes my hands to tremble as a quick image of me inhaling the scent right from the crook of her neck flashes in my mind.

"What did you say?" she asks, snapping the mental image from my mind.

I take a deep breath as I pinch the bridge of my nose before returning my eyes to hers.

"I owe you an apology," I repeat. "What I did today…. it was unprofessional and never should have happened. I baited you into what you said Friday night and that was also unprofessional." I watch as her eyes grow wide and her lips slowly begin in part in awe.

She probably thinks there are no remorseful bones in my body and she's witnessing a full-on miracle right now.

"While I *don't* appreciate the language you used in the hallway after class," I continue, "I am also to blame for putting you in that position. I am sorry about my behavior, Miss Fischer. You are an astounding student and with your work ethic and personality, I can assure you that you will go on to do extraordinary work in life."

I look up to meet her eyes and give her my best smoldering expression and smile genuinely. She squeezes her eyes tightly and sticks her thumb in her mouth and bites down, hard. I suck in a deep breath at the sight.

She is fucking exasperating.

I pinch the bridge of my nose again as I collect myself until she begins to speak. Then I return my eyes to her face and feel a flutter as I see the smirk on her lips.

"Thank you for your apology, Professor Moxley," she says, leaning forward onto my desk with her elbows. She flips her hair behind her shoulder and the overwhelming scent of her perfume fills my nostrils again. "I really have enjoyed working with you this semester and I hope your next assistant is half as good as I have been. Perhaps you'll treat them with a little more respect than I've gotten from you."

She stands up and abruptly leaves my office, moving her hips with her walk a little more than usual as she collects her items from her desk and walks out the front door. I can feel the tightening in my groin on my pants and slam my fist on the desk—shutting that automatic response to a beautiful woman down immediately. My heart is racing and the scent of her perfume everywhere in my office has my brain a foggy mess.

Dammit, I'm in trouble.

Apparently, if there is one thing in this world Professor Moxley is passionate about, it is the eradication of toxic substances. My fingers rush along with the keys today trying to keep up with his overly enthusiastic lecture over the Toxic Substances Control Act. Over the past two weeks, after he apologized for belittling me in his classroom, he has become almost an entirely new person to work for— and with. He's cheerful, friendly, and most importantly— personable. Most nights we work together in his office now going over the questions for the final exam. He works on the computer on one side of his desk and I work across from him on the other side. He's taken an interest in my studies and spends the time discussing what my plans after graduation are and what I plan to do with my Anthropology degree.

He had seemed surprised, or taken aback at least, when I said my goal was to become a paleontologist and continue to discover fossils and new species, but will likely choose to start as a curator in a museum. He even offered to write me a glowing recommendation letter for the future. Oddly enough, I've started to look forward to the nights we spend working in his office.

The more time we spend together, I can't help but notice the flutters in my stomach I get whenever he breezes by me and I get a whiff of his cedar and amber cologne. He often rolls up his dress shirts while we're working and exposes his muscled forearms as his biceps

47

are tugging at the thin fabrics, a part of the male body I've never had the slightest inkling I was attracted to—before now. I swear I even catch him staring at me from time to time, whether we're in the lecture hall or just working together in his office— but to notice that he's staring at me, I'm clearly staring at him as well. Not to mention, I've really paid attention to that taut ass underneath his form-fitted pants more than I used to.

These thoughts are becoming completely inappropriate for someone with a boyfriend. Even if it is a boyfriend you barely see anymore now that he's filling in at a law firm when he's not in class.

My cheeks flush with my thoughts as I gather the items from my desk, watching as Professor Moxley dismisses the group and struts down the stairs towards me. He's pulled his hair into a bun today at the back of his neck and has not shaved for a few days, allowing his stubble to become prominent once again across his chiseled jawline. I can't help but smile back as he leans against my desk, feeling the flutters rise in my stomach as his eyes glance over me.

"You look nice today," he remarks with an added wink. "Big plans tonight?"

I chuckle because it's Wednesday; he knows the only thing I'll be doing tonight is grading papers in his office. His seemingly flirty smile pulls at my heart and I toss my hair over my shoulder as I lean across my desk towards him.

"Oh yeah, great big plans...," I murmur. "My boss is this genuine hard-ass that makes his assistant work the night Thanksgiving Break starts."

I laugh as his jaw drops and he holds a hand over his heart in an exaggeration of my words hurting his feelings.

"A genuine hardass you say? That doesn't sound like him," he winks, I feel my knees weaken.

Push those inappropriate thoughts back down, Lyla. He's just being friendly since you so clearly like to call him terrible names.

"No, he's definitely a hardass, but it's okay because I think I'm getting him to soften up a bit," I wink back at him, unable to help myself, and turn to head out the back door. "See you in a few hours, Professor."

I can almost swear I hear him whisper "soften up my ass" as I stride through the door, a tingling spreading through my legs.

Happiness and euphoria wash over me as I walk through campus today. Texas in the fall, while all the leaves are changing and falling, is breathtaking. The air is still warm during the day but cooler at night, the perfect subtle change to the constant rain back home in Washington. Unlike many of the other students, I'm not going home for the break this year. My brother, Tyler, had mentioned offering to fly me out to his house in Rhode Island for the holiday. Not wanting to rush a trip out there I had politely turned him down, insisting that a quiet night at home with Parker is all I needed. I'll get together with Tyler at Christmas and that is soon enough, anyway.

Turning down the street filled with small, local businesses, I pop into a café to grab a coffee before going home. Parker hasn't responded yet after I asked if he was almost there so I figure I have time to spare.

"A grandé Mocha Latte, please," I say to the barista as I hand her my credit card. I lean against the counter as she prepares my drink, pulling my phone out to text Parker again.

ME: Are you still coming over before my office hours?

Immediately upon sending, I hear a ding from another phone in the quiet café and peek over my screen as I giggle at the coincidence.

What the fuck.

My giggling quickly subsides, the noise getting caught in my throat. Parker is sitting in the corner with another blonde woman leaving a trail of kisses down his neck as he strokes the side of her face. I can feel the water welling in my eyes as I stand there. My feet feel too heavy to pick up and carry myself out of the shop. The only sounds I can hear is the hissing of the steam coming from the machines behind me— everything else is jumbled noise, completely inaudible. I grip my phone so tightly my hand begins to hurt.

"Ma'am," the barista says from behind me, "here's your coffee."

"Um, thanks," I say, barely above a whisper with my throat choking on the words.

I reach behind me for the cup without taking my eyes off Parker. Betrayal, anger, and deceit ripple through my veins. Before I rush out the door, I turn on the camera and snap a picture of them kissing. I run back out to the busy sidewalk, holding the coffee steady as I push my way through the crowds of people. I send the picture in another message to Parker with a simple "fuck you" message and turn off my phone.

I can't go home. I don't want to go back to the empty apartment right now. He'll come there looking for me and he'll want to fight and cause a scene.

Aimlessly wandering, letting my feet carry me as my mind is in a fog of chaos and hatred, I find myself in Professor Moxley's office. It's empty so I throw myself into my chair and bury my head in my arms—trying not to think twice about the fact this is where I instinctively came for comfort. I let myself sob into my desk as my heart feels as though it is being ripped from my chest. The sound echoes through the empty room and the sound of footsteps in the hall elude me as I crumble. I lose track of time, not caring about who could

51

walk in and enjoy the show of the naive student crumbling because their boyfriend was caught cheating on them.

My relationship has been a complete sham for who the hell knows how long. How long has he been going behind my back? Why not just end it with me if he was that unhappy? Were there signs of him wanting out that I missed? Is this why he never wanted to move in?

"Dammit!" I shout, pounding my hand against the desk.

The sobs explode from inside my chest, ripping through my body as I curl over onto my desk again.

"Miss Fischer, what are you doing here so early?" a deep voice says from above me.

Goddammit. Not now, not already.

"Lyla, are you okay?" he asks.

I shake my head no as I try to take a deep breath, wiping my tears away before looking up at him.

I can sense the heat from his body as it reaches my skin, he crouches down next to my desk—his elbow so close to mine as he props it on the edge. His hand brushes mine lightly before he hesitates, then pulls it away.

"Wanna talk about it?" he asks, offering a half-hearted smile when I peer through my curtain of hair at him.

"It's stupid college kid stuff, it'll be fine," I say.

"Clearly it isn't fine."

I lift my head, wiping the water streaks from my cheek as I stare at him. His smoldering cerulean eyes pierce my soul as I look into them, feeling the warmth of his skin drawing me to him. His hair is still pulled back and I find my fingers itching to trace the protruding cheekbones covered in stubble. I take a deep breath before hanging my head as I work up the courage to divulge my personal life to him.

"Seriously, talk to me, let me listen," he says, placing a soft, warm hand on my arm, his brow pinching together in concern. "I'm sure I'm the last person you'd want to confide in but I am here for you if you'll allow me to be."

"I caught Parker kissing another girl in the coffee shop on my way home after class. I took a picture and sent it to him and didn't want to go home so I came back here instead. I'm sorry, I know I shouldn't be in your office when you're not here but I didn't know where to go. My friends still have classes or have left for the day and I didn't think he would assume I would come here if he wanted to talk," I explain in one long breath.

His thumb is rubbing against my skin as though he's trying to console me discreetly. His cologne pierces my nostrils and I close my eyes as I inhale it deeply, letting the smell remind me of the forest back home. My cold. clammy hands relish in the heat from his hand on my arm. I struggle to keep them clasped together instead of reaching for him, relishing in his warmth.

"Come into my office," he says, extending a hand to help me up. I take it as the heat from his hand surges through my body, tingling my core, and sends my heart into a frenzy.

You're just sad and he's trying to be nice, it means nothing else.

I sit down at my usual spot but instead of grabbing a stack of papers, he reaches into his bottom drawer and pulls out two glasses and a bottle filled with amber liquid.

"Didn't you just threaten to report Parker for public intox not that long ago?" I blurt out at the sight in front of me, then quickly cover my mouth.

"I don't condone this, nor should I have told you that I would report him. However, I think you could use a night off," he says, winking at me. He pours a small amount into each glass and hands one to me, raising his as I take a small sip. The scotch burns my mouth, trickling down my throat, but fills my insides with the heat.

"Thank you," I squeak. "Is there something I can work on?"

He chuckles and shakes his head, he turns his computer screen towards me and scoots his chair back to where we're next to each other with only the desk between us.

"Let's take the night off, it is the beginning of the break, right?" he says. "Wouldn't want that boss of yours to be remembered as too much of a hardass."

I choke on the sip of my drink, laughing into the cup as I sputter.

54

He turns on a video quickly identified as a documentary on the early findings of dinosaur fossils and I stare at him with an awestruck smile. He raises his glass again, I lean across the table to clink the glasses together as he smiles back at me. He grabs a pair of tortoiseshell rimmed glasses and puts them on, turning back towards the screen as the room darkens around us. I use the darkness to steal glances at the man I used to despise, the man that drove me so crazy it led me to argue with a professor— now becoming the man that picked me up in my darkest hour without hesitation.

Sitting in my office with the lights off, watching a documentary while drinking scotch on campus with a student— it's all very wrong, but for the first time, the company of another woman feels right.

"Do you enjoy being a professor?" Lyla's quiet question snaps my attention away from the screen.

She has spent the majority of the documentary commenting on the different species being uncovered and searching for inaccuracies during the interviews with the paleontologists. She had sipped her first glass slowly, but the alcohol now in her system seemed to lighten her mood over the past hour and shine a light on a new side of her.

"Indeed I do, Miss Fischer," I inform her. I haven't been able to stop myself from stealing glances at her. She's becoming mesmerizing as the alcohol flushes her cheeks and the way she ends up smiling every time she yells at the speaker in the documentary. With both of our arms resting on the desk, they're close enough to feel the heat emitting from her skin— *too close. I wonder if it's as soft as it looks.* My heart pounding in my chest every time her arm slips a few centimeters closer to mine on the table is enough to warn me that what I'm feeling now is going to get me in trouble. "Why do you ask?"

She takes her time as she inspects her fingernails, swirling her drink around in her glass as her glassy eyes look around the room.

"You were a lawyer before, right?" I nod, she shrugs. "Maybe that's why you always act like you have a stick up your ass."

56

She fights back a laugh, leaning over so her head rests on her arm as her hair spills across the desk. I rub my chin, taken aback by her sudden abrasiveness.

"Does it seem like I have a stick up my ass tonight?" I ask, leaning in closer.

"Hmmm.....," she ponders, wetting her lips as she gazes up at me. "I guess not, but in general on any other given day.... Abso-freakin-lutely." A husky laugh bellows out of my chest as I double over, my hand smacking the edge of the desk at her honesty. "So I can say that you have a stick up your ass but I can't call you an asshole, is that right?"

Her teasing tone keeps me laughing, tears beginning to brim the corners of my eyes— I wonder when the last time I laughed this hard was. As I settle down, wiping the water from behind my glasses and fixing my eyes upon her, she breaks into a captivating grin. Sitting up, she toys with a piece of her hair without breaking eye contact. Leaning even closer in, I cock my head with a wicked grin and answer her.

"That's right, Lyla. You can tell me I have a stick up my ass or call me any name in the book or say anything you damn well please to me, as long as it's not in a hallway full of students and faculty members. Does that sound like a decent enough arrangement?"

Her cheeks flush at my words, or perhaps our proximity as I'm now mere inches away from her face. She nods slowly, taking in a few short breaths before picking up her glass and polishing off the rest of the scotch.

"I don't think they're still in South America while they're filming this," she huffs, crossing her legs dramatically. I clench my thighs together as I hyperfocus on her wet lips as she wipes the drop of scotch from her mouth and licks it slowly off her finger, sending a flutter through my groin.

"What makes you say that?" I ask, my voice rough as I raise my glass for another sip.

"Because just look at them!" she exclaims. My eyebrow raises in confusion as she chuckles, letting her head drop into her palm on the desk before sitting up and tossing her hair back again. "They're barely tan, it's too dry of a climate for them to still be there. Hardly anyone has an accent that they keep interviewing. It just doesn't add up!"

She shrugs with a smirk and turns her attention back towards the monitor. I watch as the glow of the screen reflects off her skin, seemingly paler than weeks before. Seeing her in tears when I walked in this afternoon had cracked the walls I have built up for so long and I felt compelled to offer her comfort.

"What? Is there something on my face?" she asks.

"What? No?" I say, confused.

Her lips purse as she crosses her arms, the sudden movement of her body sends a breeze towards me and sends a chill down my arm.

"Then why are you staring at me?" she asks.

Fuck. She caught me this time.

"I just…," I started, biting my lip to buy myself some time before continuing, "I just zoned out there for a minute. Sorry."

"Okay then, weirdo," she winks. "The documentary is over. So…. I guess I should go…."

"Can I ask you something first?" I ask hastily, not wanting her to go yet.

She shrugs, nodding her head as she wipes her palms against her thighs.

Fuck, what am I doing?

But it still feels so right, so does that make it wrong?

"What did you see in Mr.Bennett?"

Her eyes widen at my words, her mouth opens, and closes as she struggles to find the best answer and I watch her expression change from confused to angry.

"I met Parker when we both started here, the first-week classes began and we became quick friends. Well, us, and Lucy, and Brian. We'd all come from out of state, trying to find our footing in a new city. We enjoyed the same sports, spent our time exploring around town, and just eventually it merged into something more."

"That doesn't answer my question, though," I tell her. "What did you see in him? Was he good to you?"

"I mean, in the beginning, sure I guess so," she bites her lip, staring at her hands twisting in her lap. "I think I just assumed our relationship was losing the sizzle that we had in the beginning and we were finding complacency, though he never seemed as ready to take it any further. He wouldn't move in together, no matter how convenient it would have been for either of us. He prefers drinking and going out while I would rather spend time at the museums or watching a movie at home. He never gave me any grief about my extra workload or when I would skip out on a night of drinking, though now I have to wonder if this was the first time he had cheated because of that. What he did today, it makes me feel the need to question a lot of our relationship and see if there were any signs I missed along the way— see how long he's been fucking me over and probably laughing about it behind my back."

The back of her hand flies up to her eyes, wiping away whatever tears were beginning to fall again as I feel my heart shudder in my chest. As she sits her hand on the edge of the desk, drumming her fingers along the wood I reach out and take her hand in mine. Her body jerks in response, her eyes shooting to my face, seeing the sorrow in my eyes.

"Are you sure you want to go?" I ask.

Her eyes drop as she takes her bottom lip between her teeth.

I groan internally, the warmth of the scotch spreading through my veins— and other parts of my body sensing how enticing this woman across the desk from me could be.

"I mean, I'm probably going to go home to Parker beating against my door begging to explain since I shut my phone off as soon as I ended it with him and haven't turned it back on since," she explains.

"Why don't you turn it back on so we can assess the situation properly and then make an informed decision on whether to watch another movie or go home?"

She nods and steps out the door to grab her phone from her purse. As she sits back down across from me, she twists her hands together on the desk with the phone next to her as it powers on. My foot is tapping anxiously against the tile floor but if she's noticed, she hasn't brought it up. Instantly, her phone begins to ding multiple times in a row. I watch her shoulders rise and fall with her deep breaths as she reaches for the phone. I watch intently as her expressions change from annoyed eye-rolls to angry pursed lips and finally I see the water begin to well in her eyes as she bites down hard on her lip and slams the phone down on the desk. She buries her face in her hands, her shoulders bounce as she silently sobs into her palms.

What the fuck did that little douchebag say to upset her?

"Can I see?" I ask. She nods without moving her hands from her face. I grab the phone off the desk and scroll through the messages he's left.

PARKER: Shit, Lyla baby, that isn't what it looks like.
PARKER: Let me explain. I'll be at your place in ten minutes.
PARKER: Come on, let me in so we can talk about this!
PARKER: Dammit Lyla, just open the goddamn door. She means nothing to me. She's just someone that works at the office.
PARKER: Fine, you don't want to talk? Fuck you.
PARKER: Don't bother contacting me again. Anything I have in your apartment you can have. I don't want anything that you've touched, it's tainted now. Have a fantastic fucking life, bitch.

I take a deep breath, squeezing my eyes shut as I squeeze the phone tightly in my hands. No one deserves to be spoken to like this, especially not this bright, talented, young woman sitting in front of me.

I know exactly what she's feeling right now, I've felt it myself. She doesn't deserve this shit and that asshole sure as fuck doesn't deserve her.

I delete the messages from her phone as I stand up and walk around the desk and crouch down in front of her. I sit the phone down quietly as my heartbeat echoes in my ears and I reach my hands out—placing one on her knee and the other on the side of her face.

"Look at me, Lyla," I murmur.

She shakes her head no but I can hear her deep breaths rattling through her chest now.

"Please," I beg, my thumb brushing against her temple.

After another deep breath, she pushes her palms against her face as she slides them away to face me. Her eyes are bloodshot and wet streaks run down her cheeks. I use my thumb to wipe away the lone tear left in the corner of her eye and give her a soft smile. The long black lashes cover most of her eyes as she stares at the ground where I'm crouched. I slowly move my trembling hand down the side of her cheek and place it under her chin to lift her face to look into my eyes. I feel her sharp inhale as our eyes meet only inches apart.

"I know the pain you feel right now. I've felt it. You deserve far better than to be treated like someone's fallback plan. He didn't love you or he would never have been in a position for another woman to kiss him," I say. Her lips part as she assesses my words, but I'm not done yet. "You should be with someone that recognizes how incredibly talented, beautiful, hardworking, and intelligent you are. That person should want to worship the soil at your feet, to take on the responsibility of holding your heart, and follow you anywhere."

I almost expect her to slap me, which she would be right to do at this moment.

I take a deep breath as she blinks quickly, her eyes darting up and down my face. I stroke her bottom lip with my thumb softly sending a flutter through my chest. Sitting this close to her makes my cock feel like it's on fire, throbbing and pressing against the seam. I would do anything to wrap her in my arms right now if she were any other woman and it wasn't going to cost us both our future. As my eyes slowly move down the front of her body, she moves and wraps her hands behind my neck and in a split second, her lips are crashing onto mine.

Shocked and frozen in place, my mind explodes in a haze as she presses her lips harder against mine. I can taste the Scotch on her lips but I fight back a moan as she twists her hands into my hair. Her cheeks are still wet from crying and the throbbing in my groin is overpowering my ability to think straight. As quickly as she pulled me in, she pushes herself away before I have the chance to react—properly kissing her back.

"Oh my god, I'm so sorry," her hand covers her mouth. She runs out of the room before I can stop her because I'm still frozen in my place on the floor.

"Wait!" I finally yell, standing up to run after her, but she's already gone. Her footsteps have disappeared through the hall. I lean forward against the door, smacking my palm against it as my forehead pressed against the cool wood.

What the fuck just happened?

But no, she was just upset. She had been drinking. Maybe she hadn't meant to do that at all and was just reacting to the combination of those things and I was just the closest person to her at the time. Yes, that's it. She hates me, doesn't she? Sometimes the lines between hate and lust can get blurred, that's what happened here tonight. I trace my lips with my finger, smiling at the sight of a slight tint of pink lipstick coming off onto my skin.

Maybe she hates me, but that kiss sure didn't feel like it— at least not to me.

I scrape the bottom of my pint of Cherry Garcia Ben & Jerry's clean, licking the spoon dry, before tossing it into the trash can filled with the remnants of the junk food I have eaten for the past forty-eight hours. My apartment is filled with the scent of leftover pizza and fried chicken, pints of ice cream fill my freezer— all the worst foods for my body during the worst three days of my life.

I guess this is the kind of life I live now.

I fill a glass of water and return to my couch to continue my binge-watching of *The Vampire Diaries*, groaning at every swoon-worthy kiss and Damon's slew of innuendos. I could turn the show off, switch to something happier or less sexy, but I deserve to feel every ounce of shame and guilt and unhappiness after what I've done.

Was kissing Professor Moxley that big of a mistake?

That's an absurd thought, of course kissing him was a mistake. He's a professor first of all, and secondly, he gets under my skin and makes me angrier than anyone I've ever met in my life. Just because he said some nice things, gave me a few drinks, and helped me through a hard night doesn't make him a hero— it just makes him human. Tyson Moxley hates me as much as I hate him, human instinct beating out the rage at the world or not.

Hate and passion can walk hand in hand, leading to the best love story sometimes.

66

I ball my hands into fists as I pull my knees to my chest, watching yet another sex scene unfold on the screen. Water isn't going to erase this memory today, but wine might. I stand back up and go to my fridge.

Empty. Fuck.

If I want wine, I'm going to have to leave this apartment. I didn't intend on doing that until Monday at the earliest. Throwing myself back down on the couch, I find my phone—still on Do Not Disturb mode with only Tyler set to send anything through— I check the time. It's only shortly after one in the afternoon and there would still be plenty of time to come back and wallow in my misery if I leave right now.

Maybe I should go to the Natural History Museum, too. That always makes me feel better.

Now that isn't a bad idea. No one would be at the museum the day after Thanksgiving, which I had so luckily gotten to spend alone after the fiasco with Parker and choosing to skip out on Friendsgiving. With Parker and I sharing a group of friends since starting here, I hadn't felt inclined to put myself through the misery. The only friend that has always been solely my own is Lucy, but she had skipped classes this week and gone home to Alabama early.

I should tell Lucy what happened with Parker at least.

I hesitate, fingers hovering over the screen. I've only touched my phone long enough to wish my parents and brother a 'Happy

Thanksgiving' yesterday and had then immediately placed it back on the table, face down, to ignore. Tyson had done the decent thing and deleted the messages Parker sent me before handing me back my phone in his office, clearly not wanting me to torture myself by having to see them after leaving. I should thank him for that if he's willing to be within a classroom radius of me— or speak to me at all.

Screams emitted from the television as I watch the blood pour out of a body and chuckle at the fake effects. *Maybe getting some fresh air would do me some good if I'm laughing at death, even if it is fake.*

I mumble profanities to myself as I force myself down the hall to my bedroom and rustle through my closet to find something to wear. Past the point of talking myself out of leaving the apartment, I grab a set of red lace underwear from my dresser and slip into it as if sexy lingerie will improve my mood. I push my legs into a pair of black skinny jeans and a long-sleeve green shirt, quickly run a brush through my hair, and apply a light coat of mascara and lipstick. Pleased with my ability to look like I haven't spent three days crying and eating like shit, I slip into my black Vans and order an Uber from my phone. The crisp Texas autumn air hits me as I walk out the door, pausing to stand in a ray of sunshine to let my body soak in the warmth as I wait. I close my eyes, lifting my face towards the light, and spin in a circle—something is calming about the sunshine here that I never got in Washington.

68

A horn startles me, signaling the arrival of my car ,and I slide into the backseat as they say hello and take off towards the museum. The mesmerizing city buildings flash by through the window as I'm resting the side of my head against the panel. Choosing Houston over a college closer to home has always been my best chance at a future with a full scholarship, but feeling all alone in a big city will make anyone a little homesick.

No one back home is missing me, though. Mom and Dad are too busy with work these days and enjoying having even fewer responsibilities with Tyler and me both gone. Tyler and Cassie are settled into their new house, living a happy life as newlyweds. The friends I once had, gone.

Never, in all of my twenty-four years, have I ever felt so alone.

Perhaps that's why I let myself think differently of Professor Moxley, even if it was just a momentary lapse of judgment—for those few hours, I didn't feel quite so alone in the world.

"Here we are, ma'am," the driver says as we pull up to the front of the Natural History Museum. I slide out of the car with a quick "thanks" and head towards the large glass doors. The cold air inside the building sends a shiver down my body as I show my pass to the attendant and wander through the exhibits. I always save the paleontology exhibit for last, but after walking through the Pompeii and African Wildlife exhibits I just want to retreat to my first love— Dinosaurs.

Walking into the room and being surrounded by the large, fossilized specimens has a way of feeling like home.

One day, I want to discover an entirely new set of fossils. I want my work to be on display in a museum just like this and I want to contribute to the discovery of history.

"Miss Fischer?"

His deep, husky voice sends a chill down my spine as I stand frozen in place. My heart rattles my chest, a spark into my core.

What the fuck is he doing here?

"Lyla?" he says, his voice growing closer, his steps headed towards me.

I struggle to breathe, collecting myself into composure, and turn to look at him. His glorious figure stands there in a pair of dark wash jeans and a plain white shirt under a well-fitted black leather jacket. His thick, blonde hair frames his freshly shaven face. The sight of him sucking on his bottom lip serves as a memory of how soft his lips felt against my own, no trace of regret dances in my mind.

"Professor Moxley," I whisper.

The heat rises to my cheeks as he takes two steps closer to me. My heart pounds against my chest as I blink quickly and look back to the mountain of bones in front of me— immersing myself in focusing only on the smooth fossils instead of the chiseled man beside me.

"We're not in class-," he begins to say as I cut him off.

"I'm so sorry about what happened Wednesday!" I shout, my hands flying up to the sides of my face to hide the flush in my cheeks.

He chuckles, taking another step closer to me. I force my eyes down to stare at my shoes and pull at the hem of my sleeves, letting my hair fall in front of my face. My skin can sense how close he is and I feel the warmth in my cheeks spreading over my skin. He reaches a hand out and places it beneath my chin again as my stomach is filled with flutters. He pulls my chin up to look at him— *just like in his office before I stupidly kissed his beautiful face.*

"Don't be sorry, Lyla," he demands. "And we're not even on campus, so call me Tyson."

He winks, I gulp, and my knees weaken in place as I refrain from reaching to place his hand on the side of my face. His woodsy cologne is surrounding my nostrils and fogging my mind as I look into his deep, cerulean blue eyes. The dim light of the room makes them darker but I swear I see a flame resting in the expression on his face as he slowly licks his bottom lip.

"Okay, Tyson then," I murmur. "What are you doing here?"

Discerning the heartbeats in my chest from the butterflies wreaking havoc in my stomach becomes a chore, one solely to focus on as I watch the amusement flicker across his face.

Cocky, arrogant bastard is most likely enjoying fucking with my head. Trying to figure out the best way to humiliate me again or find a way to use it against me in the future. I said I was sorry, what else does he want from me?

71

Amid emotions, a trickle of anger begins to spread across my body as he takes his time in forming a response. So much time, that I huff and return my eyes to staring at the meticulously designed room filled with life-sized dinosaurs, his hand still resting on my cheek singing the skin with his warmth.

"Turns out that documentary we watched sparked my interest in dinosaurs, fossils, and how they could possibly be so fascinating," he replies, stroking his thumb across my cheekbone as he withdraws his hand. Though I hadn't wanted it in the first place, my body yearns for his touch again.

"Really? You're into all the environmental stuff but you didn't find fossils interesting?" I ask, an accusation bitter in my mouth.

He lets out a deep laugh as he shrugs.

"I guess you got me there," he says, leaning in closer to me, brushing the loose strands of hair behind my ear. His breath is hot against my ear as I squeeze my eyes shut and try to steady my heart, focusing solely on taking enough air in to fill my lungs. "Perhaps it was just the company that sparked an interest and I realized I had nothing to contribute to our conversation involving these species and was hoping to remedy that before our next time together."

Pain lingers in my ears from the sound of my heart pounding in them. My palms are clammy and my knees could give out any second, but I hold my body still as he takes a step back with a smirk on his face. With his eyebrow raised, daring me to make the next move, I straighten myself up and smirk.

Two can play this game, Tyson.

"Let's learn about dinosaurs, then," I say.

He holds his hand out in front of him, gesturing for me to lead the way. The feel of his eyes on my body as he walks behind me blazes through my clothes as if he's scouring every inch of me, and I stop at the Tyrannosaurus Rex collection.

"Behold, the most basic of all dinosaurs!" I exclaim, sending him into a rolling fit of laughter. "Today, you could find this dinosaur sporting a fashionable pair of UGG's while sipping on their favorite fall beverage."

For the first time in days, a genuine smile spreads across my face. We walk through the exhibit together, hands brushing against each other's and arms touching, as I rattle off interesting facts about each dinosaur—making a point to emphasize that the Triceratops is my favorite.

"How cool would it be to just headbutt someone when they piss you off?" I laugh.

Professor Moxley stops, reaching a hand out and grasping my arm. He pulls me closer to him and holds me in place as he stares at my face. His hand cups my jaw gently as his thumb traces my bottom lip, his eyes focused and filled with concern.

"Have you been crying again?" he asks.

I struggle out of his grasp, looking towards the display as I bite my lip. I'd done my best to hide the remnants of the weekend's bloodshot eyes before coming today, but not well enough.

Of course, I have, idiot. I kissed my professor the same day I caught my boyfriend cheating on me in a moment of weakness and then ran out of the room and now he's standing here in my favorite place in the city and the only thing I want to do is kiss him again no matter how wrong it is.

"You have, haven't you? That's why you won't look at me," he says. "Did that little shit say something else to upset you?"

I snap my eyes back and glare into his. His lips have pressed together into a thin line and I feel the heat from his grip on my arm. His narrowed eyes give a sense of sincerity to his concern and I laugh.

I fucking laugh so heartily that it consumes me with rage.

"Actually, no. He hasn't said a single goddamn word to me," I retort. "Not that I've given him the chance since my phone has been off since I got home Wednesday."

His face softens, his lips parting with a sorrowful glistening in his eyes— as though he's no longer plotting to murder a student. His head lowers as he takes another step towards me, I hold my stance firmly and let his chest brush against mine. With my chin held high, I bite the inside of my lip to keep the seething insults in my mind from being hurled at him.

"Were you crying because of what happened in my office?"

74

I nod, choking back the tears that instantly form in my eyes. I squeeze them shut as I wrap my free arm around my stomach, in the mere inches of space between us and my fingertips brush against his abs.

I should have just stayed home. This isn't how today was supposed to go. I should have just stayed in and on the couch until Monday.

"Why would you cry about that?" he asks, stroking my cheek with his knuckles. I feel him step close enough for my breasts to press against his jacket, my arm firmly stuck between us. His cologne swirls around my nose as I take another deep breath, inhaling every last drop.

"Because I... I shouldn't have done it," I manage to choke out. "It was wrong and out of character and you're just so damn gorgeous and I lost myself in the moment and-"

His lips crash against mine and I stumble backward, my arms falling to my sides— only to be caught by his hand around my waist. Every sense of right and wrong is tossed out the window and I yank him closer by the front of his jacket with one hand and intertwine the other fingers into his hair. His tongue slides across my bottom lip as my chest erupts in maddening, jolting pleasure and I part my mouth just enough to let it in. He swirls his tongue against mine, flicking the tip softly and I moan into his mouth. The hand he's slipped around my waist slowly slides down before slipping into the back pocket of my jeans.

"Does this feel wrong to you?" he murmurs through broken kisses, holding onto my face as I open my eyes to find him staring right into mine.

Instead of answering with words I can't form in the heat of this moment, panting with pent-up desire, I press my lips to his. His hand slides down my face, lightly tracing my neck with his fingertips and I lean my head back exposing more of the skin as his fingers curl into my hair holding it back. His lips lightly press against my collarbone and work their way up to my ear. Unable to move, gasping with pleasure and holding him to my skin with my fingers dug into his scalp—his hand snakes down the back of my neck, down my spine leaving a trail of heat where he's touched.

Panting and moaning, I twist my head to meet his mouth again and quickly force my tongue into his mouth. This time it's him that moans as his hands grasp my ass and lifts me into his arms, my legs wrapping around his waist in response. I clasp my hands behind his neck, burying my lips into his as he carries me through the room and into a dark corner, pressing my back against the wall.

"Dammit, Lyla," he growls, letting his hands dig into my skin.

I can feel the outline of his hardness against my hip as we're pressed so tightly together, forcing myself to restrain from my need to throw my head back and beg for more. With my hand sliding down the front of his chest, finding a hardened set of abs where my fingers land, I feel my wetness throbbing inside my jeans. I slip my hand

76

under his shirt against his heated skin and trace the pattern of his muscles. His sharp inhale as my cold hands touch his skin sends a heightened wave of desire through my throbbing wetness.

"Tyson," I moan.

"I've got you, baby," he whispers, his teeth nipping the delicate skin of my neck, his panting in sync with my own.

"This is…," I gasp, his mouth brushing against my sweater on my breasts. My thighs squeeze tighter, pressing us closer together.

"This is what?" he whispers, gently biting my nipple through my sweater, waves of passion burn through my body as I pull him closer. "Is this not what you want?"

I struggle to breathe, gasping for air through the thick heat around us. His lips work their way back up my neck, nibbling and biting as each touch makes my need for him increase.

"No, I don't know…," I say, and then his teeth press down on my bottom lip as he chuckles. "Fuck, Yes. Yes, I want this. God, I want this."

Her confession, the desire rippling through her moans, fails my restraint. The room around us disappears, all that matters is us— the hunger we clearly feel for each other.

Lyla's fingers drag across the waistband of my jeans, my hardened groin pressing against the fabric as she smiles behind our kiss. I hold her firmly against the wall with one hand still on her firm ass in the pocket of her jeans. I squeeze gently as my free hand wanders up the inside of her shirt to her soft stomach—the moans from taking her nipple in my mouth through her shirt still echo in my head. Our hearts pounding in rhythm and the taste of her in my mouth is quickly spiraling out of control. I want her— no, not just want— my body needs her.

I suck on her bottom lip before sitting her feet down on the floor, stepping back from her as I gasp, shaking my head to erase the fog, and attempt to control my urges. She stays pressed against the wall with her eyes closed, her mouth hanging open with one arm having fallen to her side limply— the other still resting in the waistband of my pants. A reminder of how far I let the situation go. Her chest is heaving in search of air as I reach out, pushing her hair behind her ear and grazing my nose along the side of her neck. The struggle in my mind, the war in my heart—they rage on, a battle of right and so fucking wrong. I'm not sated yet, I still need more of her—all of her. Wrong wins. I nibble on her earlobe before whispering into her ear.

"You never gave me a chance to kiss you back the other night," I whisper. Her breath is hot against my neck and I take a deep breath, inhaling her floral perfume as it mixes with my musk. "You should probably remove your hands from my pants, Miss Fischer, before someone gets the wrong idea."

She rips her hand away, shrugging as her face flushes red, and the corners of my mouth turn upwards. She peers up through her lashes with needy, hungry eyes as she bites her lip again. I can't resist that fiery gaze, not that I'm trying very hard. I suck in a deep breath and press my body against hers again. I lightly press my lips on hers and drag them down her jawline and neck before she leans in, grasping my hair in her hands, and pulls my ear to her lips.

"Maybe I want to give them the wrong idea," she whispers.

"Fuck," I mumble, the uncomfortable tightness in my pants is making it hard to be rational.

I tangle my hand in her hair and pull her lips back to mine urgently, pressing her harder against the wall as she desperately moans into my mouth. Thrusting my tongue through her soft, open lips and swirling the tip against hers, I nip her bottom lip once and pull away. She quickly puts her hand directly against my erection and squeezes, her eyes blazing. An exasperated moan leaves my throat, my breaths short and unfulfilling.

"Christ, Lyla," I growl. "What are you doing?"

When I look at her face again, a smug smile forms on her lips. Her hand wanders, rubbing her palm down the front of my hardness and squeezing the inside of my thigh. My pounding heart rattles my core, leaving my mind to irrationally want more. I grab her hand and push it back to the wall, her eyes widening as she gasps. My chest heaves, panting as I hold her back and force myself back to my senses. The longer I let this go on, the harder it will end up being to stop and if I want her—ever, at all— this isn't where it will happen. Brushing my lips up her neck, nuzzling my nose against the delicate skin I whisper into her ear.

"Not here," I say.

She rips her hand from my hold, balling it into a fist as she squares her shoulders. Her eyes pierce mine with rage and desire. I know I've pissed her off—again. I hold her waist, gently pulling her into my arms, and feel her turn to stone at my touch. My heart sinks, desperately wishing that we were anywhere but this museum, in public.

"Lyla, we can't do this," I whisper, pressing my lips into her hair. "Definitely not here."

"Fine, then let me go," she demands, using her hand to push between us, forcing me away from her.

I try to pull her back to me but she twists herself out of my grasp and glares back at me with a murderous look. She inhales a deep

80

breath, her shoulders rising as she composes herself and runs her fingers through her hair. I grimace, waiting for her to start screaming at me and wondering which name she'll call me today. I deserve whatever she chooses, I'll let her scream at me until her throat is hoarse and I can haul her out of here, take her somewhere more private to finish what we've begun. Instead of screaming, yelling, or even speaking to me, she lifts her hand and wiggles her fingers as she waves goodbye with narrowed eyes. As she stalks away with an exaggerated sway in her hips, I run a hand through my hair and clasp the back of my head.

Should I chase after her?

Her black hair bounces against her back as she turns the corner out of the exhibit. Without any more hesitation, I turn on my heels to sprint after her. Catching up to her quickly, I grab her shoulder and spin her around to me. Her amber eyes are brimming with tears as she covers her mouth with her hands, shaking her head in defense.

"Lyla-," I start, but she shakes her head faster.

"Just let me go," she pleads. "I'm sorry, just please let me go."

Tears fall from her eyes but instead of reaching up to wipe them away, I pull her into my chest and wrap my arms around her. I nuzzle my face into her hair as she sobs against my chest.

How many times am I going to make this poor woman cry?

"Lyla, please," I plead. "Let me explain, for once just let me fucking explain, instead of running from me."

She twists, pushing herself out of my embrace, and glares at me, fury burning in her eyes. Her hands are balled into fists at her sides and I hold my hands up in surrender. Again, I've let myself lose control of the situation and she's back on the defensive.

"What on earth is there to explain?" she whispers, angrily. Her body shudders with every word. "I'm a student, you're a professor, this is all a load of shit that can't happen, and it never should have, right? Tell me I'm wrong."

"You're not wrong.... dammit," I whisper, "But that isn't why I said not here!"

She sucks in her lips, crossing her arms in front of her as she waits for me to continue.

"I said not here because we're in a fucking museum. We're in public. Public nudity is a felony, Miss Fischer," I hiss, my face inching closer to hers with every word. "I said not here because I don't feel like having to explain ourselves to the police. Not once did I say not at all because you felt exactly what you did to me, dammit. You have no fucking idea how badly I want to throw all common sense and reasoning out the window and bury myself in you against a wall right here, right fucking now.

"I had to force myself not to chase after you on Wednesday, knowing there was still a good chance of another faculty member being in the building, and the idea of you running out of there that upset with me has killed me since," the honesty spills out of me as her

82

eyes widen. "Lyla, you kissing me ignited a fire that I haven't felt in a very long fucking time and I quite honestly do not give a damn if it's wrong in anyone else's eyes because I refuse to deny how right it feels. If you don't feel that—want that—then fine. Go. I won't stop you."

I clasp my hands behind my neck, squeezing my fingers tightly together as she mulls over what I just said. My heart is pounding as I watch her face soften and then turn into a frown. She takes a deep breath and steps forward, pressing her lips against my cheek.

"Goodbye, Tyson," she whispers, turning around and walking away through the exhibit.

"Are you serious?!" I call after her.

"I'm going home."

"After all that I just said, that's all you have to say? Nothing else?" I growl, walking faster to keep up with her. She stops but doesn't turn around to face me so I halt my steps, shoving my hands in my pocket instead of reaching for her.

"You just dumped a shit load of confusing bullshit on me, Tyson," she seethes. "I got cheated on, my relationship ended, and I kissed my unattainable, closed off, asshole of a boss all within the same day— just for that same asshole to show up here, now ruining my favorite place in this city, and spill his usually closed off heart out to me. Excuse me if I'm a little fucking overwhelmed right now."

She continues walking, never once looking back at me over her shoulder. As I watch her disappear out of sight, it dawns on me just how far I let it go today. I never once intended for this to happen, I never planned to kiss her—hell I hadn't even expected to see her. Seeing her in her element and the joy in her eyes when she talked about the different species and fossils, it just hit me how desirable she is. Being with Lyla had been easy and the first time I had enjoyed myself and the company of another person in many, many years—I let that rule out any logical part of my brain.

Suddenly, everything that is wrong with our situation doesn't matter anymore because the other part of our story that matters is how we feel about each other—and my inability to control how I feel about Miss Lyla Fischer, is dangerous for us both.

The first half of this week has gone by in a blur. Monday was so overwhelming with needing to play catch up during Professor Moxley's class and our office hours —which I did not sit in his office for— that I barely had time to think about what happened at the museum. Tuesday I found myself filled with regret, thinking that I should apologize for being so forward, but alas changed my mind. He had come strutting into his office with his hair back in a tight bun, his thick tortoiseshell glasses, and crisp black pants that hugged him in all the right places— suddenly I had felt no remorse because I was in fact, not sorry for my behavior. Wednesday, again, was a day filled with catch-up between the lecture hall and office hours. He invited me to sit in his office so that we could go over the exam together but I feigned a need to recheck a group of pop quizzes, a feeble attempt to avoid him.

Now, it's Thursday and I'm sitting in my Foundations of Anthropology Theory class daydreaming about how I would love nothing more than to feel his lips against mine again. Chewing on the end of my pen, I let my mind wander down a dangerous path of dreams.

His lips, his hands, his tongue... His chiseled abs uncovered, my naked breasts pressing against his chest. His tongue swiping over my stiffened nipples...

I shudder as I imagine his tongue against that sensitive area. My cheeks grow hot, flushed from the idea of him. The memory of his touch sends a tingling jolt through my body, focusing on my throbbing wetness.

Stop, office hours are too soon after this class. You can't be thinking about this or he'll see it written all over your face.

I squeeze my thighs together in my seat, wiggling to relieve some of the needed friction as my mid-seventies professor drones on about Cultural Anthropology. I've already completed this course but a second completion is necessary for my Master's Degree. I feel a twinge of sorrow for the first-time students that are holding on to his every word, blissfully unaware that they'll be right back here within a few years— if they're anything like me. Poor Professor Timmins has been using the same coursework and exams for the past fifteen years and I don't see that changing until they hire someone to replace him.

What seems like hours later, he finally dismisses us as he glances at the clock and realizes he's gone over our allotted time by fifteen minutes— again. I throw my notebook into my bag and hightail it through the building, stopping at a food truck for a quick dinner and arrive at Professor Moxley's office only three minutes early for office hours. He's already seated behind his desk but peers through the doorway at me as I confidently strut across the room and toss my bag where my chair should have been— if only I had been paying more attention to realize it wasn't there. As my bag lands with a thud on the floor in the space my chair usually is, I cringe hoping my laptop didn't take the impact. Professor Moxley lets out a deep laugh from inside his office. I freeze, glaring at the spot where I usually sit without bending over to grab my bag and shallow breaths heave through my chest. Biting the inside of my cheek, I know he's trying to find another way to get under my skin—a power trip move to keep me close to him.

"Where the hell is my chair?" I shriek, my body shaking angrily as my hands balled into fists as my nails dig into the skin.

The sound of his chair pushing out from under himself echoes through the room, footsteps growing louder as he stalks around the corner of his desk, and leans against the door frame. His cologne follows him, announcing his presence before I turn around to look at him.

"Why don't you come and look?" he laughs, gesturing into his office with a smirk so wide on his face I would love nothing more than to smack it right off his perfectly structured jawline.

What a sight that would be, my perfect handprint across his neatly shaven face today.

I cross my arms, raising a dramatic brow, and lean against the side of my desk with no intention to go any closer to him. My fingertips drum along my bicep, the silk fabric of my shirt soft beneath them. My tongue presses against my teeth, sending searing pain through it as I hold my stance, refusing to give in to his *charm.*

I bet he would love it if I slapped him. He seems like the kind of guy that would be into that sort of thing. Maybe I should try it and see what happens.

He snickers again, raising his brow to match my challenge and using his entire hand this time to attempt to wave me into his office — where I assume my chair is now taking up residency.

"Where is my damn chair, Professor?" I ask, more sternly this time. He shrugs, his smirk turning into a full smile. He looks elated with how this is panning out, as though he's baiting me into another argument. I swear, that man must get off on pissing the world around him off.

"Why, Miss Fischer," he retorts, "I am unsure of which chair you seem to be missing exactly, or how one misplaces their chair, but as it turns out," he steps aside letting me peer past him into his office, "there seems to be an extra one in here you're welcome to work at tonight."

"No," I seethe. "I'd rather stand all fucking night than work in there."

He tilts his head, stepping towards me as my nails dig into the skin under my shirt. My lips are pressed into a narrow line, the heat of anger ripples through my veins as I take shallow breaths, avoiding succumbing to the scent of his cologne.

"Suit yourself, Miss Fischer," he whispers, leaning in close enough to let his lips brush my ear.

With a wink, he turns around and heads back behind his desk— returning his attention solely to the papers in front of him.

"Fuck you," I mumble under my breath. Angrily, I grab my bag off the floor and stomp into his office—feeling like a toddler having a tantrum the entire time. Stopping at the threshold, I place my bag down gently on the floor inside the door and cross my arms again.

"I'm not working in here unless you tell me why you want me all up in your personal space to begin with," I demand.

I watch as his shoulders move up and down as he lets out a deep sigh, placing his head into the palm of his hands as his elbows rest on the edge of his desk. He runs his hands through his hair, slowly leaning back into his chair and I notice every stretch of the fabric against his chest and biceps. I bite my lip, knowing where my mind will wander, again, if I let it— which I'm trying hard not to.

Stay strong, you can do this.

"Miss Fischer, perhaps I just thoroughly miss your company as we work so well together in the evenings," he says, pinching the bridge of his nose.

"You're an asshole."

"That does seem to be your favorite name for me, lately," he retorts. "Maybe you should come up with a new one soon. That one is getting predictable and just doesn't sting anymore."

I fight hard to keep my face like stone, refusing to let the corners of my mouth turn upwards as he fires off his remarks. This has become a fun game, seeing how far one of us can go before the other loses their shit.

"Maybe it wouldn't be necessary to use that name—or any others—at all if you ever did anything worth removing it from my vocabulary."

His eyes squeeze shut, jerking his neck to each side. Amusement spreads through my insides, watching him squirm as I hurl insults at him.

"Lyla, please, stop," he begs. "I was trying to have a nice evening. I just want to work with you tonight, please."

"You're joking right?" I scoff. "We hardly ever get along, let alone work 'so well together'," I use finger quotes as I reiterate his words back to him as my lips press into a thin line.

"Dammit, Lyla. Just sit down," he yells, slamming his hand on his desk. Startled, I straighten up, my eyes widening at his outburst, and walk slowly towards the chair, sitting carefully as I hold my breath. He takes a deep breath, leaning forward on his desk as his eyes soften in apology. "I'm sorry, fuck I'm so sorry. I didn't mean to yell. I just do, in fact, miss your company."

"Are you sure that's all you miss?" I tease, not ready to let him off the hook that easily. "I'm not in the mood to be feigning niceties, Professor Moxley."

His eye roll would usually send me into a fit of laughter, but not tonight. Turns out I'm not only hot for a professor but I'm also

90

irate and begging to piss him off enough to send him into a hate-filled passionate lovers quarrel this evening.

"Dammit, you are absolutely infuriating," he says, shaking his bowed head. "You know that, right?"

"And what are you going to do about it?" I murmur leaning forward on the edge of the desk.

His head snaps up, eyes blazing as they move from my eyes down to my lips. He takes his bottom lip in between his teeth as he squeezes the edge of his desk with his hands so hard his knuckles turn white. In a swift movement, he pushes himself back from his desk and with a few large strides he's right next to me and I'm on my feet ready to face off with him. My heart thunders in my chest as my skin tingles from the deep inhalation of his cologne trickling through my senses. My nails dig into my palms again as I brace myself for the words about to spew from his mouth.

To my surprise, he takes a deep breath as he places his hands on my hips and I gasp as he pulls me towards him. There's no way he can't feel the thundering beat of my heart through my breast pressed firmly against his chest—the mental image of us naked that I created in class today starts playing in my head. I peer up through my lashes as he presses his forehead against mine and sighs. Wrapping one arm around my waist, he lifts his other hand and traces it down the side of my face before cupping his hand under my chin. His fingertips leave a

91

trail of warmth where they have touched— liquifying my insides in the process.

"If you don't want me to kiss you, now would be the time to speak up," he whispers, his breaths shallow and quick.

I gulp, reaching a hand up the backside of his neck, and firmly tangle my fingers into his hair as I take a deep breath. I let my lips brush the side of his jawline, feeling his body stiffen at my touch. I gently bite down on his earlobe before loosening my grip on his hair.

"I don't want you to kiss me," I whisper into his ear.

Startled, I drop my hands from Lyla and take a step back as she loosens her grip on my neck. The heat of her flesh against my own and the way her nails were digging into my hair lingers on my skin. Mouth askew, I stare into her eyes looking for a glimmer of hope but all I can see is pain and sadness, hollow eyes void of happiness. The rims of her eyes are red and beginning to water as she sucks her bottom lip in between her teeth. I reach my hand to brush the sole tear running down her cheek away, but her hand swats mine as she shakes her head defensively.

"I can't do this, Tyson," she whimpers. "I may be able to confidently hurl insults at you and push your buttons, welcoming any challenge you throw at me, but I'm not the same person that I thought I could be at the museum."

Her head drops as she focuses solely on her shoes, tapping her flats against the tile floor of the office. She crosses her arms around her chest, wrapping them around her as if they are a shield and she's ready for battle— but I'm not here to fight her.

Perhaps if I could only fight my feelings for her we wouldn't be in this situation, to begin with. If only I had kept my mouth to myself in the museum this would be a different scene playing out tonight.

Seeing her pain, it breaks something inside of me that I didn't know was still there. My throat tightens as I watch her, feeling the distance between us spread further than the few physical feet.

93

"What do you mean you're not the same person?" I ask, dreading the answer.

She takes a few deep breaths before quickly wiping her cheeks with the back of her hand and meets my gaze with a furrowed brow.

"I mean I'm not the kind of person that takes this kind of a risk, Tyson. I don't choose the bad guy, I don't walk the line of right and wrong. I do the right thing, I get the best grades, and I have always had a plan for my future," she shakes her hair over her shoulder, lifting her chin. "I assure you that I am not some astronomical slut that regularly tries to take off a man's clothes in public, especially not a man that is as far from attainable as one could be. Most importantly, I don't sleep with assholes," she declares. The corner of my mouth lifts slightly at her confession, part of me wanting to remind her about Mr.Bennet being far more of an asshole by cheating on her than I have ever been—but not here, not right now.

"Miss Fischer, I can assure you that the thought of you being anything less than a proper woman has never crossed my mind," I tell her. "As for the rest of it, I never expected that I would be the kind of person that would take this risk either. I never used to be. I haven't felt anything for another woman, like I said before, in a very long time. This is a shitty situation to say the least, but we can either figure out how to navigate it together or we both deny what we're feeling and walk away."

Her lips press into a thin line as she mulls this over. She opens her mouth a few times, closing it abruptly before forming the correct words. The seconds pass slowly as I let her weigh the options in her mind, on her own terms. This isn't only about me, it has to be her choice.

"I'm not the type of person that just climbs into someone who, essentially, is a stranger's bed without getting to know them first. I'm not saying I'm a prude, but I can count the number of partners I have had on one hand and I will not sell myself short."

I beam with pride as I watch her cheeks flush. My heart flutters while my groin twitches in approval in her blush.

This woman will be the absolute death of me.

"Sit down, Lyla," I instruct, my voice gentle, gesturing towards the still empty chair with a smile. "Let's break the rules again tonight." She stands there, her eyes fixated on me as I walk around the desk and pull the restocked bottle of scotch from my bottom drawer, setting the two glasses out once again.

"I'm…. erm, not sure….. that's a great idea," she chuckles, still standing as she watches me. "Turns out I make bad decisions where scotch is involved."

A profound laugh bellows out from my chest as I fill the first glass for myself.

"I assure you, Lyla, no funny business will happen for the rest of the evening and I will even cut you off after two glasses if need be."

95

She nods, I pour her glass a couple of inches full and slide it towards her, watching as she sits down slowly. Leaning back in my chair, I prop my feet on the corner of the desk and take a small sip from my glass. Lyla erupts in a fit of giggles watching me let loose.

"What the hell are you doing?" she asks, covering her mouth with her hand as she doubles over.

"Tonight, I want to just be your friend. I want you to feel comfortable with me, Lyla. I'm happy to be an open book if that's what you need," I raise my glass to her. "Ask me anything your golden heart desires and I will answer honestly."

She cocks her head to the side, her brow furrows as she raises the glass to her lips, sipping slowly as she taps a finger on the outside of the glass.

"Why?"

"Why what, Lyla?"

"Why do you want me to get to know you?" she asks sternly. "What is the point of this?"

Because I can't imagine not having you after coming so close.

I can't imagine losing you.

I can't see you cry, not again.

"Because I don't want you to feel as though I'm a stranger, Lyla. I'm drawn to you in a way that is entirely new to me and it scares me a little, not being able to control it. I respect you as not only a colleague but a person. I owe you this much if I ever want the chance to explore this complex chemistry between us."

Her brow tightens, furrowing closer together as she sets her glass back on the table, crossing her legs and resting her elbows on the exposed skin of her tanned knees.

"You don't owe me anything," she says. "But I like this game, sounds like a good chance to see what's underneath the asshole's stone-cold exterior. It's been a long week and to be honest, I don't much feel like working so I'll play along under one condition."

"Name your price, Lyla."

"We have to take turns asking questions."

This is going to cross a line somehow, but whatever she wants is what I'll work with.

"Do you want to count asking why I want you to get to know me as your first question or should we start now?" I ask, playfully.

"We'll start now, that was just a clarification question about what the hell is going on," she smiles. "Why did you decide to start teaching?"

I wince.

Ouch, going straight to the deep shit. Not even a transparent favorite color or food question first.

"Teaching was never really my plan, but practicing law didn't work out the way I had planned after some unfortunate events," I pause, trying to gauge a reaction across her blank expression. "At the time, I was pretty bummed and I can't say that the first few years of students I had were given my full potential, but after time I settled into a routine and it fell into place," I felt myself go into a mindless haze as images of my drunken outburst in court following the affair and Ivy's childhood room after collecting dust during my supervised visitation. I shake the thought out of my mind, inhaling sharply as I continue. "There's an exhilarating feeling when a student comes back or sends a letter years later acknowledging a lesson you've taught and they have used in their career."

Lyla lifts her glass to her lips slowly, processing the extensive line I've just given her as I hold a forced smile, hoping she doesn't press into the subject of the unfortunate events. Some things are meant to be left in the past.

"It's your turn," Lyla says.

"What do you miss about Washington?"

"Wow, that was quick to think of," she jokes, a soft smile spreading her lips as she peers around the room. She's quiet for a few minutes, I watch as she looks lost in her thoughts before shaking her head with a laugh. "I think I miss the trees the most, honestly. Everything here is so flat, or it's just an expansive stretch of massive buildings."

She shrugs, taking another sip as I wait for her to continue— or ask me a new question.

"Don't get me wrong, I love Texas. This was my dream school because the opportunities to be selected for a dig trip are far more extensive being this close to South America, where most of them happen these days. I love that there is sunshine almost every single day, but I do miss the cooler weather back in Washington."

That's it? There's no missing family or anyone important back home worth mentioning?

"Why did you choose to teach Environmental Law?" she asks.

"That's easy," I say. "As you are interested in finding out more about the history of our planet, I am equally as interested in preserving it for the future generations."

"I didn't realize we had so much in common," she chuckles. "Why did you not mention a person, or place, when I asked what you miss about Washington?" I ask her, unable to refrain from my curiosity.

Waiting patiently, I sip from my glass as she chews on her lip.

"I need to preface my answer by saying I have a great family, I really do, but having parents that show up when you need them and having parents that only provide are two different things. I had the latter. They worked and they provided and we had everything under the sun we could ever want, besides our parents' love and affection. My brother moved to Rhode Island the same year I moved here, to Texas," she divulges information, articulately as if she's never spoken of her family before. I lean forward, hanging on to her every word,

99

reassuring her that I'm just as invested in this conversation as she is, that every piece of her past is important. "Sometimes I go home for the holidays, but it's usually more of a hassle to coordinate around their schedules. They're in the business of luxury real estate sales and they have always believed people to be more generous and ready to buy around holidays, so I just visit my brother instead or hang out here."

She shrugs, taking a sip from the now close to empty glass, and slides it back to me. I open the bottle, pour it half full, and close the bottle before sliding it back to her.

"I don't have daddy issues if that's what you're thinking in that beautiful head of yours," She gasps as the words come out, covering her mouth with a hand behind a fit of giggles.

I laugh, genuinely and deeply, along with her.

"As good as that is to know," I chuckle, "that is entirely not what I was thinking."

She smiles, tilting her head to the side as the flush in her cheeks disappears.

"What did you do before you became a professor?"

"I worked at my father's firm in Dallas as a partner, but it didn't work out long term," my response is brash, my voice cooling at the recollection of my time there.

Lyla remains calm, collected as she ponders, her lips pursing slightly. My hands clench as I force the memories away.

100

"Where would your dream dig trip land you?" I ask, curiously but desperate to change the subject.

"Argentina, hands down," she says with a smile so wide I can see both rows of her teeth. "Between the dig sites and the rainforest, there would never be a dull day throughout my career. Not to say I won't eventually want to settle down, but I have a list of things I want to have done with my life before that."

A piece of my heart feels as though it's been turned to ice as she rattles on about her list and what she wants to do before she settles down in life.

Because while she's full of hopes and dreams, I've already lived that part of my life and I'm past that, but am I ready to settle down — again? Will I ever be at that point?

"Would you ever want to go to Argentina, Tyson?" she asks, her eyes ablaze as the scotch begins to flush her skin.

"Is that your question, Lyla?" I murmur.

She nods, smirking as she leans against the desk.

"I would, actually," I reply. "I've been to Europe, to Canada. I've been to Mexico and Russia. I love a new adventure."

A little adventure never hurts anyone.

"That's good to know," she murmurs, shooting a sultry gaze in my direction.

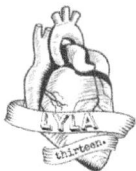

Heat glides through my veins— whether that's from the amber liquid in my glass or my body absorbing the information that Professor Tyson Moxley would enjoy my dream of Argentina. I watch as his muscles expand the fabric of his shirt, lifting the glass to his lips with a sly smile as he watches my every move. I'm suddenly very aware of his eyes on my face, my skin, and my body. My chest begs for air as it's all escaped my lungs and I'm reeling in shock— enough to forget to take a short breath.

"I want to pass on my next question," I say, needing to recollect myself. "I'll take two questions later."

He nods, understanding without any explanation—the way he's looking at me right now, knowing that I'm a mirror image back at him, it explains itself.

"How did you end up as my TA this semester," he asks. "Why not assist someone within the Anthropology Department?"

I chew my bottom lip. Knowing how the last few months have panned out, I would bet that it was fate rather than my forgetfulness that brought us together.

I don't think that is the answer he is looking for though, fate— he's a grown man, he doesn't possibly believe in fate.

"Honestly, Professor, I'm here because literally no one else wanted to be and I was out of the country until right before the term started and I was assigned to you," I let out a sigh. "It makes me

102

sound unprepared and like I didn't have my shit together, but I merely forgot to send in my request to work only within the Anthro or History departments and ended up here. Not that I'm not grateful, you're a brilliant professor and this has been a great experience."

His feet drop from the desk as he turns his chair to lean in closer to me, reaching a hand out before quickly withdrawing it— as if he had wanted to place it on my hand, or arm.

"Sounds like we were meant to find each other, Lyla," he winks. "Fate, even, some might say."

My heart erupts, thundering so violently in my chest I feel as though I've run a marathon. My palms are clammy as I attempt to pick my glass up to shyly take a sip but sit it down in fear of dropping what is likely an expensive crystal.

"Do you believe in fate, Professor Moxley?" I squeak.

"Is that your question, Lyla?" he murmurs, leaning in closer.

He promised no more funny business or touching tonight.

I squeeze my thighs together as I stare into his soft, cerulean eyes behind his thick-rimmed glasses. A strand of hair has fallen from behind his ears and my fingers tingle with desire to push it back, to feel his soft skin against mine again. I nod, unable to form a coherent sentence.

"Yes," he smirks, "I do believe in fate. I believe there is always a larger reason that the universe pushes people together," His eyes look away, lost and empty for a moment before continuing, "or even away."

The room feels small. I feel as though I've been lifted from my body and I'm staring down at this scene unfolding in front of me. Not only is Professor Moxley, Tyson, a grown man with an understanding of the law and a passion for the environment— he's also one with his spirituality and beliefs that more than just our actions affect our everyday life.

This is the kind of man you savor, the kind of man you spend every waking moment with, and enjoy every second of it.

"Do you resent your parents for not being more involved in your life?"

His question startles me, an unexpected and very personal shift in direction. I lick my lips, tasting the bitter scotch on them as I debate over his question. We agreed to be honest, open books—but I don't know an honest answer.

"Tyson, I truly don't know how to answer that question," I whisper.

"Try, please," he says, his eyes pleading with mine. My throat feels dry as I swallow, nodding my head.

"I don't think that I resent them, not anymore. Maybe I did when I was a kid, never having my parents there to cheer me on at a competition or hearing their applause at the honor class dinners. The other students would run for their families, be embraced with open

104

arms, and showered with flowers and balloons, but I was always alone," I admit, tears brimming the rims of my eyes. "When we got older, Tyler would make an effort to be there for me when he could, but I always felt like I was taking away his free time. It wasn't his responsibility to be our parent but he took on that role once he was old enough to realize we didn't have any. I guess I just got to a place along the road that I stopped wishing they would show up, learned to be proud of myself, and not give a shit about the other kids and their happy families."

This time, he doesn't hesitate when he reaches his hand out and places it on my forearm, the gentle touch sending a surge of electricity through my body. I quickly wipe my tears away with the sleeve of my shirt, choking them back down in my throat as I meet his eyes again. He looks sad, his own eyes wide and remorseful— enough that I feel the desire to walk around the table and wrap him in my arms. He probably wouldn't stop me, even though he should.

"I just can't imagine," he mumbles, "I can't imagine having a child and not desiring to be a part of every aspect of their life."

His voice drops at the end as he blinks quickly, refocusing on a painting on the wall behind me.

"Do you want more kids, Tyson?" I blurt out, covering my mouth, again, from my word vomit once again as my cheeks burn. "I mean, I know you have Ivy since we talked about it in class but did you ever want more?"

105

"Lyla, I'm not sure how to answer that, but, as we are being completely honest tonight and you already know that I have a sixteen-year-old daughter, I'll try, " he says, resting his face in the palm of his hand and turning a picture frame towards me. I'm met with a picture of a stunning blonde perched in front of the Eiffel Tower, clearly the real one, with her hair in a high ponytail. There is no denying the resemblance between her facial features and Tyson's. I gasp, looking between the picture and the contorted pain in his now scrunched together face. "I met Ivy's mother in high school, in our sophomore year, and was head over heels for her. I was the son of a rich lawyer growing up and it had never felt like the people around me cared about me— but at the time I thought she did. We became inseparable. She fell pregnant with Ivy when we were nineteen and I proposed immediately. I thought I was doing the right thing." He sighs, shaking his head in his hand before running the hand up through his hair and gripping the back of his neck. "My parents, they helped us out a lot. They made sure we attended our classes and got a further education, selfishly because my father wanted me to take over one of his practices one day."

"What happened?" I whisper.

And do I even want to know?

"I thought we were happy, but my job left little time for life at home. She grew unhappy with me but relished in the life of high society living. She had an affair with her personal trainer when Ivy

106

was six and left, taking almost everything with her— including our daughter, spinning the situation in her favor and ending my relationship with my parents as well. There was never a chance to think about having more kids with Sloan and I haven't been in any form of a relationship since. So, to answer your question honestly, I don't know if I would want more kids at this point in my life. It would be a bridge to cross if there was ever a time to cross it."

It was my turn to reach out and take his hand, rubbing circles with my thumb against the corner of his hand in comfort. It takes all of my willpower this time to not walk around the desk and sit on his lap, to pull him closer to me, and allow his pain to become my own.

"Please, don't think lower of me because of my past, Lyla," he begs. The pleading is clear in his eyes as he holds my gaze. "I may not have handled that situation with delicacy, I screwed up more than once in those first years following the divorce but I have tried to be the best father I can be to my daughter in the time I am allotted with her. I love my daughter, Lyla," the sight of him fighting back tears breaks my heart. Watching this man crumble, thinking that I could ever think less of him for something in his past that was not even his fault, shines a light on how deep the feelings I've pushed down have come to be. "Ivy has been my everything for so long, and I never let myself feel anything real for someone since Sloan left."

I nod, unsure of what I should say with this revelation. A part of me thinks this is his way of confessing that he has real feelings for me, but a small part also wonders if the desire to feel close to someone only runs skin deep.

Why would he entertain me with these raw, honest answers if he wasn't finally ready for something more?

As if reading my mind, he begins again.

"I can't begin to explain myself and my actions over the years, Lyla. I've become hard and cold towards others but then you came along and challenged me. You've brought out a fire that has been out for so long inside of me. Perhaps not always in the best way," he winks, "but this, what I feel when I'm with you, I want to keep it."

"I want it too, Tyson," I admit. "I don't know what it is, but I want it."

He smiles, picks up his glass, and downs the rest of his scotch as I watch, astonished and intimidated.

Can I be the right person to put the broken pieces of him back together? Or will we just end up destroying each other in the process?

My thighs ache, feet burning as I pound against the moving platform of the treadmill trying to calm myself from the evening in the office with Miss Fischer— Lyla. She hadn't gone easy on me as I had expected, not even a little bit. She had asked the hard questions— the future, the past, my hopes, marriage, kids. Instead of reeling back in after my confession over Ivy, she spoke extensively with me about how each piece of the past creates our future. Lyla spoke as if she has lived a thousand lives— each more meaningful than the next. If we had met in passing at the museum and she had spoken with such wisdom, such knowledge, I would have melted in place. Never, not in all my years, has anyone been able to surprise me as much as she continues.

I wipe the sweat from my forehead, pushing the loose locks of hair back as they stick to my skin. I'd stuck to my word, never once touching her more than a soft brush of the hand; a warm touch when she touched on a particularly sore subject matter. Learning that her parents were as involved in her life as mine provided common ground, something to further bond over. While mine may have cared more while I was younger, my failed marriage and career have long since lost the majority of their respect towards me. Lyla spoke highly of her brother, Tyler, who lives in Rhode Island and spends most of her holidays with him. She spoke of her dreams to travel, discover— but most of all, to continue to learn.

Her ambitions in life are not ones small enough to be bottled and stored away for a future time because each day, every fucking day, she is taking strides to fulfill them. She thinks of her future—not everyone else around her— first, a characteristic I have long admired and so rarely found. A woman that knows not only what she wants out of life but how she plans to achieve it, that's a woman worth pursuing.

She's a student, it's still wrong, but fuck. It's worth it, she is worth it.

When we spoke of Sloan, she didn't shy away or show any sign of discomfort— as if it was a pain she knew as well. Her eyes remained soft and inviting as I spilled, perhaps too many, details of our past. How Sloan had been the apple of my eye, I had been smitten and felt loved in return, of the years we spent tangled in a web of what I can now see was full of greed and unhappiness. She reached for me, she held my hand as I opened up, for the first time to anyone, about the end of our marriage— the affair. She was kind as I explained wholeheartedly how the end of my career came from my wrongdoings as I coped with the loss of my family.

I turn the treadmill off, stepping to the floor and bracing myself as I slide against the cool walls. My chest heaves as my lungs gasp for air, sweat pours down my chest that I don't bother wiping away. The sweat trickles through the prominent abs, leaving the ridges full of condensation and tickling the skin. Bent over, resting my palms on my knees as I cool down, my dampened hair sticks to my neck sending a chill down my spine.

For years, I have allowed the past—allowed Sloan—to control my life in every way. The memories have haunted the idea of starting over, of finding someone new to share a life with— just for Sloan to find a way to destroy it, like everything else good in my life. After all this time, am I to believe fate hasn't been the reason Lyla Fischer has come into my life and ignited the spark long lost inside me?

And what will Ivy think when she is introduced to Lyla if that is what either wishes for the future? What will Sloan make of me finally moving on and out of her hold that she has prided herself on for years?

Sloan never once struck me as the conniving type until the divorce lawyers were called in. She acted as though she believed I would stay, despite her ongoing affair, and let her be happy in her way while keeping our family intact. The loyal man inside of me had wanted that, tried to see the good in that event— but the prideful man won. I couldn't bear the thought of going to an event and having the knowledge of my wife's affair floating around us, trying to tune them out as we meander our way around a room. Sipping champagne with colleagues, with clients even, and the air heavy with deceit. Having to spend each moment at the office wondering if, or rather when, I would come home to find another man in our bed— the bed we shared each night.

Ivy, of course, has grown more loyal to her mother with each passing year. She's spent her formative years growing used to the lifestyle of the rich and mighty, letting Sloan's claws dig deeper into her skin. Eventually, I fear there will be no room left in her heart for me. The time we spend together is minuscule compared to the time she spends elsewhere— whether with Sloan or her high society friends. I notice the changes, even the slight appearances, where she has found herself in all her mother's flaws. I wish I could introduce her to the Sloan I met in college. Sometimes I wonder, would Ivy recognize that version of her mother? Would she be as disappointed in the person she has become as I am?

I stumble with aching limbs to the shower adjoining the equipment room. I let the cool water rinse over my body as I lather myself in suds, washing away the night. I can still taste the remnants of scotch left on my tongue. Lyla and I had three glasses each, she had insisted on one more after I told her only two, as we divulged our souls and I made good on my promise to be an open book. With every new topic, I expected her to run out of the room screaming that she was in over her head, that she could never love a man like me— but it never came. In fact, she left me with a warm, tight grip of the hand, a smile so perfectly pink and wide as she thanked me for being honest. She wished me a great night as she gathered her belongings. She waved as she reminded me of the topic for tomorrow's class— as if she is the teacher and I am the student. I saw her glance back over her shoulder once with a flush on her cheeks barely noticeable in the full moonlight shining through the windows as we had once again stayed long past the allotted office hours.

As I dry my skin of droplets of water, slide into a loose-fitting pair of boxers, and lay into the oversized bed I wonder— will there be a night in the future that I am no longer going through the motions? Is there a future where my nights don't land me in this large house alone? The thought of a life after Sloan has long felt out of reach, a risk I was never willing to take—until now. I wonder, concocting sweet dreams in my mind until my eyelids grow heavy, the moon glowing through the windows as I drift into sleep with images of a life with Lyla Fischer by my side.

My Friday morning routine was usually no different than any other morning— until today. The late night with Professor Moxley had made me restless and eventually, the sun rose as a pot of coffee was brewing in my small kitchen. I had unearthed an entirely new side of him that was unexpected. It's not like I was unaware that he was significantly older than I, but somehow the thought of him having a life outside of teaching had eluded me. I've been in his office on multiple occasions without noticing the framed pictures on his desk of Ivy, even after discussing her in class. Perhaps that's just me being unobservant of my surroundings, or just too entranced by his appearance to notice.

As I pour a third cup of the java greatness, the beep of an incoming text pings in the distance. I drag my feet through the dim apartment in search of my phone, likely left somewhere in my tangled mess of pillows and sheets as I tossed through the night. I smile at the sight of Lucy's name— coincidentally the only person I would have imagined would otherwise be up at this ungodly hour.

> **LUCY H.:** I'M BAAAAAAACK BITCH!
> **LUCY H.:** It's almost the freakin weekend so let's get our BRUNCH ON!

Giggling, I type a message welcoming her back and let her know that my schedule for the day is filled with classes but tomorrow, our usual Saturday, works great. Brunch with Lucy has been our long-standing tradition since our first week of class— always at our favorite place, the Black Walnut Café. It's not close to campus so we usually try to go at a decent hour, plenty of time for bottomless mimosas and a recap of the week. I toss my phone back onto the bed and rummage through my closet for something comfortable to wear to class. Fridays are my favorite because there is more time to come back to change between class time and office hours, allowing me the chance to look more professional at the end of the day. The rest of the week is usually miserable as I'm either carrying around a pair of heels in my bag for the office or dressed in clothes much too nice for class.

Three loud raps on my door startle me, spilling coffee down the front of my tank top. Peering through the peephole, an unmistakable tangle of blonde hair is visible. Her knuckles hit against the door again, loud raps on the door reminding me of the scotch we drank last night still hovering in my veins as the headache thrums in my skull with every noise.

"Hey, Lucy," I groan, opening the door wide enough for her to skip inside.

"Mornin' Sunshine!" she shrieks, grabbing me with her hands and pulling me in for a hug. "Good thing you're up because we have loads to chat about." Her hair flips behind her, bouncing as she walks.

115

"No one should be this peppy in the morning, Luc," I tell her, grabbing another mug from my cabinet and pouring her some coffee.

Her bright smile could put Victoria's Secret model to shame as she opens the cabinet she knows holds my liquor and pours a shot of Kahlua in her cup with a wink. As we plop onto my worn, leather couch she curls her feet up under her and the shimmer in her eyes is impossible to miss.

"How was your trip?" I ask, raising a brow.

"Oh, it was just fine. Mom and dad were thrilled I was spending two weeks instead of just a few days at home this time," she says, waving her hand to brush the subject off. "We both know what I'm here to talk about, though."

As her eyes narrowed to slits, she lifts the mug to her lips, blows on the contents, and raises a brow at me. Panic rises, constricting the air allowed into my lungs as I grasp the hot mug tighter. The bubbling in my stomach pushes a wave of nausea through my body, forcing me to refrain from vomiting bile in the space between us.

She can't know about Tyson, there's no way. She hasn't been here and we've been careful, right? No one's seen us or we would have been in trouble by now.

"Seriously?" she gasps, shaking her head. "You're just going to pretend like you don't want to talk about why Parker is schmoozing some slutty bimbo all over his Instagram?"

Oh, shit, of course, she wants to talk about Parker.

"I wouldn't know, I blocked him on everything, including his phone number, after I caught him kissing, likely the same, bimbo in the coffee shop," I shrug. As her jaw drops a few inches, I realize I hadn't even let her know about that yet. "Shit, I didn't tell you about that. I'm sorry, it just all happened so fast and it was break so I didn't want to bother you on your trip!"

"I'm sorry," she lifts a hand, telling me to stop. "You didn't want to *bother me* after you caught that scum of the earth kissing another girl?" she asks, sternly. Her perfectly painted burgundy lips pressed together in a fine line as her thickly lined, sapphire eyes glare at me from behind her black glasses. I try to feign a smile, a small shrug, but she sees right through me. "If I wasn't the one talking you through that shitshow then someone else clearly was and I demand that you tell me who has replaced me right fucking now."

The corner of her lips twitches as she tries hard to suppress a laugh. I know she's joking around, but she can never know how right she is.

I got through it just fine thanks to Tyson Moxley, then I got drunk and kissed him in his office. Oh and then again at the museum after eating my heart out in ice cream. But don't worry, I wasn't sad because of Parker. I was just mad at myself for kissing a professor.

"Trust me, Luc," I grumble, "the only people helping me that weren't you go by the name of Ben and Jerry and come in a variety of flavors." Not quite a lie, just an avoidance of the full picture.

Her index finger taps the side of her mug as she looks me up and down, clearly deciding if she should believe my story or not.

"I'm fine, really," I say. "The texts he sent me right after it happened calling me names showed his true colors and I'm just relieved to find out sooner rather than later."

"I'm sorry, he fucking did what?" she gasps, again. "Show me. Now!"

My eyes widen as I inhale a sharp breath.

Tyson deleted the texts.

"I…. I can't, Lucy," I shake my head, flush rising to my cheeks. "I deleted them while I was angry that first night. I didn't want to see them every time I opened my phone and I knew that just by seeing his name, I would eventually start to regret not letting him explain." My hand waves in an exaggeration as I drone on and on, rambling to push her away from the topic.

"Bitch, really?" she jokes. "Do you actually think I would let that scumbag come anywhere near you? Psh. I'm disappointed!"

She takes a long swig of her coffee, giggling to herself— luckily accepting the fact the texts no longer exist and buying my story.

"I know damn well that you wouldn't, Luc," I laugh, remembering the multitude of men she has pushed away over the years. "Say, what's going on with you and Brian?"

She bites her lip, shrugging.

"Nothing, really," she murmurs. "I haven't heard from him since right before I left... I assume the shit with Parker has something to do with that, though."

"Luc, don't let my drama keep you from getting your needs fulfilled. We both know you wouldn't have settled down in the slightest unless he was doing the trick." I wink, knowing her scandalous ways and burning desire for pleasure always win with her.

"I'm sure there are other men," she remarks, "even ones that don't have cheating doucheshits as friends. I'll find one of those next time."

A twinge ripples through my heart, not wanting Lucy to give someone up that she cares about just for the sake of distancing herself from Parker's inner circle. I reach out, grasping her hand in mine, and give her a faint smile.

"You do whoever you want to do, Luc, and feel no pressure to leave a good dick if that one makes you happy and pleasured."

"Holy fuck, Lyla," she laughs, wiping tears from her eyes as she doubles over on my couch. "I can not believe you just said that!"

I laugh with her, the sounds ringing through my apartment and bouncing off the floors until both of our sides hurt in response.

"You seem… different," she whispers, finally collecting herself again.

I let out another deep, real laugh.

"You mean something different like someone who has just barely over a semester left before graduation and instead of being tied down to one place, one man and *his dreams* is now free to travel the world? I can go wherever I want, with whoever I want, and take whatever job I want now. I don't have to stay around for him or the life he's creating. It was always his way or nothing, now that I've had time to think about it all. He made all the calls, every decision down to where we ate and what clothes I wore!"

As I'm rambling, I know she's telling the truth. I am different now. I do feel free in the sense that I'm not tied down to Parker and where his life takes us, but also I've stumbled into a new version of myself.

"I'm excited to find myself again, find out who I am in the adult world without Parker as a crutch since he's always been there. This is Lyla two-point-oh and she is going to dominate her fucking dreams," I laugh, draining the rest of my coffee.

A version of me that is fine with the risks behind having more than just a crush on a dreamy professor. A version that has met someone that understands the universe is more in control than we are. Most importantly, a version of myself that is sick of living for other people's standards and more focused on me for the first time in years.

"Sure, if that's what you want to tell me it is, I'll believe you," she says with a smirk, finishing the last of her coffee in a long sip. Then she purses her lips again with the stern expression as before as she says "for now."

Taken aback by her sudden disbelief, I falter as I try to get her off the subject just as the alarm to get up for my first class goes off in the other room.

Saved by the alarm, thank god.

"I promise that's all that it is. Seriously, but I need to get ready for class so I'm not late!" I exclaim, flashing her a hopefully believable grin. "We're on for brunch tomorrow, right?"

"Duh, mimosas are calling," she winks, slipping from the couch and her feet into her shoes as she heads out the door with a quick wave.

I sigh as I press my back to the door as it closes behind me. Lucy has never been one to interrogate or question me like that, but then again she's never had a reason to before now. I don't like lying to my best friend but the matter of what is going on between Professor Moxley and me cannot just be shouted from the downtown rooftops. It was a close call, but somehow deep in my gut I know—I know that this is only the beginning. Whether this is the beginning of something extraordinary, a dalliance, or something tragic; that's the part I'm dying to find out.

I don't remember the last time I was in Dean Marco's office but it hasn't changed, besides the wilting edges of the thick bound books on his shelves. This is, however, the first time that he's summoned me here without a proper forty-eight hours notice. To say that I'm sweating the meaning of this conversation would be an understatement— but I'm perched on his navy blue armchair with my ankle crossed on my knee and a cup of coffee in my hand, my expression cordial. Dean Marco has seemingly not aged a day in the last decade and his dark skin remains untouched by even a laugh line, likely a result of never finding the humor in life. He's run his hand through his jet black hair no less than eight times since I sat down almost ten minutes ago but has yet to utter a single word. I sip my coffee, deciding how to proceed and whether it's worth the effort to rush this conversation— even with a class starting in forty-five minutes. After three more minutes, I give in.

"To what do I owe the pleasure of this meeting, Dean Marco?" I ask, offering up a warm smile in his direction. "It's been far too long since our last chat."

He groans, leaning forward on his desk with the suede elbows of his tan jacket perched on the edge.

"Moxley, I hate pulling a professor in here on such short notice but I have been given no other choice than to question your ethics and professional courtesy in person," he confesses.

122

I raise an eyebrow and stop with my coffee midway to my lips.

"I've been a professor at this university for many years and not once has my ethical or professional behavior been in question," I snarl. He nods, tapping his pointer fingers together. "What's really going on here?"

"Moxley, please," he pleads, "I am not any happier about this conversation than you are, you're a superb professor and do your job better than almost any other here, but you need to watch your tone." He pointedly shakes a finger in my direction as I chuckle. "For each year you have worked here you have also managed to lose your Teaching Assistant before the end of the first semester, had multiple students request out of your class, and now I'm hearing reports of your ex-wife attempting to bribe the board members into giving her a position within our faculty."

The hand on my knee clenches, digging my nails into the skin around it. Fiery rage begins to burn inside me as I digest this new information. For what reason would Sloan be seeking out employment, especially at this particular university, and for what purpose? I've more than taken care of her financial situation since the divorce and Ivy has been vocal about leaving Texas for her college education. It's not like the students need to enjoy my style of teaching or the mannerisms, they just need to be more prepared for the careers they are on the path to taking. Do they assume another lawyer or judge will be a ray of fucking sunshine in the courtroom? I take a sip

123

from the coffee I'm holding, recollecting my thoughts before spewing venomous words across the desk at a friend, someone that gave me a chance when no one else would after my parents had me blacklisted from any kind of a formidable career.

"Dean Marco," I start, taking a deep breath, "I assure you that I have no idea what Sloan has been up to, nor do I care. Deny her everything, accept her bribes; I assure you that I don't care and am blindsided by that part of this conversation." I switch my position, placing both feet on the ground and leaning forward with my elbows on my knees. "As for my teaching style, the students that tough it out and survive my methods of teaching all go on to achieve phenomenal careers and I receive multiple letters and emails a year thanking me for being such a hardass that they grew a backbone before their first case kicked their ass."

His lips press into a thin line, likely a result of my language in his office but it's easier to be blunt than spend a second hesitating to reword my responses for his seemingly virgin ears— though, with four ex-wives, we all know that's far from the truth.

"And what about your poor Teaching Assistants?" He asks. "Are you just as much of a so-called hardass on them as you are your students? What value are you bringing to their life, Professor?"

The corner of my mouth twitches in response. I've been harder on the assistants than the students most years, but the graduate students should be more than capable in their abilities to deal with an asshole.

"I treat my assistants with the same respect they would get from a boss in their given fields and their initiative and work ethic directly reflects on the respect they get in return."

He sighs, shaking his head in defeat. I'm too valuable of an asset to this university because even he knows the revenue our department brings in each year. While the students may not care for my methods, the other professors rave about the knowledge and students still thank me for not straying from the syllabus.

Except for this year, which I need to get back on.

"What do you believe would be the outcome of hiring Sloan? Do you truly believe you two can work on a faculty, whether or not it's within the same department, after so many years of resentment? I'm no fool, Moxley, remember that I was the one that saved your career in more than one way."

"As long as she is capable of staying the hell away from me, I see no reason why she shouldn't work here, sir," I spew. "If she wants to act like a deranged, heartbroken teenager then let that be on her. I have no desire to portray anything short of professional excellence as a long-time member of this university."

He nods, eyeing me up and down as he does so.

"And what about Miss Fischer?" he asks.

At the mention of her name, my heart pounds in my chest, a flush erupts across my cheeks and I quickly think of cold water and dead fish to shake the desire building in my body. If there was ever a more wrong time or place to divulge any hint of our relationship, I would pay to see it.

"Miss Fischer has been the best damn assistant I have ever been given, Dean Marco." My words snap out before I can catch their deadly tone. "I assure you, I was just as blindsided at her decision to leave next semester as you seem to be," I scoff, "and not to mention, unless you would like for her to teach my class that starts in thirteen minutes, I need to cut this conversation off soon."

"Mmmhm, I see," he mutters, tapping his pen against the stack of papers on his desk. "I'm sorry we had to chat like this, Moxley. I don't like these conversations but sometimes they're just necessary to hear every side of the story. I assure you, your students' grades speak for themselves and any minor emotional reactions to your teaching is something that should be handled in their own way."

I nod and stand, extending a hand to shake as he firmly grasps it in return before thanking me for my time. I turn on my heel and throw the door open as I briskly walk through the hall leading outside, making several snide remarks at students for their PDA on the way.

"Just to think I showed up today planning to have a perfectly fucking great day," I grumble to myself, weaving around the groups of students as I make my way to the lecture hall. The heat from the Texas

126

sun outweighs the chill from the autumn air as I rush across the lush grounds. My brow is furrowed tightly as I suck in my cheeks to keep from exploding at any one of the lingering eyes in my path.

The class will be receiving a pop quiz the second I walk through the door just to keep them on their toes. Serves them right for complaining to the Dean about me.

"I wonder what crawled up his ass and got stuck there," one student mutters.

They're not wrong... seriously, what the hell?

Professor Moxley had stormed into the lecture hall, seven minutes late, with a stack of quizzes in his hand. Without so much as a glance at me, he tossed them on my desk and brazenly asked me to pass them out. As I sauntered through the front of the room handing out quizzes he stood motionless and brooding, propped against his desk. His biceps were bulging out of his royal blue dress shirt as he crossed his arms. With his lips pursed and brows pinched together, I could tell someone had definitely pissed in his cheerios this morning. I could only hope his mood would improve before office hours.

As the last student hands in their quiz, he tosses them in a neat stack on my desk without looking up from his laptop. I smile gently at the young man in front of the desk, a look of solidarity against this abysmal mood we're forced to deal with today.

"You can all leave now," Tyson bellows from his chair. "Class is dismissed."

Before I even get a chance to toss my belongings in my bag, he's pushing through the staff door with such force that it bounces the door off the wall with a splattering crash. I take a deep breath as I continue to pack things away and debate heading back to my apartment before office hours instead of showing up early.

128

I could get coffee for us, maybe that would begin to remove the stick from his ass.

As great of an idea as it is, I don't know how he takes his coffee and the last thing I want to do is get that wrong today. For all I know, he could just as easily throw it at me— something I would have expected at the beginning of the year, but not now. Not after our night of honesty. *Lucy would know what to do... if only I could talk to her about it.* Regret and shame bubble inside me, I hate keeping secrets from my best—only—friend. How would I even explain this to her? *"Oh hey Luc, so it turns out that Tyson isn't an asshole. He's just had a shitty life and now I think I'm falling in love with him? Oh, and his lips are so fucking magical when they're on mine that I feel it all through my core."* Yeah, Lucy would have a fucking hayday with that story.

I make my way through the grounds of the campus, zig-zagging around groups of people chattering about their weekend party plans and which frat house will have the best theme. Campus parties were fun the first few years, but they lost their appeal after one too many late nights leading to overwhelming hangovers that not even the greasiest of burgers could alleviate the hell I felt I was drowning in. I turn my key in the lock of my apartment door and kick my shoes off as I step inside.

"Uggggghhhhhhh!" I groan, flopping onto the couch and pressing my palms to my forehead. I've dreaded going in for office hours on multiple occasions, but today feels different— more complex.

129

Whatever is going on with Tyson, it has to pertain to the conversation we had last night. Maybe I went too far, perhaps I should have played it safe and asked only simple questions.

I bet it's because I pushed to know about Ivy. His daughter is easily the most important person in his life, even if he feels like she's being tainted by his ex-wife. I should have had better control over my urge to divulge the more useful information about him.

On the other hand, he could have just said those were inappropriate questions for a student, or rather a TA, to be asking a professor if he felt that I was crossing a line. He is an adult, after all. That would have been acceptable, I would have backed off, and maybe he wouldn't have gone into alpha-douche mode today. I could have spared those students the likely low marks this close to the end of term. I groan again, grabbing my phone to check how much longer I can stall before heading to his office— either to apologize or suck it up and deal with his mood all night.

ME: Prof M is on a rampage today. Helpppppp.

Even if Lucy can't know the extent of the situation, I can still confide in her about his mood; it's not like we haven't discussed him profusely this semester.

LUCY: That man needs to get laid. Obvs not something you can help with. LOL! But seriously, maybe hand the man some dirty magazines before work and I bet you'll make his whole day.

ME: Lucy, that is the opposite of helpful. LOL. Are you trying to get me fired?

LUCY: I'm sorry, I didn't know you could be fired from a TA position. Isn't that like expelling you from a class? Is that even a thing in college?

My gut tightens again, this time realizing that I not only forgot to talk to Lucy about Parker but also my resignation from my TA position.

Fuck, I'm becoming a terrible friend.

There are exactly thirty-nine minutes left until I'm required to be there, and I no longer have the desire to wear the wedges or dress I wore to class today. Instead, I roll off the couch, landing on my knees on the floor with a thud, and slowly make my way to my closet. I grab a pair of green pixie pants and a loose black sweater, toss on a pair of black booties, and grab my bag on my way out the door. The sun is beginning to set earlier these days, the cooler evening air slices at my skin as I walk through the ghost-like campus. It's rather unsurprising how few students stop in during his hours and ask him well, anything.

I would be too afraid of beratement for not paying more attention in class if I was one of his students, as well.

I pause as I reach the building, taking a deep breath as I rub my palms together to warm my hands. Closing my eyes, I lean against the cold stone, remembering the warmth of Tyson's hand against my skin and the brightness of his smile last night. My heart flutters with the memory of his smile, the glimmer in his eyes as he listened to my life story. How the dim light in the office reflected off his skin, appearing as an aura around him.

"Lyla?"

I grit my teeth at the sound of Parker's voice, squeezing my eyes tighter before responding.

"Go away, Parker," I sneer.

"Um, okay," he scoffs, I hear his foot kick the side of the building. "It's just cold out here and I thought maybe you needed some help or forgot what you were doing. Damn, girl."

My eyes fly open with blazing rage building, coursing through my veins. My jaw clenches tight enough that my teeth hurt against the pressure.

"Even if I needed help, you are the last fucking person I would accept it from," I spit, reaching for the handle and throwing open the door before stomping away from him. He doesn't open the door and call out my name. He doesn't follow me as I race up the stairs. He doesn't do a damn thing, because he knows I'm right. He screwed up, maybe he's starting to realize that— but also maybe he's not. Either way, I couldn't care less what act of chivalry he was trying to act upon because as far as I'm concerned, Parker Bennett is dead to me.

I slow my steps as I near Professor Moxley's office, pausing to collect myself before stepping through the open door. I notice my chair is back at my own desk tonight and his door is closed, though the light is on inside. There's a stack of papers sitting on my desk with a sticky note attached to the top in his unmistakable handwriting.

Grade the quizzes from today and then you may leave.
-Prof. Moxley

What is his problem today?

I sigh, slinging my bag across the back of my chair before sitting down and grabbing my favorite purple pen from the top drawer. As I sift through the papers on my desk, placing the answer key in the middle with the ungraded tests on the left of it so I can add the finished ones to the right side; I notice a second sticky note. My heart races, hoping the second note is a form of an apology or at minimum, an explanation.

It's not.

Don't even think about using the purple pen.
It's unprofessional.

"Asshole," I mutter, flipping off the closed office behind me before tossing the pen back into the drawer and pulling out a red one in its place. I hope he sees me, comes out, and starts a fight. If he needs to let out some steam, scream, or fight, I'm the right person to take it from him. I tap the pen against the edge of the desk and settle in for the night— grading the pop quizzes that I could have prevented and feeling the burning glare on the back of my neck from Tyson's eyes through the windowed wall behind me.

This morning's meeting with Dean Marco put me in a deplorable mood and not so unlike myself, I took it out on the people I seemingly care about the most— my students and of course, Lyla Fischer. Instead of facing her and discussing the situation like adults, I left notes on the work I needed her to complete this evening. Hiding away, I locked myself in my office, alone, to work on the final exam while having a heated texting conversation with my ex-wife.

SLOAN: Why wouldn't you want me to work at the Uni? It's not like I'll be in your department or interfering, you just have always loved it so much and I thought it would be a nice change of scenery.

ME: Sloan, you haven't worked since we graduated and whatever you're up to, I want no part of. Leave my job and my life out of whatever devious plans you have going on inside that head of yours. If you need money, I'll give you money.

SLOAN: Don't patronize me, Tyson. You know I don't need money, I'm just bored and Ivy is gone all the time so I'm alone.

ME: Yeah, I have no fucking idea what that feels like. My wife packed up and took our kid with her years ago.

I'll pay for that last part, but I've had it with her bullshit tonight. She won't tell me what job she's going for or why she wants to work at the university to begin with. She's up to no good and if I don't put a stop to it now, I can only imagine the hell that will break loose once she sinks her claws into some poor student that can't resist her charm.

Just like Lyla can't resist me, nor do I want her to keep trying to resist the passion.

No, I refuse to admit that I am to Lyla what someone else would be to Sloan. Sloan is the devil incarnate and every able-body, male is better off as far away from her as possible.

SLOAN: Is that supposed to be a jab, Ty? I don't like it. Don't make me tell the lawyers you're being unfair.

Goddammit, Sloan. This is her favorite card to play that she always wins. Once a screw-up in a courtroom, always a screw-up in life in the eyes of a judge around here. I know better than to push her buttons but we've managed to stay as far away from each other as possible over the past few years. We don't interfere with each other's personal life and we talk on only a needed basis. If it doesn't involve Ivy, we don't talk about it— until today. Her decision to descend her wrath on my territory has set me off in a red hot fury that is destroying everything in my path.

I peek up through the window, watching Lyla diligently grading the quizzes from this afternoon— the ones I forced on the students due to my bad mood. She's swaying back and forth in her chair, bouncing her head to a clear beat that she likely has playing from the speaker on her phone. I'd watched as she scanned the notes I left her, I could feel her frustration over my dislike of her favorite purple pen as she pointed her middle finger upwards. Oh, what I would give to be back to the routine of last night where we enjoyed the company of one another and talked freely.

But under no circumstance can Lyla know about Sloan coming to work here, not until it will affect her life in any way.

Plus, even if Sloan was to work here, the chances of her crossing paths with Lyla are scarce. The Dean, despite his questioning, wouldn't dare to put us anywhere within the same department and she has nothing to contribute to the university as it is. Unless she is serving as a part of the administration, she has no skills to qualify her for a position.

The sun descends and the outer office begins to grow dark, Lyla switches on the lamp in the corner of her desk as she works her way through the quizzes. She's been taking her time, likely in hopes that I will open my door and ask her to join me. Any other night she could have finished the quizzes and left an hour early but tonight she's still here fifteen minutes after office hours have officially ended. I admire her in that sense. Her desire to see me for a better man than I have been for the last ten years, the kind of man that is capable of love and a future with a woman worth his time— but that's the problem. I'm not that kind of man. I sealed my heart when Sloan left and the only person that's been allowed in since has been Ivy. My daughter, my blood— my everything.

I grasp the back of my neck in the palms of my hands and squeeze my eyes shut. I reminisce about the previous night. Lyla's warmth in her eyes, the way she would shift her body closer as she asked a particularly insightful question, her lack of embarrassment while grilling not only a man way too old for her but a professor— essentially her boss.

And therein lies the problem. This… whatever this is… it's wrong on so many levels. I'm over a decade older than Lyla. This is wrong, so wrong.

But it feels so right. Fuck, does it feel right.

My heart swells as I think about the way her lips felt against mine, the way her fingertips grazed my skin and left a burning trail where they touched. My cock twitches in response to these memories and I fight my urge to run out the door and wrap my arms around her, apologizing for my sour mood and asking her to spend the night in my bed where I can make it up to her time and time again.

But that would be wrong, it would be unethical— but most of all, it would be dangerous.

138

With Sloan inserting herself into my life again, there is sure to be an immense amount of backlash, inevitable excruciating chaos. Lyla is innocent. She doesn't deserve to be thrown into this mess as a pawn in whatever devious scheme Sloan is cooking up.

Three knocks on my door, a simple sentence from her mouth and I'm melting in my seat.

"Can I come in, Professor Moxley?" Lyla asks.

"Sure," I say, sourly, watching as she enters with caution. Her cheeks are flushed as she twists the sleeve hem of her sweater in between her fingers of one hand, a stack of finished papers in the other. Guilt spreads through me.

"These quizzes are finished," she mumbles, raising her hand with the papers without looking at me. "I just wanted to drop them off before I head out."

I point to the basket on my desk, unable to form the right words to ease her pain. I suck in my cheeks, feeling the tension between us is driving me crazy. She can't possibly understand what's going on in my head, and I'm not ready to explain— not yet, not until I have to.

She drops the papers in the basket and turns around, slowly walking towards the door. She grabs the doorframe in her hand just as I avert my eyes back to the computer screen in an attempt to finish the exam. She stops, waits a few seconds, and then looks over her shoulder at me.

"I don't know what's going on with you today, but I'm sorry if it's because I overstepped last night," she says. My heart drops to my stomach. She thinks this is all her fault and I'm still unable to form the words to tell her that no, none of this is her fault. I watch as her shoulders rise and fall with a deep breath, her knuckles are whitening with her grip on the frame as if she's holding herself steady and bracing her mind for the words she's about to say. "I don't deserve to be treated like this. We're adults, Tyson. If something I did upset you, you should have the balls to talk to me about it."

With that, she walks away — slamming the door behind her. My heart stops as my lungs remind me that I haven't taken a breath since she walked into the room. She gathers her bag and glares at me through the windowed wall, her bottom lip between her teeth. I can feel her guilt, her pain. What I can't do, is bring myself to stand up and walk out that door. Not even to relieve her guilt, to tell her that she's right.

She is right. She doesn't deserve what I've dished out today, and I still don't have the fucking balls to talk to her about any of this shit. I'm acting like a moody, douchebag of a teenage boy, all because I feel as though my ex-wife is still holding my balls in the palm of her hand.

"I'm so sorry, Lyla," I whisper as I watch her walk through the doors and out of sight.

"Can we get two flights of mimosas to start with?" Lucy asks the waiter, batting her eyelashes while flipping her long, blonde hair over her shoulder with a pearly smile that would knock the wind out of any man. As his jaw drops, he proves that he is no exception to her charm— not surprising. She chuckles as he walks away, peeking back over his shoulder with his cheeks flushed. I close my eyes and shake my head.

"Luc, can you make it through one brunch without giving a waiter a boner?" I laugh. "It's too early for this shit."

She throws her head back, letting out a melodic laugh that would echo off the walls if we were inside. Even for Texas, it's an unusually warm day for December so we're sitting on the patio in only a light jacket. As Lucy studies the menu, feigning interest in ordering anything other than her usual waffles, I lean back in my chair and let the sunlight warm my cheeks. I hadn't slept well after my snarky remarks to Tyson in his office before I left for the night, but today wasn't going to be ruined by thinking about him. No, today was about spending time with my best friend and dissing my ex— her new favorite hobby.

"Geez, Lyla," she complains, jokingly, "what has crawled up your ass already this morning?"

I shrug as the waiter returns with our trays of flavored mimosas—original, strawberry, watermelon, and pineapple—

decorated with corresponding fruits. He winks at Lucy, winking as a stripe of color comes to her cheeks. She picks up her strawberry glass and pops one of the fruits between her full, red lips while looking him right in the eyes before he scurries away.

Poor kid.

"That was so, so not nice, Lucy," I laugh.

She shrugs, dismissing her actions without another thought, and wiggles her fingers at another group of muscular men across the patio.

"He'll be fine, Lyla," she sips her drink, now drumming her fresh manicure along the iron tabletop. "However, you seem to not be fine and I'd like to talk about that instead of being reamed for exploring my options in the male department."

As the still flushed waiter returns, I take a sip of the pineapple mimosa as I ponder over her question as she rattles off her order of chicken and waffles, before telling the waiter I would like the Nutella smoothie bowl. *I can handle ordering my own food, Lucy.* I try not to look irritated at her actions, it's not like this is the first time or I was planning on ordering something different— she just knows me too well. He takes our menus and scurries back inside as Lucy leans onto the table, propping her chin up on one hand, and stares at me.

"It's nothing, Luc," I say, trying to shrug her off. "Parker just showed up outside of Ty-Professor Moxley's office, before office hours yesterday and it got under my skin more than I thought, I guess."

Fuck, that was a close call.

She groans, dramatically, and smacks her other hand on the table.

"What the hell did he want?"

"He said I looked confused, thought I needed some help as though I'm some incompetent girl unable to survive on my own."

"Fantastic, just fucking peachy. Perhaps he would enjoy my foot up his ass for those misogynistic views of his?"

I snort, suddenly glad I'm here with Lucy— and her lack of a filter. An unexplained weight lifts as I take another sip of my drink, gauging the disgust written across her face. Lucy had been *Team Parker and Lyla Forever* up until she saw him with the bimbo a few days ago and ever since she has been sending a constant slew of hateful jabs at him and all the ways he wasn't right for me.

He never cared about what you needed in life, your plans, or what you wanted to do after college. He was so self-absorbed. Was he like that in the bedroom as well? I bet he's got a tiny cock and lacks oral skills too. Those kinds are always the biggest douchebags.

I smile, remembering that conversation as she gulps down the last of her first mimosa before picking up her next.

"Anyways, I didn't give him time to elaborate before I walked away and slammed a door in his face."

Lucy's nose crinkles as her lips push into a fine line.

143

"Yeah, well, I'm sure you were just preparing to work with that big dick of a professor you've somehow not killed yet," she retorts.

You have no idea how right you are, Luc.

Yet, even knowing how terrible to deal with Tyson had been yesterday, that doesn't stop me from coming to his defense.

"He's really not that bad anymore," I mutter.
Lucy gasps and her glass slips just a fraction in her hand. She tightens her grip on the glass as she looks between her almost accident and my face, searching for a sign of insanity.

"What the hell did you just say?"

I roll my eyes, twisting the hem of my sweater in between my fingers.

"I said he's really not that bad anymore," I repeat, sternly. "Seriously, now that I've gotten to work with him for a while I think everyone makes him out to be a lot worse than he is. He was just having a bad day yesterday, that's all. We're all entitled to those."

Yeah, sure, keep telling yourself that. Even if he was a Grade A Asshole after a perfectly pleasant night.

Lucy scrutinizes my face for several minutes in silence. I try to keep a poker face, though my heart is pounding through my chest up to my ears. I start glancing at the other patrons or watching an occasional pedestrian— anything to showcase my nonchalance about this conversation.

144

"Lyla, I need you to listen to me very carefully," she says, reaching across the table to take my hand in hers. I raise an eyebrow at her gesture, watching her eyes grow wide. "I think you're developing a form of Stockholm Syndrome for Professor Mucho-Douche."

Suppressing a laugh, I manage to ask her what the hell she's talking about.

"Seriously, think about it!" she exclaims. "You work with him *every night* and you spend more time with him than anyone else. Isn't that what happens when people are kidnapped? They start to develop feelings for their kidnappers and feel sorry for them after so long together? You're definitely with him more than anyone else these days and I think it's having the same effect on you!"

Holy shit, she's being serious right now. What the hell is wrong with her?

"What the fuck did that waiter slip into your drink?" I laugh. I can't help the laughter rising from my chest and out of my mouth, so loud that the other patrons are beginning to look at us.

"What?" she asks. "Tell me you can see it, Lyla. Everyone, and I mean everyone, hates Moxley. He acts like a God and just because he looks like one too, doesn't give him the right to treat the rest of the world like shit."

The waiter returns, forcing Lucy to remove my hand from her grasp to make room for our plates of food. I stir my spoon around my bowl, mixing the ingredients as she cuts her waffles into bites.

145

"I think he's just old enough to not give a shit what anyone else thinks of him," I say, once again defending him.

Lucy shrugs, digging into her waffles and swiping whipped cream with her finger off one waffle and seductively licking it off while maintaining eye contact with yet another waiter across the patio.

Goddammit, Luc. Give it a rest.

"Whatevs, Ly," she surrenders. "Just don't say I didn't warn you when you fall under a spell and think you're falling in love with him!"

I chuckle, taking a spoonful of my smoothie concoction into my mouth and removing the spoon with a *pop*.

"Don't worry, Luc, that's not going to happen," I assure her. "How about instead of picking apart my not-relationship with my *boss*, you tell me about your vacation."

Lucy's face lights up, launching into a story recollecting her time spent with her family— fabulous and extravagant, as always. I listen with intensity, with the probing question suddenly nudging the back of my mind.

Am I falling in love with Tyson Moxley?

146

ME: Ivy, where the hell are you at? It's almost two in the morning.

I wait several minutes, hoping for a response but one never comes. I groan, tossing my phone on the couch beside me as the fire begins to die out. The time I get with Ivy is already too short as it is and suddenly she's been cutting it even shorter by staying out with her friends until unholy hours in the morning on my weekends. Sloan doesn't give her a curfew so it's likely that all hell will break loose if I try to enforce one when she's here— so I just don't. Ultimately it is my own damn fault that I lose even more time with her.

We'd had a nice dinner together before she left. I'd made her favorite—beef and broccoli—and we had talked about her applying for early admission to various colleges around the school. Ivy has always been intelligent, but the fact she is already completed with her credits and far enough along that she could graduate at the end of the semester and start college in the spring had taken me by surprise. If anything, I wish she would have told me sooner so I could have tried to convince Sloan to let me have more time with her before she heads out— knowing that once she leaves, there is little chance of her making an effort to see me.

Minutes tick by, feeling like hours as each movement of the clock hand seems to slow down the longer I stare at it. At half-past

147

two, with no response, I retire to my bedroom in a worse mood than I had been in when I'd left campus yesterday. Lyla had, once again, rightfully put me in my place for acting like an asshole, but I have yet to bring myself to apologize to her. She deserves an apology. I just don't know where to start.

Sorry for unloading my personal shit on you, even though you asked. Sorry that even the Dean thinks I'm a shitty human being, and he's not wrong. Sorry that my ex-wife is still a raging bitch and trying to fuck with my life ten years later.

The truth is, there's a lot to apologize for— more than she could ever understand. Restlessly, I toss and turn between the cool sheets as thoughts of Lyla and all her perfections linger in my mind. The way her cheeks flush when she's uncomfortable, the perfect pink of her lipstick that matches her flush just right. The way she doesn't wince as we sip sub-par bourbon in my office, the way her hips sway just right as she's strutting away when she's feeling sassy. My cock again twitches in my boxers as I groan, reaching down to feel the hard member and relish the way a few simple thoughts about her send my body into a frenzy it hasn't known in years.

I hear the door open and slam shut shortly after three, waiting to hear Ivy's bedroom door close before drifting off into a dreamless sleep,

"Dad, seriously, take it down a few notches," Ivy snarls, reaching for a mug and filling it to the brim with coffee, her eyes squeezed shut.

"What? You don't like feeling as though you're at a Guns 'n Roses concert first thing in the morning?" I laugh, flipping a pancake on the skillet as she groans.

"No, not really," she says, likely with an eye roll that I luckily can't see as I'm facing away from her. "But I also wouldn't want to be at one of their concerts at any time of day."

Payback for showing up at three in the morning, clearly having been out drinking underage, is a bitch. Even bigger of a bitch than your mom.

I sit a plate of pancakes down in front of her, watching with amusement as she covers her mouth and forces a few bites into her mouth.

"Something greasy would be better for that hangover," I chuckle, pulling a sheet of bacon and sausage from the oven with a wink. "I usually wouldn't allow such foods on the same plate as my pancakes, but for this, I'll make an exception. Just this one time." Her eyes widen as her fork slips out of her hand as I place a few extra greasy pieces of each on her plate. Clearly, she thought she was being devious and her hangover would go unnoticed.

"Dad, I-," she sputters as I hold a hand up to stop her.

"It's fine, Ivy," I sigh. Her shoulders soften as I plop my plate of pancakes down next to her and take a seat. I run my hand through my

149

hair before facing her, placing a hand on her arm. "Okay, let me rephrase that. It's not fine, not at all. I don't want you out drinking, you're underage and it's dangerous. I can't even begin to explain the anxiety that I felt last night while you were out with god knows who, doing who the hell knows what. I'm trying to not be overbearing or an asshole, but I hated not knowing if you were safe.

"But I also know that you didn't drive so you were at least smart about it and if anything, that's something I can tolerate for now. You're going to be heading off to college in, most likely, just a few weeks, and I know you'll be doing the same, or worse, there."

She pulls together a smile, resting her head on my shoulder. For one split second, it feels like she's a kid again and her world revolves around me— just like it used to. She used to insist I tuck her into bed every night and read her the same story about a princess fighting her dragons and saving herself from the tower she was locked in. She thought the world shone right out of my ass back in the day until Sloan ripped us apart.

My chest tightens as I press a soft kiss to the top of her head. I've been robbed of so much of her life, something I'll never forgive Sloan for no matter what hell she brings into my life. Her choice to rip apart our family was not one I handled in the right way and losing Ivy had been my punishment. When Ivy had turned fourteen and we had gone back to court because Sloan was insisting that she needed more money, she was given the choice of who she wanted to live with— of course, she chose Sloan. What girl wouldn't want to live with their mom at that age? Puberty had happened years before but her body was flooding with hormones and feeling too uneasy about talking to her dad about boys.

"I feel like shit, daddy," she mumbles.

I chuckle lightly, trying not to jostle her head as she keeps it nuzzled in the crook of my neck.

"I don't doubt that one single bit, baby girl."

"Why do people even like drinking if you feel like this the next day? What's the damn point in a few hours of hazy fun?"

She groans, taking small bites of the bacon from her plate and chewing slowly to hopefully ward off any nausea.

"Maybe they just don't drink as much as you did last night," I murmur.

"Ughhhh.....," she sips her coffee, slowly, before putting her forehead onto my shoulder. "I think I'm going to throw up."

"You know where the bathroom is."

She barely moves her head as she agrees.

"Just promise me, you'll never hesitate to call for help if you put yourself in a situation where you've drunk too much, okay Ivy?" I plead.

She lifts her head so her chin is resting on my shoulder and nods.

"You got it, daddy," she says. "I need to go lie down until I head back to mom's, okay?"

I swallow hard, wanting more time with her but nod towards her room with a forced smile. I clean the dishes up as she trots off to her room, hearing the thunk of her hitting the bed as I load the dishwasher. When the kitchen is finished up, spotlessly clean, I sit down to watch the afternoon football games until it's time for Ivy to leave.

Once again, it feels like I'm losing her all over again as I listen to her pack her suitcase two hours later and ready herself to head back to her mother's, where she will spill all the details of where she was last night while I'm left in the dark.

In the dark is where my soul has been resting for the last decade, but when an image of Lyla flashes through my mind once again— the darkness begins to fade with a new light. What a world it could be if she could pull me back from the monotone shades of grey and black I've let myself live in for so long? What if, for the first time in years, this is what hope feels like?

Can I live in a world where I find and allow myself to love again, just to have it all ripped away like before?

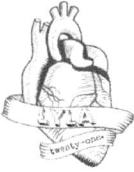

"Yes, Ty, I'm still planning to come out for Christmas," I say, assuring my brother that I don't intend to blow off his family for the holidays. "Good, cuz I'm dying to see you, sis," he chuckles. "It's been so long that I might forget what you look like now."

"Ha ha," I reply, sarcastically. "You know I can't wait to see you guys and I think I could use a change of scenery. Texas is just not quite green enough for me these days and I can't believe I'm saying it... but I might miss snow!"

Tyler gasps loudly through the phone speaker. Clear as day, I can imagine he's dramatically covering his chest with his hand in surprise with his mouth gaping in surprise. I'd never been a fan of the snow growing up, but as I've gotten older I think back on it now and realize that's because I knew we were going to be alone more often as our parents traveled more during the winter.

"Okay, now I know Texas is messing with my little sister and I need to get her out of there as soon as possible!" he exclaims. I hear Cassie calling him to head to bed, it's later on the east coast than it is in Texas, and he assures her that he's coming.

"Go to bed, Ty. I'm just going to watch an episode of *The Office* and head to bed myself," I say, flipping through my list until I find one of the Christmas episodes to watch tonight. *Dwight's obscene Christmas traditions are just what I need tonight.* I can hear him shuffling, mumbling to their Schnauzer about heading to bed, and finally, the sound of a washer starting before he tells me goodnight and hangs up.

Late on the east coast, apparently, has become almost eleven for my brother as he gets older. I settle in with a glass of rosé in my favorite yoga pants as the theme song to my favorite show begins, leaning back into the plush couch and wrapping a thick blanket over my lap. Ty and I had always watched this show together growing up and it used to make me want to work in an office. I went as far as to get a job as a receptionist one summer and swiftly realized that real life is nothing like television, that kind of drama doesn't keep life interesting at all. My friends back home had always said I was too old for my age, which typically drew me to the older crowd or led to being a loner. The boys in school were never mature enough for my liking which meant I didn't date much before meeting Parker, and that obviously went well for me.

Lost in a fit of laughter as a typical cheesy line makes me lose it, I almost miss the sound of my phone going off. As I pick it up, I don't recognize the number minus the local area code. Swiping it open, I almost drop the phone in surprise.

1(713)555-0243: Lyla, I owe you an apology for my behavior Friday.

Goddammit, Parker. Of course, he would go as far as to use someone else's phone to get ahold of me. Fucking asshole.

> **ME:** Fuck off, Parker. I don't want your apology, just leave me the hell alone.

I smirk as I hit send. It feels good to be a little classless for once. Being wise and mature beyond my years is for the dogs after a glass of wine on an empty stomach tonight. But, instead of respecting my wishes, my phone dings again.

> **1(713)555-0243:** Not Mr. Bennett, but I would be interested to know what pain he has been causing you. Also, what a mouth on such a usually proper girl like yourself.
> **ME:** If this isn't Parker, then who is it?
> **1(713)555-0243:** Miss Fischer, are you telling me that more than myself and Mr. Bennett caused you grief on Friday? If so, I'm afraid I will feel even worse about my behavior than I already do.

"Oh, *holy fuck!*" I yell, dropping my phone on the floor and spilling wine down the front of my shirt in an effort to retrieve it. "How the hell did he get my number?" I wipe the front of my phone off on my pants to keep the sticky sweetness of the rosé off the screen.

ME: Prof. Moxley? How did you get my number?
1(713)555-0243: You gave it to me on our first week in the office, in case I was ever unable to reach you via email or in case of an emergency. This apology felt like an emergency.
ME: An emergency? Two days after it happened? Doesn't sound like much of an emergency to me.

I add a shrugging emoji, pleased with myself, and hit send before adding his number into my phone with a discreet T.M identifier instead of using his name. I flip the TV off, dumping the remains of my wine into my mouth, and toss the glass into my dishwasher as I head to my bed. I strip my wine-covered shirt and toss it into the overflowing laundry basket in the corner of my room, a reminder that I didn't do it this weekend while I had the chance, and make a mental note to start a load before class in the morning.

T.M: You are, as usual, correct— but that does not mean I am not sincere in my apology. You were correct, you did not deserve my lashing out and as much as I would like to say it won't happen again, I won't make a promise to you that I am not one hundred percent sure that I can keep. Just please, understand that my behavior on Friday had nothing to do with you in the slightest.

156

I reread his text over, and then over again. *There he is, there's Tyson from Thursday night.* This makes my heart soar, butterflies flutter in my stomach. My fingers flit across the screen as I type a witty reply.

ME: As much as I would like to accept your apology, I am not willing to say something to you that I do not one hundred percent mean. Actions speak louder than words can ever read. If you want me to accept your apology, you better find a way to earn it.

With a smug smile, I bury myself under my covers as an image of Tyson curled between his sheets bellowing out a deep laugh at my latest text forms in my mind. An image forms of the rock-hard abs I felt in the museum reminds me that he's built like a magnificent piece of art. *A piece of art that I would like to lick.* Another ding snaps me out of my dirty thoughts.

T.M: I plan to do just that, Lyla, however long it takes. Don't push me away, give me a chance to apologize.
ME: One week. You have one week.

Where the hell did that come from? I'll just assume the quick inhalation of the wine is to blame. At least it sounds good and gives him a week to sweep me off my feet with some likely elaborate apology.

> **T.M:** Thank you, Lyla. Get some rest, please. I'll see you tomorrow.
>
> **ME:** I'll hopefully see the Tyson that I enjoy being around tomorrow, I don't so much care to see the other guy. Goodnight.
>
> **T.M:** I'll do my best to be the nice guy when you want me to be. Sweet dreams, Lyla.

With a storm raging in my chest between how wrong this situation is becoming and how right it makes me feel, I settle in for the night. Tyson Moxley is confusing the hell out of my heart and mind, but I think I like this feeling. This feeling, this hope, and excitement— I could get used to this. *Sweet dreams, Tyson.*

Lyla surprised me with not only her witty responses last night but even in responding at all. She had assumed I was Mr. Bennett at first though which leads me to believe he is still causing her problems— something I intend to get to the bottom of and put an end to. If a grand gesture apology is what she wants to smooth this miscommunication over, that is exactly what she will get. I just haven't figured out precisely what that will entail. Luckily, she's given me a week to come up with something and I can gauge exactly how pissed off she is for today.

As she flits through the staff door, donning a tight, red pencil skirt and a black, long-sleeve silk blouse that molds to her body in all the right places, she seems genuinely happy to be here. My heart flutters as I watch the way her black heels carry her tanned legs through the room with unwavering precision. She waves at a few of the students as she sets her laptop up at the desk next to mine, but manages to avoid eye contact with me completely—the corners of her mouth upwards in a smirk. The scent of her perfume travels through the breezy room, straight into my nostrils, causing my chest to tighten as my mind remembers having her so comfortably in my arms before.

"Ready whenever you are, Professor," she says, startling me out of my daze and reminding me that we are in a lecture hall full of students. My expression falters as I gulp, standing up from my desk and walking behind her just close enough to feel the warmth of her

159

body on my exposed forearm. *I can play this game too, Lyla.* I swear I even see her spine straighten with the proximity, feeling the draw of her skin to mine.

Straightening my tie, I clear my throat and welcome the class for the day. A few mumbled responses remind me that while I might feel different, the student body still sees me as the raging asshole I've always been in the classroom. I manage to rattle through the lesson on conservation and the laws that some lawyers will try to get around in a courtroom with ease. Fingertips flying across keyboards, the loud and erratic sounds of keys tapping fill the room in my silent breaks to ensure everyone has time to catch up. Being called an asshole by Lyla and chastised by the Dean recently have caused me to reevaluate the way my time is spent in the classroom— obscurity for a seasoned professor. I focus on taking more time to pause, taking in the questions the students ask, and just paying attention to the facial expressions of the students today than I ever have in the past. I let them go on time, another rare occurrence most days, and watch as most students leave relaxed and smiling— definitely a first. I relax against the desk, nodding towards students as they wave before heading out the door. *I could get used to being respected instead of feared.*

"I think you managed to go an entire class without berating a student," Lyla murmurs. I spin around, grinning as I place my hands on the edge of the desk. Flashing her pearly smile between perfectly pink lips at me sends my heart into a thunderous beat. She walks

160

around the desk, slipping her bag over her shoulder and letting her fingertips trail up the side of my arm. Inhaling sharply, I'm hit with another draft of her intoxicating perfume and focus only on the heat from her body so close to mine. Her breasts brush against my bicep as she pulls up to her toes, whispering in my ear. "I hope that isn't what you call a grand gesture of an apology though. I'm not that easy, professor."

She winks smugly before slipping out the staff door without ever giving me a chance to speak as I'm still coming down from the high of her scent.

I grab the stack of papers from my desk, shoving them into my bag, and sling it over my shoulder. I pause at the threshold of the door, remembering that I had asked her about her favorite food last week. My excitement builds as I head across the grounds in search of the taco truck that makes the street tacos she couldn't stop talking about. We work during typical dinner hours and I can only hope that she doesn't take the time to eat before coming in tonight.

Twenty-five minutes of scouring the campus later, I stumble across the green and red painted truck with a line formed almost fifteen deep. I groan on the inside, knowing I'm probably the only person in a hurry to get somewhere while the rest will happily wait all night for this food. *It's all for Lyla though, it's to do something selfless for someone else and to repent for your actions. She deserves this.* I wait out the line, answering some emails on my phone and checking in with Ivy—

hoping to hear back about an early admittance letter. When it's finally my chance to order, I settle on two bags full of tacos, chips and salsa, and churros before quickly jogging across campus, bags of food in hand, to—hopefully—beat Lyla into the office.

The sunlight begins to fade through the windows as I pull her chair into my office and clear off my desk, putting all the food out and I drink in the aroma of decadently unhealthy food. I can hear her heels clicking down the hall, she's whistling—a sound I've never heard her make before—which makes me wonder what has put her in such a good mood today.

Cuz it sure as hell can't be all just for me.

I lean against the doorframe of my office to appear casual, just as she walks through the main office door, blocking the sight of the food. Her walk slows as she nears me, but as she pauses in confusion, looking around for the source of the scent, a smile explodes across her face.

"What have you been up to, Professor M?" she asks with a smirk. I shrug, unable to keep myself from smiling back at her.

"New nickname that doesn't involve a derogatory term?"

"Would you prefer something different? I'm sure if you give me a few seconds I can come up with something," she laughs. "I just wanted to test this one on for size but I'm more than willing to accommodate your desire for something more vulgar."

I bite the inside of my cheek, warm happiness spreading through my veins as she steps within arm's length of me. Close enough to feel my body being drawn to hers.

"I think," I take a step towards her, watching her straighten up with the proximity, "that I rather enjoy the change."

Her shoulders rise and fall quickly, her eyes meeting mine with a fiercely playful glint.

"Are you going to tell me why the room smells like tacos?" she whispers.

"Why don't you come to see for yourself?"

She turns quickly and goes to sling her bag onto her desk but in haste, I reach to grab it before it lands and nod my head towards my office.

"With me, tonight, Ms. Fischer," I wink. "There is a lot of work to be done on the contents sprawled across my desk."

Her cheeks flush, her mind clearly as in the gutter as my own with that innuendo.

The closer Lyla gets to me the more my body reacts. My skin tingles at the heat protruding from her body, my heart thunders in my chest. I suck in a deep breath as I turn back inside the office and she follows me inside. I sit her bag down by the door, fully aware that she won't be needing anything inside of it this evening.

"Holy shit, " she mumbles.

Her hand grasps my forearm and the heat singes where she touches. I look over my shoulder, taking in the sight of her pink lips parted and eyes wide in surprise. A warmth spreads through my chest as I instinctively jerk my arm closer to my body, pulling her against me and grasping her waist with my other hand. Instead of pushing herself away, she steps in and traces her fingers down the side of my jaw. I brush my lips across the skin of her forehead, gently pressing them as I feel her inhale sharply and her grip on my arm tightens.

"I owe you much more than dinner from a food truck," I whisper, "but I'll spend the allotted week apologizing for my behavior."

I step back from her, releasing my grip on her waist as her fingers loosen around my arm and she stumbles backward to her chair before taking a seat slowly. I retreat around the back of my desk and take a seat, watching as her eyes scan the food with a greedy shine in her eyes.

"If tacos are only the beginning of your apologies, I look forward to seeing what else you come up with," she winks, picking up a churro and biting down slowly between her lips. As she chews the bite, her eyes flutter closed and a soft moan escapes from her mouth sending a bolt of lightning through my body. I suck in a deep breath, dipping a chip into the salsa and licking the excess off with my tongue while looking into her eyes as they reopen. She sucks in her lips to suppress a grin, a warm flush rising over her cheeks as she crosses her legs in her chair. "I never knew chips and salsa could be so damn sexy."

With a chuckle, I pop the chip into my mouth and swallow before leaning across the desk until I'm mere inches away from her face, tracing my fingers through her hair and pushing it behind her ears.

"Miss Fischer, let me show you just how sexy eating can be."

"I just feel like I'm suddenly a new and improved version of myself, Lyla Fischer two-point-oh," I tell Lucy as we stroll towards the lecture hall. All day Monday I had felt invincible, as though I could take on the world—alone— just because of some wine-infused text messages to Professor Moxley. I'd worn my favorite heels that gave my ass the perfect lift in my pencil skirt for an extra kick; even though my feet were killing me today, they were worth the effort yesterday. He had not only been attentive and pleasant, not just with myself but the entire class, but he had gone out of his way to apologize for his behavior last week.

"Well I bet it's because you're no longer being held back by one-hundred and eighty pounds of a rock-solid asshole," she retorts, lifting her latte cup in salute.

Just go along with it. She doesn't know better.

"That's probably true," I roll my eyes, shoving her arm playfully as we come to a stop at the main door. As an art major, Lucy refuses so much as to set foot inside the law building— as though the politics discussed inside would "harsh her vibe" as she calls anything she doesn't want to do.

"Trust me, I know it's true," she says. "Clearly he knows it too since he's shown up where he knew you were going to be."

166

"Welllll, that's his problem," I click my tongue against my teeth. "I don't need his apologies any more than I need my mommy and daddy's acceptance these days."

"You fucking go, girl!"

We clink our cups together as I check my phone, noticing there are only about ten minutes left before I need to be in the office. Part of me is excited to see Tyson, especially after enjoying dinner and watching another documentary last night.

"You know I can't come in there," Lucy says, interrupting my thoughts before I got around to remembering Tyson slowly licking salsa off his finger. "I'm working on my final project and I can't risk taking those law cooties home with me right now." She shudders dramatically, wrapping her arms around herself in the process.

"When are you going to tell me what this final project is, Luc?" I ask with an eyebrow raised.

"When it's finished of course," she laughs. "Tooooooodles! Say hi to Professor Dickwad for me!"

I wave her off with a forced laugh and pull the door open, closing my eyes as I take a deep breath before stepping inside.

I wonder what Tyson will have in store for me tonight, not that I expect anything else from him. Going out of his way to get the dinner last night was more than I anticipated out of an apology from him.

I climb the stairs carefully, taking my time as I head in the direction of his office on the third floor. The hallway is deserted, which isn't unusual for the evening lately, but with finals coming so close I had expected other professors to begin working later in the evenings.

I wonder what the other professors would think if they saw me working inside his office with him for these hours. Would they assume something inappropriate is going on? I mean, not that it usually is but I do have bad enough luck that if something were to ever happen again, someone would definitely walk in on it.

While lost in thought, I've managed to walk past his office and am now face to face with the law professor's bulletin board in the hallway that showcases each person and a few things about themself. I scan each picture carefully, then check again— Professor Moxley is nowhere to be found.

"Wonder what that's about," I wonder aloud, then turn back and head towards his office. Before going through the doorway, I take another deep breath and reassure myself quietly. "I am strong, invincible, and smart. I can be flirty and sexy while also retaining my dignity in this situation."

I nod, then head towards the back of the room but quickly notice that my chair is back at my desk— but his door is closed and the room is dark.

What the hell.

Confused, I place my bag on the side of my desk and press my ear to the door but no sound comes from within. I knock twice, receiving no answer. Biting my lip, I pull my phone out of my pocket and check my emails in case I missed one stating that office hours were canceled— for the first time *ever*.

With no missed emails or text messages, I sit down and fiddle with my pen before searching through the stack of papers on my desk trying to find something to occupy my time.

Because there would be no end to the berating if he were to show up and I'm not here, even if he's late for once.

Minutes tick by slowly, each movement of the hand on the clock dragging as though it was pulling itself up a cliff by its fingertips. My mind begins to wander, questioning if he's gotten hurt and if there's reason to be concerned. I could just try texting him, but if that is the case I wouldn't want the wrong person to find our recent message exchanges. I struggle to begin checking more quizzes, he had at least given the students the option to take them home to complete them. At the end of the first hour, I smugly pull open my drawer to exchange my pen for my fun purple one instead. *If he isn't here, he can't dictate what color I grade in.*

A small box rests inside my desk drawer with a piece of stationery neatly tucked into the top with a piece of ribbon. My fingers tremble as I lift the box from the drawer, noticing the unexpected heaviness as I place it on top and remove the note to read it first.

I apologize for my absence this evening, Ms. Fischer, and

hope this will suffice as an extension of my apology.

-T

I blink, rereading the note three times, taking account of how he not only didn't touch base on where he was instead of being here but also that he didn't say that I was allowed to leave. I pick the box up and hold it in the palm of my hand as it grows moist with the heat radiating between my skin and the box. After pulling the top off the box and sliding the paper away, I gasp as I lift a palm-sized, quartz Triceratops figurine from the box. My heart swells as my eyes brim with tears, biting my lip to hold them back. I notice there is another scrap of paper inside the box.

P.S. - Because I know they're your favorite, and the T-Rex

is as basic as a PSL and Uggs.

My laughter echoes through the room as I fold the note and stick it back into the box, then trace the details on the figurine with my fingertip. The flawless stonework and weight in my hand make me realize that this was something he must have found before the weekend, or paid an exuberant amount of money to get it here after my demands of apologies.

"He's definitely off the hook now....," I whisper, grabbing my phone and texting him before I lose the courage.

ME: Apology accepted, you're off the hook.

The clock nears eight and I pack up my belongings, carefully placing the figure back inside the box and wrapping it up carefully. Even if someone notices me carrying the box across campus, no one will think twice to ask me what's inside. I don't fear for someone trying to mug me, though this is far more priceless and valuable than anything inside my apartment at this moment. As I turn the lights off in the office, closing the door behind me, I grip the box tighter and descend the stairs.

The crisp, evening air stings my skin as I step outside and I quicken my pace towards home. Houston is rarely known for being chilly, but tonight the only thing warm is the flush on my cheeks as I think about the special present I've gotten from a soft-at-heart professor— a professor I have fallen for, with no way to stop myself. The wrongs and rights of the situation are a constant, raging war between my heart and my head. For one minute, I let myself think about what happens if it all goes south if the world found out about our secret and everything became a dumpster fire of chaos.

Would it all be worth it? Is he worth it?

As I hear the beep of my phone, I pull it out of my pocket and read the newest message.

> **T.M.:** Maybe you're letting me off the hook, but I'm not quite done apologizing yet.
>
> **T.M.:** You deserve more than cheap apologies and secrets, Lyla. I can only hope that one day there will be a way to deserve your forgiveness.

I smile, tracing the message with my finger before returning the phone to my pocket.

It would, without a doubt, all be worth it in the end — secrets or no secrets.

FIVE HOURS EARLIER:

"Are you sure we can't do this any other evening?" I ask, tapping my foot impatiently against the hardwood floors. "I have office hours tonight, Sloan."

Her cackling through the phone sends a wave of annoyance through my body, heat rising in my veins as she orders someone— likely a maid—to clean up the mess she's made in the background. The last thing I want to do tonight is have dinner with Sloan but she insists that if I want to know why she wants to work at the university, I have to be willing to have dinner with her in person. I grimace as I imagine spending the evening with her instead of Lyla, mentally hoping there's a way out.

"Awwww, come on Ty-Ty, it'll be so much fun!" she insists. "We both know that you want the juicy gossip I'm just dying to spill."

Her overly sweet voice through the speaker echoes through the empty room, a shudder rippling through my body reminding me of the cold-hearted bitch she is inside.

Fun is not what I would call it, especially not at the last minute.

"Fine," I huff, slamming the drawer shut on my desk. "But we're meeting in the city, you are not to come to the house and neither of us will be drinking."

At least we won't be drinking at dinner.

"I have a different proposal," she says.

173

Of course you do.

"What, Sloan?" I grumble.

"Take out at your house and a single glass of wine, and I'll agree that the amount of time we spend together is only three hours," she insists.

"And at the end of the three hours, I can push you right out the door?"

"Sure, if I've given you the answers you want before then and you're not begging me to stay longer."

Under no circumstance could anything you say make me want to spend any more time with you. Not a fucking chance in hell.

"Takeout that you bring with you, one glass of wine, you will answer my questions before the end of the first hour and you leave at the end of the third," I demand.

"Sure thing, Ty-Ty," she chuckles. "I'll bring Chinese, be there in an hour!"

She hangs up before I get a chance to respond and I slam my fist down on the desk. I had been looking forward to giving Lyla her latest form of apology in person, but perhaps leaving a note would suffice. I turn the carved Triceratops between my fingers, admiring the craftsmanship in the etching of the quartz. Lyla had insisted that it was her favorite dinosaur and I scribbled out an amusing reminder of that conversation and how she felt about the T.Rex and placed it inside the

174

box before wrapping it back up and scribbling a note apologizing for my absence for the top of the box.

I place the box inside her desk drawer, the one with her purple pen that she loves and will definitely use in my absence, and walk back out the door before anyone can stop me to chat while the other professors are wandering the halls.

I could have just canceled the office hours completely, given Lyla the night off even…

But I won't, because I want her to find the present and in a twisted way I look forward to hearing her response. For the strangest reason, I'm excited to hear from her this evening— hoping that the figurine will spark enough inside of her to initiate a conversation with me first. It's weird, sending a text to a student as a professor, so I've just been choosing to not spend my free time talking to her as much as I would like. Within the next month, she will be out of my office and on to bigger and better things in her life and could easily forget about me.

But will I ever forget the way she has begun to thaw my insides? Or the way she has sparked life back into me after so many years in the darkness?

Of course, I won't, because Lyla Fischer is going to be the one that fixes me— in the same way, Sloan was the one that destroyed me.

I slam the door of my Camaro, turning the radio on full blast as I peel out of the parking lot and down the main road towards my house. The afternoon traffic is light, allowing plenty of time to make it home and remove anything of value from the main rooms of the house. While I'm at it, I might as well just remove anything that she could easily pick up and throw if tonight's dinner were to turn into yet another fight. Groaning, I pick up the few scattered picture frames and assorted Texans football memorabilia I have strewn throughout the house and lock it away in my bedroom. Thankfully, I have no reason to impress Sloan. so I grab my favorite pair of grey jogger pants and a blue long-sleeve shirt from the closet. She always hated when I wore sweatpants while we were married, now considered a luxury of comfort in the evenings, and the sooner I manage to get her out of my house, the better.

As I grab one of the cheaper bottles of Pinot Noir—her least favorite— from the wine rack and two old wine glasses from my cabinet, the knocking on the front door begins. Her signature four taps and a pause start a battle in my core. I don't want to let her back in this house but I also can't give her the chance to blindside me at work. If I'm able to control the evening, keeping her at arm's length and pushing her out the door the minute our three hours are up, there's minimal chance of her further damaging my life. I put some paper plates on the bar and thread my fingers through my hair as I walk towards the knocking as she grows more impatient, the sound getting louder.

"Time to get this the fuck over with," I mumble.

I muster up the best fake smile I can across my face and open the door, blinded by the setting sun as Sloan steps through like she still owns the place. Her icy blonde hair falling past her shoulders, the tight, silk black blouse, and a pair of coral dress pants that hug her thighs too tightly.

"Oh my goodness, I have just missed this place so much!" she exclaims, holding the bag of food in one hand while pressing her other hand to her left breast with her mouth agape.

"It's your own damn fault you ever left, Sloan," I retort, jabbing at the way she walked out on me years ago.

"Oh hush now, Ty-Ty," she smiles, wrapping her hand around my arm as I cringe at her touch, yanking my arm away from her. "Let's not spoil this evening by living in the past and look towards the future instead."

She turns, strutting towards the kitchen, clicking her tongue at pieces of artwork I've hung in the past few years, pointing out how certain decor doesn't match the flow of the house. A house she hasn't lived in for over a decade, one that she unquestionably would have no clue if something matched the rest of the house. I follow her, begrudgingly, into the kitchen as she starts rummaging through cabinets until she finds the real plates and starts dividing the food up as I open the wine, pouring my glass to the brim.

"We just can't ruin our fine dinner with an obscenity like paper plates, Ty," she chastises, sitting down next to me at the bar and taking

177

a sip of her wine. I watch as she struggles to keep her face together, knowing she hates the wine she's just sipped, but she plays it off well. "This is nice. It has just been far too long since we've had a meal together and quite frankly I've missed it."

"Well, that makes one of us," I mumble, twirling my lo mein on my fork and popping it into my mouth. Her eyes narrow as she stabs a piece of shrimp off her plate.

"Could you just try to be pleasant for a few hours?" she barks.

I shrug, taking another bite of my dinner and a long sip of wine. She shakes her head and continues eating in silence. Knowing what she's up to is important in due time, but for now, watching as the annoyance spreads through her is more amusing. Perhaps if I can keep this up, she'll tell me her evil plan *and* leave before the first hour is up.

Time passes, five minutes to ten, ten to twenty. She refuses to begin another conversation, clearly aware of how uncomfortable and unhappy I am about being backed into a corner with her. I throw my fork down on my plate, crossing my arms as I turn to face her. The corner of her mouth lifts as she slowly places her fork on the counter, flipping her long strands of hair over her shoulder and placing her hand on my knee. Instead of her hand feeling warm, like Lyla's, it feels like frostbite piercing my skin.

"Are you now prepared to have a civil conversation, Tyson?" she asks, batting her eyelashes at me. I take a deep breath, nodding as I swallow the last remaining shred of my phony pride.

"I'm sorry for acting out, Sloan," I apologize insincerely, "but it still hurts to see you and remember everything that I lost."

Her face brightens, though she contorts her lower lip into a dramatic pout. She traces her fingers along the side of my face, running them through my hair, freezing the skin with each touch. She taps my chin twice with her thumb and squeezes my knee before leaning in to whisper in my ear.

"I guess that means you'll be happy to know why I'm here."

Two can play this game, Sloan.

I twirl a strand of her hair between my fingers, letting the tips graze the side of her cheek as she leans into my touch. I lean forward, careful to limit my breaths as I'm edging closer to her skin, the overbearing jasmine and cherry perfume burning my nostrils. She sucks her bottom lip between her teeth as I slide a hand down her arm. "Why don't you tell me why you're being so secretive about something you're just bursting to tell, sweetums."

Using her favorite pet name sends a shiver down my spine in disgust but will surely work in my favor. She inhales deeply as she bites back a smile. Her greedy eyes look over my body, feeling them undress me inch by inch in her mind. As she gets closer, her lips brush their way up the edge of my jaw until she's against my ear and her hot breath singes my neck.

"I made a huge mistake leaving you, and I will never love anyone how I love you," she whispers. "I want you back, sugar buns."

Those six words are all it takes for the ice to spread through my body, affixing my limbs to my chair in shock as my body goes numb.

ME: Are office hours happening today or can I save myself the trouble of walking back across campus?

I hit send, not giving a single shit if I sound like an asshole because in my eyes that's about all that dick-hole *Professor Tyson Moxley* has been this week. Not showing up to hours on Tuesday and sending a cryptic message that evening when I thanked him was fine—really, it was. Yesterday though, he didn't even show up or cancel his class. I floundered in front of a classroom full of students who had been prepared to receive their essays back from the previous week. Expecting that he would show up with another apology for his office hours, I trekked through the rare, autumn rain on campus and sat in the office for a total of four and a half hours. The longer I sat there, the angrier I became until I stormed out of the office.

My grip on the phone is so tight that the skin of my palm begins to burn from the pressure. It's only twenty to three, plenty of time before hours are supposed to even begin—if he plans to be there. I won't be leaving this apartment until—if—he replies. I pace the length of my apartment, counting every step as a calming mechanism, but check my phone every few steps and undo any progress I make to not let the anger overtake me today.

181

Maybe he's hurt or something, should I be worried? Is there someone I should call to check on him? What if he just up and disappeared without so much as another word? Would I be ok if that happened?

I freeze, thinking about the possibility of a life with Tyson suddenly not in it anymore— no explanation, no goodbye.

My life was fine before he came along. It's not like I've ever needed a man to feel complete in life. Parker, I foolishly had believed to be someone worth my time. I enjoy spending time on my own more than other women my age, in no rush to settle down. There are plenty of places I want to go—goals to check off my list—before I ever start to think about settling down.

But Tyson had started opening up, making me believe that he was capable of being more mature and different than the others.

Isn't that what they all do, though? They say whatever they want you to hear, break down your walls, and eventually get into your pants before they leave. Not that he had gotten to that satisfaction yet—maybe he never will. He certainly seems to have lost interest in the chase.

Is that all I've been? An unattainable goal?

I shake my head in frustration, now I know I'm starting to sound like a crazy person.

"Seriously, Tyson, just fucking answer your goddamn phone!" I yell, throwing my phone onto the couch.

As if some higher power can hear my request, my phone dings. I gulp, stepping slowly towards the spot on the couch it landed, and close my eyes as I reach down to pick it up. It dings two more times before I take a deep breath and peer through my eyelashes just enough to read the messages as I flop onto the couch.

T.M.: Not tonight.
T.M.: We will have class tomorrow.
T.M.: I apologize for my absence, Miss Fischer.

"What the fuck?" I grumble, pinching the bridge of my nose and rereading the messages. My fingers are flying across the screen as boiling rage fills my veins.

ME: Of course, now I'm Miss Fischer again.
ME: An explanation would mean more than your apology.

Not that I'll ever get one that holds any amount of depth. The man is a fucking emotional tomb.

I pick up the remote and turn The Office back on before grabbing a bottle of wine from the counter. Without bothering to grab a glass, I screw the top off the cheap bottle and sit back on the couch taking a large gulp before my phone dings.

"Go away, asshole," I groan, reaching for the hunk of metal and roll my eyes as I read his latest message.

> **T.M.:** Perhaps one day I will be able to give you the explanation I promise you deserve. For now, it's better this way.

Another large gulp of wine down, I wrap my arms around my knees and pull them to my chest.

> **ME:** What the fuck is that cryptic bullshit supposed to mean? If this has something to do with anything I've done or said, seriously grow up and talk to me about it. Don't avoid me like a scorned teenage boy.

In all of the years I've been in Houston, even in the first few weeks when I knew no one, I have never felt as alone as I do right now. There isn't a soul I could even call and explain the situation at hand; of fighting with my Professor Boss-Man that I've kissed a few times and we've both managed to make it a dumpster fire of confusion. Lucy would be the least judgemental, but why tell her about something that I don't even understand? She would want details that I can't give her and the self-confidence that she has does not extend through me the same way.

"Get your ass on Google and find out where the motherfucker lives. He's still a male and if you want answers you are perfectly capable of showing up and demanding them for yourself. Don't let him coerce you with googly eyes or cryptic messages into backing down, girl. You can do this and you can win because you are a badass woman and women hold the keys to the world through their vaginas!"

My eyes burn as I fight back tears and hear Lucy's voice in my head. I know the latest impulsive message riddled with anger would likely be the last one of the night. I close my eyes, leaning back into the cushion and focus on deep breaths, and counting to twenty. I picture sitting on the edge of a warm beach and dipping my toes in the ocean water. Sounds of seagulls flying overhead, waves crashing against the land, and the scent of salty air in my nose.

Just as my heart rate begins to even out, my phone dings and it begins pounding again as I reach for it.

> **T.M.:** Please believe me when I tell you
> that my actions this week have nothing to
> do with you, Lyla.

My face flushes in anger as I bite down on my lip.

ME: Oh, so now I'm Lyla again when you
want to sound nice and caring? Well,
maybe you don't remember but actions
speak louder than words, Professor
Moxley.

Too far, way too far.

Still, I hit send and realize that even if he was beginning to
open up before, it doesn't matter anymore. He's clearly sending the
message that he's over whatever he thought—or pretended—that he
felt towards me.

*Because the truth of it is, I'm just a silly student that never mattered
at all.*

T.M.: Dammit, Lyla. I understand that.
Just give me a chance to apologize,
again. Even though I don't deserve the
chance.

"You sure as absolute hell do not deserve that chance," I
complain.

ME: You have one chance to show me how
sorry you are, Tyson.

Anger consumes me as I grab the nearest throw pillow and scream into it, tears streaming down my face. In all of my life, I have never dealt with someone capable of infuriating me as much as Tyson. He brings out a side of me that I didn't even know existed— one where hate and love can coincide, thrive together even. As I take a deep breath, shoving my feet off the couch to the ground, and stand up, the phone dings again. I pause, my hands balled into fists at my side, and shake my head before reaching for it.

> **T.M.:** Can you meet me at the North Entrance of Blaffer Art Museum? ASAP?

I swallow hard, letting my heart slow itself before I reply.

> **ME:** If you promise to explain, yes.

I run towards my bedroom, peeling off my office clothes and sifting through the closet in a hurry, and tossing them around the room.

> **T.M.:** I will tell you everything, Lyla.
> **T.M.:** Bring a jacket. It's going to be chilly.

"Dammit, Lyla," I mumble. "Where are you?"

It's been close to an hour since I asked her to meet me and she had, for some lucky reason, agreed. I'm starting to think she's blowing me off, which would be justified and reasonable payback after the hell I've put her through lately. There is no reason for her to hear me out or a single chance to explain—not that any explanation involving Sloan and her blowing up my life this week will ever be good enough.

How am I supposed to explain something I don't even understand myself?

On Monday, life was finally coming to a peaceful and happy junction for me. Clearly, Sloan could sense that I was on the verge of being happy and had to find a way to completely fuck it up— take her back or let her take the job. She's feigning sadness over the possibility of Ivy heading off to school and unsure of what she will do with her free time and big, empty house. Her desire to return to her roots and rekindle our relationship is built around the mere idea of being completely on her own—except for the staff she keeps on hand, pretending they don't even exist.

What kind of psychopath gives someone that kind of an ultimatum?

Sloan does. That's the kind of psychopath she is now and making any kind of a decision about her ultimatum has driven me to near insanity.

188

Another ten minutes and my heart drops as I see her emerge around the corner dressed in a pair of light wash jeans that hug every inch of her legs and hips. A leather jacket dons over her shoulders and I chuckle, waiting for her to recognize me perched against my motorcycle—wearing my leather jacket. It was a risky move, bringing the bike and not knowing her stance about riding on one, but I know Decision Day is coming with Sloan. I can't stand the idea of never getting the chance to have Lyla on the back, her arms wrapped around my waist and her chest pressed against my back. I readjust the crotch of my pants as it begins to tighten before shoving my hand back in my pocket as she finally looks my way and her perfectly pink lips turn upwards. As she strolls towards me, her black hair bouncing around her face and eyes covered by large sunglasses, my lips curve into a smile and I grip my custom handlebar tightly to refrain from reaching for her.

"I don't think you're supposed to be parked here," she says, her face moving slowly as she takes in the sight of my bike while chewing on her lower lip. She stands beside me, letting her fingers graze the soft leather of the seats and smooth black paint on the back of the bike. "I like this, I like this a lot."

"I guess it's a good thing I'm not planning on parking it here," I wink, putting my sunglasses on and straddling the seat before beckoning for her to climb on. She hesitates, fidgeting with the hem of her jacket as her teeth bite down harder on her lip. "Please, Lyla. It's better if we talk away from campus."

I watch as her shoulders rise and fall through her three deep breaths before she takes a step forward, resting her hand on my shoulder as her weight shifts between each foot. The heat makes my entire body react, sparks flying through my skin. I want to pull her into me, press my lips to hers, and hold her tight—but not here, not right now when I have so much to atone for. I'll take the win of getting her to climb onto the back of my bike for now.

"I've never been on a motorcycle before," she says, her voice small and timid. I smirk, run a hand through my hair, and stand up enough to reach up and rest my hand on the side of her face. She leans into my touch, brushing her lips against the palm of my hand as I trace my thumb along her cheekbone.

"You will always be safe with me, sweetheart."

She gasps but nods as she takes another step and squeezes my shoulder as she lifts a leg over the side and sits on the seat behind me. Sitting with her hands resting on her legs, her knees squeezing either side of my thighs—I believe this is, in fact, her first time on a motorcycle. Chuckling lightly, I pick each hand up with my own and wrap them around my waist, twisting my head to face her.

"You have to hold on, Lyla," I tell her.

She nods quickly and tightens her arms around my stomach as I start the bike with a roar. I give her the thumbs-up sign and see her

190

nod from the corner of my eye. After checking traffic, I pull out and let the wind blow my hair. Being on the bike has always felt freeing and acted as my fortress of solitude. I would take it out when Sloan was picking a fight, threatening me in one way or another over the years. In the first months after the divorce, I didn't so much as even start the Camaro, strictly riding the bike everywhere I went. Not any of the fondest memories this bike holds compares to the way it feels to have Lyla on the back with her hair whipping around her face and feeling her laughter rumble through our bodies as we wind through the city streets towards Hermann Park— somewhere far enough away from campus, somewhere without prying ears, for me to beg for her to hear me out.

My hands grip the handlebars tighter as I focus on the road with the warm pressing of Lyla's body against my back. Years and years of spending my time in seclusion, locking my heart away in a box and throwing out the key, I've forgotten the tenderness of another person's touch. The longer I'm away from others, the easier it is to be on my own and appreciate the silence. Sloan had been my first true love, Ivy had quickly taken her place in a different way— until they both left, leaving me cold, alone, and heartbroken.

As we near the park, Lyla has become more comfortable, resting her head on my shoulder. Every so often her lips brush the side of my neck and I hope it's intentional, reveling in her gentle caress. Even the wind hasn't been able to mask the scent of her perfume as

191

she's this close to me and it's intoxicating; sending overwhelming urges through my body to turn around. I could take her back to my house, throw her on my bed and keep her there forever. I could keep her—us—a living dream if that was an option.

But it's not, because Sloan could still find a way to ruin even that piece of happiness for me. She has spent years manipulating our daughter and twisting her vines of wrath through every crack in my life, ensuring that I am miserable at every turn. So why does she suddenly want to feign an interest in rekindling our love? What benefit does she see at the end of this road?

And is there a way to shield Lyla, sweet, innocent Lyla, from her wrath if I choose neither option? Can I shelter her from Sloan if she ends up on campus? Or I could let Sloan back into my life and pretend to love her again, letting Lyla be free to go and live her life, fulfilling every last dream and I can cheer her on from the sidelines.

But is the path resulting in the lesser shitstorm a life that I can find a will to live with and for?

I park at the Japanese Garden, pushing the kickstand down and offering Lyla my hand to help her off first. I quickly notice the grin spread across her face as she tries to tame her windblown hair before lifting her sunglasses on top of her head. Suddenly, I can't fight it anymore. I kick my leg over the side of the bike and grab her waist, pulling her right up against me.

"Lyla, I need to kiss you. Now," I plead. "Unless you tell me not to."

She gasps before nodding, giving me the permission I need. I crash my lips onto hers as I tighten my grip on her waist. Her hand reaches behind my head and her fingers dig through my hair to pull my lips into hers. I push her lips open with my tongue, sliding it inside her warm mouth and gently flicking her tongue as she moans into my mouth. My heart pounds through my chest, thundering in my ears as I lose control. Our kisses become more urgent as she pulls me closer with every grasp— and then she pushes me away, flushed and disoriented. With our heavy breathing filling the silent void, her wide eyes stare into mine as I take my sunglasses off and sit them on the bike.

"I can't do this, Tyson," she mumbles. "I thought I could.. as much as I want to... I just can't. Not until-"

"Not until I explain," I cut her off. "I understand."

She nods and I take her hand into mine, leading her to a gazebo overlooking the pond and pull her down next to me, rubbing the side of her hand with my thumb.

"Promise me that you'll hear me out," I plead. "Until the very end."

She turns towards me, propping a leg on the bench and resting her unoccupied hand on my thigh.

"I promise," she says, squeezing my thigh in reassurance. I take a deep breath, then I begin to tell her my story.

Tyson talks, I listen.

"I met Sloan in high school, she was a transfer
student and her foster family moved here from
Louisiana. I was immediately drawn to her looks and
charm," he admits. "As a Houston native, I took it upon myself to offer
to show her around. We spent so much time together that it was
almost inevitable for us to fall in love at such a young age. We both
ended up coming here, to U of H, after we graduated but she fell
pregnant with Ivy during our freshman year."

I nod, watching his face fall as his eyes glaze over with
memories of his haunting past.

"We were so young, so fucking young, Lyla. Sloan was ecstatic
which made me elated to be going through such a life-changing
scenario with a woman that wanted nothing more than to be a mother.
Her foster family was clearly out of the picture at that point. They cut
her off the moment she turned eighteen and never bothered to check in
on her. My family became hers and shit, they just adored her. She was
the daughter my mother never had. They doted on Sloan throughout
her pregnancy, ensuring that she had everything to be happy and
comfortable as they created a home for us within their own home.
They offered to help with Ivy as soon as she was born, allowing us to
finish college and get our degrees. My father and grandfather started

195

their law firm many, many years ago and I was expected to follow in their footsteps. I did so without a second thought because that was the life planned for me and at the time I wanted nothing more than my own father's approval.

"When Ivy was four, we moved out and began our life as a family together, in our own home. I was already practicing at the family firm and Sloan was able to stay home with Ivy, giving her the mother figure in her life that Sloan had always wished to have for herself. I thought motherhood was perfect for Sloan after everything she had been through. She always seemed so elated, loving, warm — until Ivy started school. When she was no longer home every minute, every day, Sloan grew hateful, bored, and lonely. She spent more time drinking and picking fights with me, questioning where I was if I had to work late, and eventually finding other men to entertain her time. I had my suspicions, I wasn't completely oblivious to her extracurricular activities but I tried to look past them."

His hand squeezes mine tightly as he shakes his head, an angry growl coming up from his throat before he continues.

"It took me finding her in the bed we shared with her personal trainer before I had the sense enough to tell her to get out. I never expected her to take Ivy with her, not in the capacity that she managed to at least," his voice breaks as he sucks in his lips.

I lean into him, offering a reassuring peck to his shoulder as he composes himself. He rests his forehead against mine, quickly stroking my jawline with his hand.

"I didn't handle the affair maturely, Lyla," he whispers. "I'm not proud of the way I behaved, the way I acted out. I drank constantly, I rarely showed up to work because I couldn't stand to look my father in the eyes after he berated me for leaving the mother of my child. He emphasized that I was disgracing the family name and when I finally had enough, I did the one thing I was sure to rid myself of his toxicity for good. I showed up drunk to court one day."

"Oh god, Tyson," I murmur.

"I always thought my mother had enough love in her heart to forgive me, even if it took some time and she would come to terms with losing Sloan as her faux daughter... but she didn't, she hasn't. I haven't heard from my parents in almost a decade. Ivy and Sloan spend most of their free time with them. They spend more time with my daughter than I do, honestly. Unfortunately, I screwed myself over in the beginning and was barely allowed supervised visitation for the first few years. It gave Sloan plenty of ammunition against me as the years went on, using anything and everything she can against me when it comes to our daughter. Being a father was *everything* to me and Sloan ripped my life apart with her affair. Instead of working through it, healing, or finding a way to move on... I just stayed in that broken state for the last ten years."

"I have given Sloan everything she's ever asked for, before and after our demise. Yet, she took everything from me that I didn't even know I had," he says. " She weasels her way through my life and destroys everything in her path. She has been doing just that for the last decade, crushing whatever small pieces of myself I attempt to put back together. I've spent the last decade building up a wall around myself because the idea of letting someone get too close is terrifying. The only thing I've ever wanted is for Ivy to eventually not see me as the villain in this story."

I hold his hand tighter as a single tear falls from his eye. He flicks it away with the back of his thumb, then presses his lips to my knuckles.

"There are so few pieces left of me that if anything else is broken, I may never be able to put myself back together again," he sighs.

I scoot closer to him on the bench, letting my knee rest against his warm thigh. The desire to pull his head to my chest ripples through my body as I watch his face fall more with each passing minute. I run a hand down the side of his face gently, pushing the hairs behind his ear that have fallen forward. He musters half a smile and takes a deep breath, squeezing my hand as I wait patiently for him to continue.

"You are a good person, Tyson. One day, Ivy will see Sloan for who she is and come to terms with it. From what you've told me, you are the hero in this story," I tell him. "Sometimes the hero looks like the bad guy, in the beginning. You just have to get through their rough backstory to find their true identity."

The corner of his lip tugs up as the tension releases from his shoulders, letting me know my words have pulled at his heartstrings.

"The moment you came into class the first day, it was like a spark ignited from inside of me that had been out for far too long. I couldn't look at you and not feel drawn to the desires that had laid dormant in my soul. I've never been drawn to another person the way that I am to you, Lyla," he sighs. "That's why I have been the biggest asshole in the entire universe towards you."

I raise an eyebrow in confusion, my lips pressed together. My usual slew of responses are resting on the tip of my tongue but I don't dare let one slip, not now.

"Lyla, I know that my behaviors have made no sense, but I can assure you that my unintentional jackassery is a mere result of my inner turmoil and confusion," he lifts my hand to his lips, pressing softly before resting our intertwined fingers on the side of his face. "You are a fearless, exquisite, confident, persistent, and intelligent woman. A rare breed, that deserves to be cherished and treasured, to be raised upon the tallest pedestal and worshipped. But Lyla, as much as you deserve every moment of someone's attention and love, I just *can not* promise that I can give that to you."

199

My heart sinks as his eyes squeeze shut. I can see the pain warping his expression as I bite back my tears. The realization that this is not only an explanation but also a likely goodbye, is beginning to dawn on me. *This is the risk you take when you fall for the wrong, older, and off-limits man.* You risk feeling so blissed out and courageous one minute, then free-falling off a cliff without a parachute the next. The silence feels like free falling out the side of a plane, waiting to find out if I'm going to crash into the darkness or have a hero swoop in and save me.

"It's not that I don't want to give you all of that Lyla, but complications are arising that could ruin everything for not only me but you as well."

He readjusts, placing a leg on either side of the bench so that we're now facing each other, and grabs my face in his hands. His blazing eyes staring into mine, as though he can see through my mind and into my soul. He chews on his lower lip for a moment before relaxing and pressing his forehead to mine. I close my eyes and get lost in the scent of amber and pine on his skin, the warmth of his skin against mine— because now I'm sure, this is goodbye.

"What complications, Tyson?" I whisper.

I feel the rise and fall of his body with a deep breath, my heart crashing through my chest as I feel the darkness closing in. I'm seconds away from crashing, and he's not trying to save me.

200

"Sloan applied for a job at the university. She was offered the job last week after I met with the Dean the previous Friday," he croaks. "She came to me on Tuesday with two simple, at least in her belligerent mind they're simple, options."

With my throat clenching shut as my lungs scream for air, I'm unable to give them, I wait. I can't open my eyes to look at his face for fear of losing the small amount of control I've held back my sobs with. Inside, my mind is screaming and telling me to run— that Tyson Moxley is about to break my heart before I ever realized it was his to break.

"What are your options?" I struggle to say, without taking a breath.

He shakes his head, fighting a battle unbeknownst to me. He struggles as he chokes on the words he tries to form, forcing them back inside. He wraps his arms around me and pulls me flush with his chest. I can feel the pounding of his chest on my shoulder as his lips graze the top of my head, through my hair. He holds me close as I hear him stifle back his sobs.

"My options are to let her take the job, where she will inevitably find a way to ruin my reputation and career, again. Plus, she will likely find out about you, my feelings for you, and ruin your life as well," he pauses, another deep breath, another squeeze of his arms around my body. "Or I can forgive her for her past actions, take her back, and reunite our family once again."

The darkness closes in as I feel my body weakening. My heart shatters, the ringing sound of silence fills my ears as I lose the will to fight the tears any longer. The warm liquid burns down my face as I press my face into his chest, gripping the sides of his jacket so hard the zipper rips into my skin— but if this is the last time I'll ever feel his body against mine, the pain is worth it in the end.

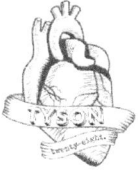

I hold Lyla in silence, the air surrounding us so quiet I can almost hear as her heart shatters in her chest. Her hushed sobs, her face buried against my chest bring tears to my eyes. Pressing my face into the smooth silk of her hair, I inhale her perfume and lose myself in the warmth of her body. She's been quiet, she's been more patient than I deserve— but in the end, my explanations will never be enough. Ultimatums were always one of Sloan's specialties to bend the world to her advantage.

"Lyla," I murmur, stroking her cheek gently with my fingertips."Baby, I'm right here."

She pulls away from my chest, wiping her tears away with the back of her hand, and looks up.

"I have been dealt a hand of impossible choices... neither a path I wish to take," I try to reassure her.

I reach for her hand but she yanks it away, shaking her head. She averts her eyes, not daring to meet my gaze as she ponders while biting her lower lip.

"Please," I beg her, "talk to me."

She has to have questions, comments—anything— after a load of information dumped at her, but for once she doesn't seem to want to be the first to break the silence.

Sucking in her lips, her hands ball into tight fists at her side.

"What do you want me to say, Tyson?" she snaps.

203

"I need you to tell me what you're thinking, just like you always do. Be honest with me."

She erupts into a fit of laughter and I'm taken aback. My jaw drops as I watch her clutch her hand to her chest as she struggles to take a deep breath before shooting a deadly look at me.

"You want me to be honest?" she asks between the laughter. I nod as thunder pounds in my eardrums, my heartbeat threatening to shatter my chest.

She sucks in her lips, her teeth biting the insides as I see the water welling in her eyes. I reach my hand up to wipe away the lone tear that escapes but she grabs my hand, pushing it away and letting the tear fall.

"How about this for some honesty, then," she snarls.

I bite down on my tongue. Pissing Lyla off has never led to anything good between us but she needs to get this off her chest and I need to let her. Whatever she needs to say, or scream, I'll let her. She listened to every painful word out of my mouth and now, I have to do the same.

"I don't want you to get back together with your ex-wife." Lyla holds her hands up and shrugs her shoulders. "That's probably the most selfish and immature desire I've ever had, I'm probably only caring about myself and not taking the fact that your family could be whole into account but what the fuck else am I supposed to want. I've spent the last few months on a rollercoaster between hating you, liking

204

you, loathing you and just as you've started to really get me to fall for you, this is the bombshell you drop on me.

"I think she treated you like shit before and is still trying to pull the strings of your life and instead of standing up to her and for yourself, you're just letting her. Who the fuck cares if she works at the university? So she works there and the people that matter, those of us that know and genuinely care about you, won't let her destroy you. Not around there. If it's me you're worried about, don't." Her eyes are narrow to slits as she jabs a finger into my chest. "I'm a grown-ass woman, Tyson Moxley. In case you haven't noticed, I don't exactly need someone to make the hard decisions for me and try to tell me what's worth the risk in life. Because, somehow over the last few weeks, I would take that risk for you. Maybe you wouldn't, or won't, for me and that's perfectly fine. I get it. My time as your assistant is up in a few weeks and we can go our separate ways and never have to fucking see each other again if that's what you want."

I open my mouth to stop her, to say something in defense of myself—my feelings for her—but she holds up a finger, placing it on top of my lips, to stop me before I get the chance.

"If you don't think that I understand exactly how wrong this, these feelings, all of it, then you have underestimated my intelligence. If I, us, whatever this is, is something you want to fight for, we'll fight for it and we'll do it together."

"Lyla, it's too much of a risk!" I yell before she gets the chance to stop me. "If you think that I don't want you in my life, you've lost your goddamn mind." I grab her by the waist, yanking her towards me so she's pressed against my knees, holding her face in one of my hands as my thumb traces her lower lip. "I will not let Sloan swoop in and ruin your life in the same ways that she has ruined mine. I lost everything thanks to Sloan and she is ruthless when it comes to getting what she wants." I take a deep breath, watching Lyla fight to keep her mouth closed as her eyes widen. "She's given me two choices, but she only wants me to choose one of them. The one that makes our family whole again. If I just choose to let her work at the university, she'll take that decision as a personal vendetta and work tirelessly to ruin every shred of happiness and support I've found over the years."

Her expression falls as my heavy breath rattles in my chest. She runs her hands through her hair, grasping the back of her neck as she squeezes her eyes shut. Her chest rises then falls. Her mouth forms a perfect o-shape as she breathes in deeply.

The streaks of pink and orange through the sky caught my eye beyond her gaze. The sun is setting, the time has grown later in what feels like only minutes and we need to get out of here before the security finds us. We may not be doing anything wrong, but karma's a bitch and I don't need anything to cause more of a problem than we already have.

"I know this is the worst timing and there is still a fucking load of shit for us to talk about and unpack, but we need to get out of here," I whisper.

She opens her eyes, immediately darting towards the golden ball lowering in the sky, nodding in response. I stand up slowly, offering her my hand to help her up only to have it ignored, her crossing her arms instead and tucking her hands in. We walk in silence to the motorcycle, possibly the longest thirty-three steps of my life. She stops almost a foot away, careful not to come too close to me or just unsure of herself.

"Lyla...,"

"Just get on the bike, Tyson," she pleads, so I do.

She falters as she comes closer once I'm sitting down, lifting her hand towards my shoulder and then putting it back at her side. She looks at her legs, back at the bike, and then sighs as she places her hand on my shoulder in defeat so she can swing her leg over. Instead of wrapping her arms completely around me again, she grips the sides of my waist carefully. It's not how I would prefer her to hold on, but I'm not in a position to push for anything more right now when I can just take it slow and hope that she relaxes.

"Can I take you back to your place?" I ask. "I'd rather you not walk alone through campus this late."

She nods, rattling off the address of her apartment. I start the motorcycle and feel her fingers tightening on my hips as we slowly pull out of the park and drive through the city lights. I take the scenic route through the city, feeling her head rotate back and forth as she looks at the lights from the new point of view, and I can see her smiling in the mirrors. At a stoplight almost twenty minutes later, she wraps her arms around me and tucks her cold hands inside my shirt as I flinch from her icy skin.

Shit, I hadn't even thought about how cold it gets when the sun goes down.

As we wait, I reach a hand to hers through the fabric and rub gently to warm her up and she rests her head on my shoulder. She nuzzles her face against my neck, letting her lips graze the sensitive skin, and sends a shudder of relief through my body.

When I pull into the parking lot of her apartment and shut the bike off, she carefully swings her leg over and hops off. Unsure of what to do, I put down the kickstand and step off the bike so that I can face her. Lyla's expressionless face makes my heart race in the panic that this is it, this is the end.

I've lost her. She doesn't understand it now, but it's for her own good.

She takes a quick set of steps towards me, checking around us for anyone that might be watching, and throws her arms around my neck as she slams her lips onto mine. Startled, I'm slow to respond before my lips press back against hers and I wrap a hand into her hair, pulling her closer.

To hell with losing her.

Fire ignites through my veins as she pulls me flush against her chest, her perky breasts pressing against my chest. To live in the warmth of her embrace, to fight the battles Sloan throws at us together, and to have a life worth living again—it feels so fucking right. I wrap an arm around her waist as her fingers tangle in my hair, her tongue urgently flicking against my lips as I feel the wetness of a tear falling down her face. I freeze, pulling away and quickly grabbing her face in my hand to keep her from running off.

"Talk to me, Lyla," I whisper.

She looks into my eyes with such certainty that I will do anything for her at this moment.

"Fight for us, Tyson," she says. "I need you. If you need me, if what you say you feel for me is in there… I need you to fight for us because I would fight for you."

She pulls herself out of my grip and walks away. As she opens a door and slips inside, leaving me standing there in the glow of the streetlights filtering through the trees, the agony builds in my chest.

I know that I can't—shouldn't—do the one thing she needs.

Wrapped in my favorite emerald green sweater, I trudge through campus for Environmental Law and the first of sixteen final days as Professor Moxley's teaching assistant. My eyes are raw, still red and burning from the overworked tear ducts and crying myself dry. I spent the night thrashing in bed and screaming into my pillow, replaying the conversation between us in the garden. For all the times he's talked about Sloan, giving her another chance to break him into pieces has to be the stupidest decision I've ever heard out of such an intelligent man— a decision that I can't wrap my head around.

What if he doesn't want to fight for us? What if I made a mistake by walking away instead of pulling him inside and begging him to stay?

I shake my head, letting my hair cover the majority of my face as I reach the building, taking a deep breath before pulling open the door. I count my steps as I make my way towards the staff door, praying that he's running late and not waiting for me on the other side.

What if he does still love her, despite everything she's done, and he wants to go back to her?

Grabbing the handle and pushing it down, I close my eyes for a brief moment as it opens and my heart drops as I see him sitting at his desk. His broad, muscular shoulders stretch against the back of his charcoal shirt, his blonde hair pulled into a tight bun at the nape of his neck. My heart flutters as I slowly and quietly walk towards my desk,

210

placing my bag on the back of my chair and reaching inside for my laptop.

"Good Afternoon, Miss Fischer," he says warmly.

"Afternoon, Professor," I mutter, never averting my eyes from my desk.

The students begin to file inside and the room fills with noise as they settle into their seats, pulling their computers out of their bags while chatting with each other. A few yell out that they're happy to see Professor Moxley back, some ask where he's been. He waves them off with his hand, instructing them to sit down as I pull up the document to record notes on. I hear his chair pushing away from his desk as his steps grow closer, stopping next to me.

"Lyla," he whimpers, and I cave.

I look up to see the similarities in our expressions today. The dark circles beneath our red-rimmed eyes, the disheveled wrinkles in his clothes. His hair is messy in the front, falling from his bun and his face sullen. I gulp, fighting back the oncoming tears my body somehow still has left to cry. I reach my hand out, grasping onto his behind the desk, and give it a quick squeeze and a fake half-smile. The corner of his mouth lifts as he nods, squeezing my hand in return once more before stepping around the desk and beginning his lecture on conservation.

My fingers move quickly across the keyboard as my mind manages to keep up with his words, though I feel a million miles away. Instead of his usual domineering and powerful voice, his words are indignant and mellow. The whispers between the students throughout class, comments about his behaviors most likely, are left unpunished as he shakes his head when he trips over his own words. I've never witnessed him in this fashion, but my heart breaks for him as it feels as though he's losing himself.

He dismisses class fifteen minutes early and falls into his chair, burying his face in his hands as the last student leaves the room. I pack away my belongings slowly, watching carefully as he silently fights a battle in his head— his hands gripping and pulling at his hair as he shakes his head. In my head, it's a battle between what I want to do and what I should do. A fight between my mind and heart, wanting to hold him in my arms and comfort him and wanting to push him further away, letting him wallow in his self-inflicted misery.

This choice, it's his to make.

Whatever happens next, he has to decide where I fall into that equation— if at all.

My heart wins, knowing that I can't just leave him at a time like this and still believe that I'm a decent human being. I sit my bag on my desk and go to him, leaning against the edge of his desk and placing a hand on his shoulder. The warmth of his skin through his thin shirt comes close to burning the thin skin of my palm, focusing on only the tight muscles beneath my fingertips.

"What can I do?" I ask, quietly.

He doesn't respond, instead, he digs his fingernails into his scalp and drags them slowly down the back of his head before wrapping his hands behind his neck. His eyes stay closed as he breathes sharply, as though settling himself before coming up with a response. He squeezes his eyes shut and in one swift movement, his hand slams down on his desk. My body flinches as I watch his expression twist into a mixture of pain and sorrow.

"Please, Tyson," I beg. "Talk to me."

Exactly what he said to me last night.

He shakes his head quickly, his knuckles turning white from gripping the edge of his desk.

"I can't," he says, "not here."

I nod, sighing in defeat, though he can't see me with his eyes still closed. I push off the desk and quickly grab my belongings and storm out the staff door before he can stop me as my heart thunders in my ears. My feet carry me swiftly through the busy hall, managing to only bump into a few fellow students as I push towards the doors as water fills my eyes, blurring my vision. I need to get as far away from Tyson as possible— even if only for a few hours.

I find my way to the nearest coffee shop, not the one I found Parker kissing another girl in, desperate for a hot cup of coffee mixed with espresso. Running on no sleep and a lot of adrenaline can only go so far, and I'm not ready to crash just yet. I rattle off my order to the barista and scroll through my phone as she makes my order.

LUCY: OMG!! I think my project is
DOOOOOONE!!!! I can't wait for you to see it!

I smile at Lucy's excitement, knowing that she's likely
completed yet another abstract masterpiece worthy of hanging at the
Met. Natural talent in the arts comes easily to Lucy from a young age
and she's run with her obscure ideas ever since, preparing for her first
real job as a mural painter in Savannah this summer.

ME: So proud of you, Luc!! Send me a pic
later!

The barista calls my name and I grab the cup from her with a
quiet thanks. Though it's cold outside and warm here, I don't feel like
sitting still long enough to let my thoughts overpower me. Heading
back out the door for an aimless stroll, walking through the campus in
winter has never been something to brag about but is somehow more
appealing than thinking today. The trees are beginning to sag and the
grass is growing brown, a sad image when you think of Texas while
you're elsewhere. It's another unusually cold day for Texas, but still
better than a fall day in Washington. In a few short weeks, I'll be
ringing in the holidays with my brother and his wife with the
likelihood of a blanket of snow covering the ground. In all the years
I've spent going to Tyler's for Christmas, it feels like a weight being

put on my shoulders this year. Knowing what I'm leaving behind, what could happen while I'm gone, sends a crippling rush of sadness through my body.

As the sun sinks lower in the sky, I stroll in the direction of Tyson's office and step inside— even if I am a little bit early. The warm air blowing from the vents above brings life back into my numb limbs as I climb the stairs, my footsteps quiet atop the linoleum. Somewhere down the hall, through doors and walls, I can hear voices echoing, angry shouting, before I get up the stairs.

The closer I get, the slower my steps get as I realize that I know one of those voices. One of them sounds like Tyson, the other belongs to a female whose voice feels like a knife to my gut as I get closer.

"How dare you speak to me like that!" the woman shrieks.

I freeze outside the doorway, scared to interrupt whatever is going on inside and unable to breathe.

"How dare I speak to you like what? Defending myself and not letting you get your way for once in your entire fucking life?" Tyson yells.

"You know damn well that you are the only thing, the only person, that I ever wanted!" she yells back at him.

"Fuck you, Sloan," he laughs, angrily. "If that was true you never would have left and you never would have done what you have over the years. You don't want me, you're just bored. Go find someone else to play with and get the fuck out of my office."

Stunned in place but not prepared to meet his ex-wife as the sound of her heels gets closer, I turn my head and pretend to read the bulletin board on the wall beside me, the door propped open blocks me from view. The steps paused as she gets closer to the door.

"You're going to regret this," she snaps, then stalks through the door.

"You're probably not wrong about that," Tyson mumbles, his voice now closer to the door than I had expected him to be. I don't look his way until the sound of her steps fades down the stairs. He retreats into the room without seeing me on the other side of the door and I wait before going inside, not wanting to interrupt his version of cooling off— which sounds as though it involves him repeatedly slamming his door.

I swallow hard, count to thirty, and head inside with my head held high as my body feels mixed between elation and horrifyingly scared, definitely unprepared and taken aback.

I asked him to fight for us and it sounds like he's doing just that.

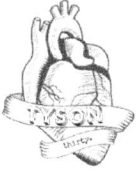

Refraining from repeatedly punching my fist against the wall is taking a certain form of self-control that I have lacked in the past, but I know Lyla is due to arrive at any moment. The fact she didn't walk in on Sloan and me fighting like teenagers was lucky enough. I can only hope that she didn't run into Sloan in the hall. Of course, Sloan had shown up unexpectedly—again—and demanded a decision be made immediately on the ultimatum she had given me. She wanted to know whether to accept the contract she was offered or if holding out for something better, something like a life with me again, is something she should be counting on. Between Lyla leaving me standing in the parking lot of her complex last night, seeing her in class today and making a fool of myself and coming to my office this afternoon— I seem to have unconsciously made a decision and then threw it into Sloan's face. Watching her expression go from smug to irate in mere seconds was almost as satisfying as the taste of Lyla on my mouth— her warm, soft lips pressed against mine. However, pissing off Sloan means that the fight has only just begun and I have turned her into a ticking time bomb against me.

In the silence of the room, apart from my still pounding chest, I hear Lyla's footsteps on the linoleum as she makes her way across the room. She pauses close to her desk but luckily doesn't knock or try to come inside. I'm not ready to unload the events of the afternoon just yet. Even if I am fighting for us, there are still so many wrong pieces in

217

this equation that I'm not ready to admit. Without Sloan interfering with my life, the mere fact that I'm a professor and she is a student is enough to ruin both of our lives— on top of the lesser problem of the age gap between us. I may not know specifics but the fact that she is a grad student means she's likely around twenty-four which puts her at twelve years younger than myself, almost thirteen.

My pen taps aimlessly against the desk as my eyes switch between staring at the blank document opened on my computer screen and out the window where Lyla has found a way to busy herself grading papers. I'll never have another assistant that comes close to the profound usefulness and intelligence that she is but if there is a chance at anything going further between us, I have to let her leave that position. I can't fight to keep her working for me and fight to have a relationship of any kind with her. When she's not working as my TA we're likely more capable of secluding ourselves—and any relationship we have—from the rest of the staff until graduation. I toss the pen across the room and pinch the bridge of my nose, succumbing to the recognition that no work will be getting done inside my office tonight. As I stand up to head towards the door, I see another person walk through the front office door and I freeze— in the months since school has started, there has rarely been a student show up during office hours.

Lyla jumps, clearly startled by whoever walked in, and quickly looks back to my office, her eyes wide, and points towards the main

218

door shaking her head. Leaning against the front of my desk, I listen carefully as I make out the voices as they grow louder.

"You can't be here, Parker!" Lyla is shouting.

Of course, it's Mr. Bennett, the only person that could manage to make today even worse.

"Come on, Ly! I just want to talk to you for a minute!" he says with a slur that sends a tingling through my skin.

"This isn't the time or place," she's yelling. "Nor is there anything you could say that I have any interest in hearing!"

There's the feisty side of her I adore so much. The side that got under my skin enough to entice me to piss off Sloan to the end of the world.

"You don't even know what I want to say but I *am sure* that you want to hear it."

I suck my tongue between my teeth, lifting off the edge of the desk, and stepping closer to the door quietly to hear better. If he is so certain that this is something she would want to hear, I would like to be enlightened as well. Given the last messages I read that he had sent her, this little shit doesn't deserve another second of her time and if he takes a step out of line I'll drag him out of the office myself.

"You have thirty seconds, start talking," Lyla is demanding. With my now obstructed view, I form an image in my mind. I can see her standing with her arms crossed, her fingers digging into the skin on her arms as her lips are pressed together tightly. The same way she's looked at me so many times before.

219

"Lyla, what happened with that girl was a mistake. I don't even know what I was thinking but I can't ever replace you. You're so fucking hot. You are great in bed, you're fun to be around, and you put up with all my shit. Fuck, I love you so fucking much, Ly. I don't want anyone else but you, ever ever again!"

My heart drops into my stomach as each of his words professing his love for her rip through me. Thinking of them in bed together, a place that I would love to take Lyla stings like a knife through my heart. He doesn't deserve her love, he doesn't even deserve to so much as look at her— *but am I any better than him?* A life with him would be easy for her if she could get past his indiscretion, his vile words, but a life with me would be complicated and full of trivial problems.

"Get the fuck out of this office, Parker," Lyla growls. "You fucked up. You can live with the consequences. I don't want you back, ever. I'm not joking. You need to leave. I can't stand the sight of your disgusting, cheating, lying face."

With those words, though spewed with venom and hatred from her delicate lips, elation soars me back to cloud nine and butterflies flutter in my chest. I step carefully, wanting to see the scene unraveling through the small window. Her arm is pointing towards the door and I can almost feel the rage flowing through her body through the walls. The sound of footsteps outside the door shuffles my own feet back around, reaching for the handle as I wait. The steps are getting closer, heavier, and more urgent.

"No, I'm not leaving. Not yet. I'm going to show you what you seem to forget you loved so much about me."

More silence, the handle gripped in my hand begins to press into the skin of my palm.

"What the fuck! Get your hands off of me!" Lyla yells and I fling the door open as Mr. Bennett is digging his hands into her waist, attempting to press his mouth against hers— against the mouth, I so desperately want to claim as my own.

"Come on, Ly, you know you miss me too," he's begging.

Without thinking, in the fraction of a second my hand is on his shoulder and ripping him away from her as she gasps. I pull him further away from her as an angry growl escapes from my mouth.

"Yo, what the fuck Professor?" he says

I squeeze my eyes shut, trying to push the oncoming rage back down inside.

"She said to get off her," I hiss. "Now get the fuck out of my office." He holds his hand up in defeat as I release his shoulder from my grip. "I won't ask again. Leave."

He stumbles back towards the door, smirking and shaking his head.

"You'll come running back one day, Lyla," he says smugly, then exits the room.

I wait for his steps to disappear down the stairs before I turn back towards Lyla, taking in her expression that seems mixed between rage and sadness. I walk towards her slowly, taking deep breaths to relax my own body before trying to comfort her. Her hands now balled into fists at her side, a single tear rolling down her cheek. Her distress sends a warm desire, a need, to comfort her and promise her that no one will ever treat her that way again— but instead, I walk past her. Back inside my office, in the blink of an eye, it seems as though the sadness fades and the rage overcomes her as she stalks towards me.

"I didn't need your help," she growls. "I would have handled Parker just fine without you coming out here and putting your hands on him, which he will absolutely tell the fucking Dean about and get you into trouble."

I cross my arms as I take a step towards her, letting my eyes penetrate her gaze and matching her expression filled with rage.

"I don't give a single fuck about getting in trouble with the Dean for pulling him off you before he tried anything else. He's lucky I didn't hurt him on purpose, and I would have without a second thought. You should know that the Dean won't take too well to his attempt at pushing himself on a woman and if he complains, he'll likely put himself at risk of getting expelled."

Her eyes squeeze into slits as she sucks in her bottom lip.

"I am a grown woman, Professor Moxley," she hisses. "I don't need, or want, you to fight my battles for me."

"Even a grown woman can accept the help she receives when she's put into an impossible situation," I state.

The anger she's holding in is sending a flush to her cheeks as she steps closer to me, so close that her perfume impales my nostrils and my mind becomes foggy.

"Maybe a grown man should know his place and when a woman needs help or when she's capable of fending for herself," she retorts. "I am a fucking Queen, professor. I am not some defenseless Princess that needs a Knight to swoop in and save her from the beasts of the world."

I fight back the chuckle in my throat.

"I have had an absolute fucking shit day, Miss Fischer. If my attempt at helping you has offended you, I'm fucking sorry. That was not my intention but Mr. Bennett deserves to have his ass handed to him and knocked off his goddamn pedestal for the things he's said to you and then having the audacity to try to win you back over. You are not a stupid woman, but I am glad that you were not naive enough to believe him. Now, if you are finished with your tantrum, why don't you act like a grown woman, a Queen as you so like to say, and thank me before leaving for the night."

"Are you out of your fucking mind tonight?" I shriek, my voice three octaves higher than I've ever heard it go before. "In what fucking world would I feel inclined to thank you for interfering in my personal conversation? One that you were clearly eavesdropping on?"

Immediately, a rush of regret hits me as the words come out of my mouth. He hasn't exactly been the only one eavesdropping on a private conversation tonight. I'm just as guilty as he is, *but I had the sense to stay out of his argument with Sloan instead of interjecting and causing more problems for everyone.* Yes, that makes me the better—more mature—of the two of us tonight. He just doesn't know that.

"Goddammit Lyla," he huffs, taking another step towards me and grabbing my face in his hands. "Can you not just accept that maybe, just fucking maybe, I got a little jealous and acted irrationally for a moment?"

My heart stops as I look into his eyes, my fisted hands letting up as my nails loosen out of the skin in my palms. His bright blue eyes are staring back at me as I gasp for air, trying to come up with an appropriate response. I'd heard him dismiss Sloan but didn't want to assume that meant he was automatically choosing me.

"You w-were…. j-jealous?" I stutter.

He closes his eyes, leaning forward to rest his forehead against mine as I breathe in deeply the woodsy cologne surrounding me, letting his scent fill my lungs and nostrils at the same time.

"Yes, Lyla, I was jealous," he whispers, my heart skipping another beat as his lips trail across my temple. "It's not something I have felt in a *very* long time and I am sorry that I lashed out like that, at you. I know that you are capable of handling yourself, but at that moment and seeing his hands on you, I couldn't control myself. The only hands I want touching you, the only lips on your skin—" His lips press against my skin harder, working his way down my cheek. "I want them to be mine."

I gasp as I reach my now shaking hands up to rest one on his waist and run the other through his hair before placing it on the nape of his neck. I press gently, pulling him closer to me as my heart races in my chest. He's choosing me, he's choosing to fight— despite the inevitable shit storm that will follow.

"Say it, Tyson."

"Lyla, I'm not perfect. Not by a long shot, but I do want to try to explore these feelings with you," he says. "If that is what you want, that is."

I nod, letting him continue.

"Before you came into my life, I was content merely existing, letting my life wither away. Then you showed up and turned my life around, made me question everything I've been doing for the last decade. Every fight we've had, every day that you have inevitably pissed me off beyond any words... it has given me a reason to fight again. It took longer to come to terms with than it should have, but I quite like it. I was cold and lifeless before you, as though my heart had become fossilized over the years and you are chipping away at the layers and discovering that maybe, just maybe, there is something still alive inside."

"Did you just make a paleontology joke while professing your feelings for me?" I ask, the corner of my mouth lifting as I struggle to contain the laughter wishing to burst from inside of me.

"Yes, I did just go there," he laughs.

I tilt my head up, pulling down on his neck until his lips are on mine. His hands on the side of my face grow hot as our lips work together, our tongues exploring gently. He groans into my mouth and the mound between my legs begins to throb. I slide my hand on his waist down and onto his firm ass, gripping gently. He gasps, running a hand down the back of my neck, and pressing his body against mine more firmly. My grip on his neck tightens as my fingers twist upwards into his hair, my lips becoming more urgent by the second as the desire intensifies.

"Lyla," he breaks our kiss, breathing heavily. "We need to stop."

"No, we don't," I say, fire burning in my eyes as I look into his. I let go of him and turn around, closing the door and flipping the lock.

226

"This is a dangerous line to walk, sweetheart," he growls as I run my eyes down the front of his body, stopping to notice the hard press of his erection against the front of his pants. "We need to be smart."

"I'm tired of being smart," I shrug. My hand slipping across the back of my shoulders, I reach the zipper of my dress and pull it down slowly — never breaking eye contact as the dress slips down my body and lands on the floor.

"Holy fuck," he groans, taking in the sight of me standing in front of him in nothing but a matching set of thin, green lace lingerie.

I step out of my dress, leaving my heels on as I step towards him and he grasps his hands together behind his neck. I press my chest against him, letting my fingers trail down the muscled torso underneath his shirt, and push myself up on my toes to whisper in his ear.

"Let's forget about being smart for the night," I whisper, letting my fingers trail lower as I nip at his earlobe. "Instead of using our brains for once, let's use our hearts."

I trace my fingers on one hand down the side of his face, pressing my lips against his neck. The other hand slowly reaches my targeted spot, dragging across his erection and landing on the button of his pants. With another deep groan, he grabs my waist and pulls me to him as his lips crash against mine in resolution. I make quick work of the buttons on his shirt as his hands explore my exposed skin, fingertips brushing the sensitive peaks of my hardened nipples, causing me to moan into his mouth. I push his shirt back to expose his chest, full of rock-hard abs and his lips brush down my neck as I admire him— soaking in every inch of his chiseled body. He sucks gently on the exposed skin of my breasts as his hands reach behind and unclasp my bra, sliding it gently down my arms. He takes a moment to look at me, his gaze worshiping every inch of my body and instead of feeling awkward and exposed, I feel sexy and powerful.

"You are so fucking beautiful, Lyla," he whispers.

"Actions speak louder than words, Tyson," I gush, heat building between us.

He wastes no time, grabbing a breast in one hand and sucking the other into his mouth—his teeth nipping at the peaks. His warm breath against my skin heats me to the core as I fumble with the button on his pants. Each flick of his tongue against my nipple, each squeeze with his hand— I'll finish before his clothes are ever off at this rate. I grab his waist, almost ripping the button on his pants as I yank them open and push them down to leave him standing there in nothing but a pair of tight boxer briefs, gently grasping his throbbing member through the thin fabric.

"Holy fuck!" he yells at my touch.

His hands push further down my body until his fingers grip the fabric of my underwear and push them down, letting them fall as he cups my ass and lifts me up. With his mouth back on mine, he

228

walks us through the room, pushing things off his desk and ignoring the clattering, breaking sounds before sitting me down and yanking to the edge. His fingers trace up my thighs and I squirm as they inch closer to my wetness, wanting to feel his touch in my most sensitive areas. As one finger traces my entrance he groans into my mouth.

"Goddamn, you're fucking soaked."

I push his briefs down and wrap my hand around his erection, gently tugging as he moans into my neck, his finger slipping in and out of me. As he carefully slips another finger inside of me, rubbing his thumb across my clit in gentle strokes, the sensation explodes through my body.

"Tyson," I plead, gasping for breath. "I need you inside of me, please."

He smirks behind my kiss, slipping his fingers back out of me and pulling me further off the edge of the desk. I hear him open a drawer, fishing around for something before I hear the sound of foil ripping and wait with anticipation as he slips the condom onto his erection. I move my hands up his chest and grasp behind his neck as he hovers over me and carefully pushes himself inside of me.

Every fiber in my body exploded when I thrust myself inside of Lyla and a seductive moan escaped her mouth. Feeling her back arch and the press of her soft breasts into my chest almost caused me to cum but I shoved the urge back down. Moving in perfect sync as our bodies quickly move back and forth, her hands twist into my hair and urge my face back towards hers. I capture her soft lips in mine as I slow my pace and enjoy the warmth of her body and flick my tongue gently. My hands slide up her thighs as her legs cross behind my waist to hold her in the perfect position and I'm free to roam her body and caress her nipples between my fingertips.

"Fucking hell, Lyla," I groan as she tightens her legs around my waist, pulling me deeper inside her.

Hearing her soft chuckle, I bite my way down her neck, sucking the skin between my teeth as I go, while she runs her hands down my bulging arms. With her chest exposed, nipples erect and lusciously pink, my lips graze on her supple breasts. I keep one hand on the small of her back and the other becomes free to tease her swollen clit. She gasps at each slow stroke, pushing her chest further up and squeezing my forearms tightly. The sight of her head thrown back, a waterfall of black hair down her back, a glistening sheen of sweat across her forehead, the flush of her cheeks, and her perfect lips parted as she moans sends me close to the edge.

"Finish for me, sweetheart," I growl, stroking her wet, swollen clit faster now and gasp as she clenches around my cock in climax as she yells out my name— sending me over the edge with one final thrust.

I collapse onto her chest, matching her deep, heavy breaths as we relish in the lasting pleasure. She lifts a hand, tracing her fingers through the back of my hair and down my spine as I bite the nipple closest to my mouth before lifting my lips to hers and slowly pull my still hardened cock out of her.

"Tyson," she whimpers between kisses, sounding almost more sexy than her screaming it as she came for me.

"Yes, sweetheart?"

I rest my forehead against hers as she catches her breath, letting my fingertips trace her flushed cheeks.

"Thank you for fighting for me."

I pull her to me, a hand wrapped around the back of her neck, holding her lips captive against my own.

"You are worth every fire of hell that I have ever, and will ever, have to walk through if it means getting to have you."

She nuzzles her cheek against my neck, moaning as her lips press against the crook.

"In that case….. can we do that again?" she asks and a laugh escapes deep from within my chest.

"Lyla, baby," I say, opening my eyes to see hers gazing back at me. I hold her face in my hands, offering three soft kisses on her lips with a soft smile. "I plan on doing that many, many more times."

A smile spreads across her face as she clasps her hands behind my neck, the quick movement lets her legs fall from my waist.

"Good," she laughs, "because I don't think I can carry on with life not having that mindblowing sex again."

"Mind-blowing, huh?" I retort, raising my eyebrow.

"Don't get too big of a head, Professor," she says, rolling her eyes.

"I think you know exactly how big my head is, Miss Fischer," I wink, then press my lips against hers quickly. "But if you'd like to find out again, I think we should find somewhere more private than my office where the night janitor is likely due anytime."

Her eyes widen as she covers her mouth with her hand. I smirk, wrapping my arms around her, and feel her relax in my arms. Inhaling her perfume, basking in the gentle warmth of her touch lets me forget about the impending doom, whether from Sloan or to my career if we're caught—just for a moment. When I loosen my grip around her, she shifts on my desk and a pit forms in my stomach as I look at her newly sunken face as she bites her lip. I tip her chin up with my finger, concern written on my serene expression.

"What's wrong?" I ask. She takes a deep breath and swallows hard as tears begin to well in her eyes. "Baby, talk to me."

"What about Sloan? Or Ivy?" she asks. "The school? The Dean? The risks? I know you said I'm worth it all, but am I? Am I honestly the person to lose everything over?"

She's throwing questions at me before I can think of a good way to answer the first one. She doesn't know about the conversation I had with Sloan today, and I'd much prefer to keep her as out of the loop as possible on that front. Ivy, however, is one fact I hadn't thought about with how little she's ever been interested in my personal life. The school and the Dean, sure they would concern her if we got caught in the long run but we could be careful. The risks? There are plenty of those in any relationship, just because ours is a little more complicated doesn't mean we can't get through them.

Her large, golden eyes stare back as I process her questions, waiting patiently for my response as she chews on her lip.

God, that's sexy to watch.

Holding either side of her face tenderly in my hands, letting my thumbs stroke her cheeks— I sigh.

"You asked me to fight for us, Lyla," I tell her. "That's what I'm doing. I meant it when I said you are worth it. I wouldn't risk it all if you weren't, as crazy as it seems right now. We can figure the rest out as we go."

Her face brightens, the corners of her lips turning upwards and I reciprocate a soft smile.

"In that case," she beams, "your place or mine?"

I pull her lips to mine and kiss her deeply, letting a soft moan escape my mouth and into hers.

I pull her gently off the desk, gathering up her clothes and handing them to her before slipping back into my underwear. I watch her dress effortlessly as I finish getting dressed and rush to her aid as she shimmies into her dress, quickly zipping her up and kissing up her spine in sections before the zipper hides the skin. As my lips brush the back of her neck, I feel her shiver and wrap my arms around her waist.

"You never said where we're going," she murmurs. "Or are you planning on taking me again right here?"

I squeeze her waist as my cock twitches, a growl rumbling through my throat. I nibble the lobe of her ear as she groans, her hands desperately reaching behind her and stroking the front of my crotch. "If you keep doing that I just might," I whisper. "But I'm planning on taking you back to my place, letting you see the real Tyson Moxley." Her hands drop to her waist as she spins in my arms, pressing her lips to mine before grabbing my hand and intertwining our fingers.

"Let's go, then," she demands.

Tyson is quick to drop my hand as we walk through the main doors of the building, reminding me that what we're doing could get us both into a heap of trouble. He's risking everything—his family, his career—for me. But what am I giving up for him? Anything?

When did I turn into the carefree, sex goddess that doesn't care about anyone's future?

"Do you want to stop by your apartment and get some things for the weekend?" he asks, breaking my train of thought.

"The weekend?" I had been assuming that he would just send me home in a few hours when he's done with me, maybe even with us.

"Lyla," he says, stopping to look at me, "once I get you to my house I don't plan on letting you out of my sight until we return to campus on Monday."

His voice is so confident, so matter-of-fact, that my knees weaken at his remark. While being in Tyson's house, seeing him in his element is intriguing— I'm not sure I'm ready for a whole weekend commitment. Unease builds in my stomach as I watch the confidence drain from his voice as his eyes scan my expressionless face. He sucks his bottom lip in between his teeth, his eyes widening with each passing moment I stay silent.

"Tyson," I whisper, suddenly unsure of how we got to this point. "I think we should see how tonight goes before you lock me

235

away in your hidden tower, alone with you for the entire weekend. That's a big step, a big commitment, and I don't think either of us really knows what we're doing right now."

I attempt a believable smile but manage a crooked upturn of the lips at the very most.

"This isn't me saying that I don't want to stay all weekend," I try to reassure him. "But we just charged into this headfirst without thinking, and I get that it was my fault, and if anything I maybe forced myself on you a little bit... but I just think we should take it a little slower from this point on. Not that I want the sex to stop! Fuck, no I don't want that to stop at all." I shake my head, laughing as my hair falls around my flushed face with the rising heat. "I just mean that let's not make any assumptions about how long it's going to be before you get tired of me or one of us comes to our senses and runs for the hills."

"Do you think you forced yourself on me?" He asks, cocking a brow. I shrug quickly, not looking up until I feel his hand under my chin. He lifts my face until my eyes have met his blazing stare, a smirk spreading across his face. "Never, ever think like that again, Lyla."

The intensity in his voice melts my insides as I watch the hunger grow in his eyes, feeling the need to have his lips on mine again puts an urgency back into my veins. But I stand there, frozen and gazing into his eyes—just wishing I could grab his face and pull him to me in the middle of this grassy common area. So I nod instead, a lump forming in my throat as his hold on my chin loosens.

236

He nods in response, tapping the toe of his shoe against the ground.

"But, I would like to grab a few things from my place," I manage to whisper. My eyes dart around the empty campus, careful to check in the shadows for any lurking students before I step closer to him and whisper in his ear. "But I'll grab enough to last until Monday because I'm optimistic that I won't have any reason to leave."

"Thank you," he breathes into my neck.

"Why don't you go grab your car and I'll head home. You can meet me there so there's less of a chance that anyone will see us together."

"I'd rather not let you out of my sight and give you the chance to change your mind."

"Don't be ridiculous," I say, rolling my eyes. "I'm trying to get us to your place quicker and inconspicuously."

"Fine," he grumbles. "I'll be there as quickly as I can."

He quickly scans the area, then pecks his lips against mine before taking off at double the speed we had started at. Giggling under my breath, I quicken my pace towards my apartment as the night replays in my head—the confidence I had exuded had surprised me, even. Maybe it was the fact that I had overheard his conversation with Sloan, something I have no intention of telling him, *ever*, or the way he handled Parker— even if I didn't need his help. If Parker hadn't reeked of tequila, I'm certain that he would have been able to tell that something was going on between Tyson and me. As far as up and

237

coming lawyers go, Parker can smell bullshit from a mile away and will easily become an asset to any firm he works for— which makes me hope he'll heed Tyson's warning and stay away from me.

I fish my keys out of my bag as I step up to my door, quickly glancing around the area before unlocking it and stepping inside— locking the door again. I've lived in Houston long enough to know that not everywhere is as safe as it seems. I peel my dress off and toss it in my laundry basket before slipping out of my lingerie and cleaning myself up in the bathroom at lightning speed before slipping into a sheer black lingerie set, tight jeans, and a loose tank top. Pulling the duffel bag out from under my bed, I quickly start throwing clothes inside and then a small bag of toiletries—just as my phone chimes from my dresser. Smiling, I grab it and sling the bag over my shoulder.

T.M.: Parked outside. Get your hot ass out here.
ME: Coming.. :)

As I check the apartment one last time, I take a deep breath to prepare myself for what lies ahead. Another ding and I shake my head as I read the last message.

T.M.: You will be. ;-)

I quickly find his classic, black Camaro parked a few spots down and I have to mentally stop myself from sprinting towards him. The darkness engulfs the parking lot at night, enough that no one looking outside towards the rumbling car would be able to make out the driver or passenger.

"Good Lord, what are we? Teenagers?" I say, laughing and holding up his last message on my phone as I slide into the passenger seat. He erupts into deep laughter, reaching over and pulling my lips to his, hungrily and urgently.

"No cold feet?" he asks, tilting my face towards him with a finger under my chin.

"Drive, Tyson," I demand, and he does.

The city lights fly past us as we speed through the streets, hand in hand on the center console. His thumb strokes the side of my hand then pull it to his lips at each stoplight. I squeeze his hand tighter, laughing at every tight turn taken a little too fast. The eighties hair metal songs are quietly playing from his radio until *You Give Love A Bad Name* by Bon Jovi comes on and I reach for the volume, turning it up and belting along— pleasantly surprised when Tyson joins in between laughter.

He slows down as we enter a secluded, tree-lined neighborhood and pull into a driveway that leads to an immaculate modern, seemingly glass-walled house. As he presses a button to open a door to a garage, I'm captivated by the stucco exterior on the few

239

walls that aren't adorned by windows and ogle the large, wooden door at the front of the house.

"It was my great-grandfather's house," he says, breaking the silence as he shuts the car off inside the garage. "He willed it to me when he passed."

"It's beautiful," I gush.

As we get out of the car, he grabs my duffel bag from the backseat and slings it over his shoulder. I stand, frozen, and stare at the motorcycle parked in the front of the garage. So much has changed since last night on our ride, that it feels like weeks have passed. The warmth of his body next to mine sends goosebumps up the back of my neck as I snap out of my trance. He stands there, smirking, and offers his hand to me— pulling me through the door and inside. Lights flip on as we step through the door and I hear the thud of our bags hitting the floor as he pulls me into him, his lips crashing against mine. He backs me up against the closest wall, running his hands down my side to my thighs and hoisting me up.

"I'll give you a tour later," he growls. His teeth trail down the side of my neck as my head leans backward, a moan escaping as he reaches my collarbone. "Right now, I want to be selfish and I need you in my bed."

I nod between kisses, his lips never breaking away from my skin.

He carries me through the house, up a flight of stairs, and through another door— our shirts falling off along the way. As he lays me onto a soft bed, his fingers are working the button of my jeans and I find myself wishing I'd opted for something with easier access as I wiggle beneath him, helping him yank the fabric down my legs, desperate for his touch. His lips trail up my thigh as he kneels in front of me, slipping my underwear off and resting my legs on his shoulders. As his tongue gently strokes my clit for the first time, I grab fistfuls of the soft blanket and gasp.

"Relax, baby," he murmurs, lips pressing against my hips. "I might have rushed while we were in the office, but I plan on taking my time tonight."

As his tongue flicks across my wetness, his teeth gently nipping at my clit, I cry out his name and succumb to his touch. I lose myself in the pleasure— knowing he's only getting started and time is on our side, for now.

For almost a decade, I have woken up alone in this bed with sunlight pouring in through the blinds at dawn. I have woken cold and lonely, though rested well enough to get by. I had been perfectly content in my mundane lifestyle— sleep, workout, eat, work, eat, workout, shower, sleep. It had become my unwritten routine and it had been fine, easy enough to follow, and safe— until Lyla.

Today, the bed is warmed and harder than usual to get out of, desire for the monotonous lifestyle drifts away. This tenacious, passionate breath of fresh air has awoken a part of my heart that I had sealed off, never expecting to want to give it to another woman again. As the late morning sun filters through the slits in the window coverings, the rays fall across Lyla's bare torso and I watch as her chest rises and falls. Each breath tickling the lone strands of hair on my chest as she sleeps, wrapped in my arms and my fingers tenderly stroking her hair,

"Mmmm....," she mumbles, rubbing her cheek against my chest.

"Morning, sweetheart," I whisper, brushing my lips into the tangled black hair splayed across my chest, letting my fingers trace down her bare spine. She sucks in a deep breath as her back arches beneath my touch. She lightly presses her lips to my chest trailing up my collarbone, to my neck, and finally on my lips as I squirm under her touch.

242

"Good morning," she whispers, nuzzling her face into the crook of my neck as her fingertips trail slowly down my thigh. "What a night that turned out to be."

I chuckle, tightening my grip around her waist. A weight lifts from my chest now, knowing that we are on the same page when it comes to the night's events means that she has no regrets—though one of us probably should.

"What a night indeed….," I mumble, circling my fingertips against the bones in her hips.

"Mmmmhmm……," she murmurs, her lips pressing against my neck as she slides her hands across my chest. "Does this mean you're finally done being such an abhorrent, pain in the ass, cocky piece of work, and ready to be nice all the time?"

Her muffled laughter vibrates against my skin as I pull her closer, lifting her chin so my lips can meet hers for a quick kiss, nipping at her lower lip.

"I don't think you'd enjoy my company nearly as much if I was nice *all* the time, Lyla."

"Why don't you give it a try and let me decide for myself?"

She takes my lip between her teeth, biting hard as her hand wraps around my cock—giving it a not so gentle squeeze.

"I guess we can try it your way," I say, gasping as her fingers brush the tip of my cock. "And if you keep this up we'll never make it out of bed today, either."

"Maybe I don't want to leave this bed," she retorts, but her fingers move upwards as they trace the indents of my muscles on my chest.

"I guess you'll never know what my famous pancakes taste like then." I roll over to pin her underneath me, her eyes widening as a smile breaks out on her face. She reaches her hands behind my neck and pulls my lips to hers. My heart hammers in my chest as I restrain myself from taking her again, taking the many rounds during the night into consideration, she's surely sore. As her thumb gently traces my cheekbone I groan in her mouth, pressing my forehead against hers.

"You can make pancakes?" she asks.

"Why don't you get your cute ass out of this bed and come downstairs and find out for yourself?" I wink. Her lips purse as she mulls this idea over, glancing down at our bodies pressed together. She lifts one leg behind my ass and presses me into her with a sly smile, her laughter echoing through the room as I let out a groan. "You're insatiable, Miss Fischer."

"Perhaps I just enjoy hearing that raspy sex voice of yours."

This time, it's my laughter in the room— a full-bellied laugh I haven't heard out of myself in so long. I roll off her, holding her hand as I lift her and she lets the sheet drop from her body. Confident and sexy as ever, she stands before me stretching her arms over her head as I bite my lip wishing we'd stayed in bed. I reach behind me and into a

244

drawer, grabbing one of my t-shirts and toss it to her as I slip into a fresh pair of sweatpants.

"Your clothes are…. somewhere…. and if you don't put something on I'm going to throw you right back into that bed,"

She smirks, slowly putting the shirt over her head and as it drops down over her bare chest it falls to the bottom of her hips— barely covering her perfectly shaped ass.

"I'll think about putting on some underwear while you whip up these famous pancakes you are choosing over sex this morning," she winks, strutting out of the room and back down the stairs I carried her up last night.

"Fuck," I muttered, running a hand through my hair as her hips sway with each step.

This woman is going to be the death of me.

As I run down the stairs, the thought dawns on me that Lyla is going to be the opposite of the death of me. Sloan had been the one to kill my spirit and harden my heart—freezing me into a routine of predictability. Lyla, now she is just the opposite. She came into my world like a hot, Texas sun in the summer as she worked her way through the cracks in my armor and brought me back to life. Lyla has become the reason I enjoy getting up in the mornings again and have become considerably less of an asshole to everyone around me, even my students owe her for the shift in my presentation. I catch up to her just as she finishes searching through her bag at the door and slips into a pair of purple cheeky underwear. Her cheeks are flushed from running through the house and the smile on her face makes my mind soar in elation.

If there was a way, any possibility, that we could stay like this, how we are in this moment, forever— I would, even if it meant giving up everything else in my mundane life.

Lyla's face is looking down but I can see her eyes watching through her long lashes, twisting the hem of my shirt between her fingertips. Her long, black hair falling around her shoulders as she taps her foot nervously against the floor. I stride towards her and pull her close, wrapping my arms around her waist as my lips collide with hers.

"Come on," I say, motioning with my head towards the kitchen. "Pancakes and coffee are this way."

"Coffee, too?" her eyes widen, surprised.

"Of course there's coffee too," I laugh. "What kind of maniac do you take me for?"

"A sexy, well-endowed, experienced one," she retorts, pressing her lips to my bare shoulder as we walk.

"Well-endowed? Experienced?" I ask. "Careful, you're going to give me a complex if you keep the compliments like that."

"Oh good God, you don't need any more of an ego boost," she says. "I take it all back, you're only average and decently ok in the sack."

246

"No take backs, Lyla," I laugh, as we walk through the kitchen door. "Have a seat, watch the magic."

Wrapping my arms around her waist, I lift her onto the wide, white marble countertop and busy myself with the coffee pot, feeling her eyes on me at every moment. With the coffee brewing and the silence between us becoming comfortable, I grab the ingredients for the pancakes and mix the batter quickly.

"Tyson," she murmurs. I turn around and she motions me with a come hither gesture. As I get closer, she lifts her legs out and wraps them around me quickly, pulling me into her. Leaning down to cup my face in her hands, she tenderly presses her mouth against mine— her tongue brushing my lower lip. If my heart was capable of exploding from a single, gentle kiss, this would be the one that did it. Something so loving, so normal, has never made me cherish a kiss more. When she loosens her legs from my waist, I peck her lips again before letting her pull my head to her chest and I listen to the pounding of her heart against my ear. "Thank you for fighting for us."

LUCY: I'm heading to Brunch now, see you soon!

LUCY: I'm here, you on your way?

LUCY: What the hell, Lyla? Where are you? Are you blowing me off?

LUCY: I'm officially concerned. You haven't missed a Saturday Brunch in years.

LUCY: And you're not home?? Did you just disappear without any warning?

LUCY: I guess call me if you need an alibi. Smooches.

"Oh shit," I mutter, scrolling through Lucy's messages. I hadn't even thought about our outstanding brunch date when Tyson asked me to come for the weekend. Lucy isn't stupid, she knows I wouldn't just disappear or run away. My erratic change in behavior, disappearing without a warning is so unlike me that she will be keeping a closer eye on me after this.

"Everything okay?" Tyson asks, his lips pressing gently against my neck as he wraps his arms around me from behind. Instinctively, I lean back into his touch and sigh. His lips graze upwards as a flutter erupts in my chest, warmth spreading through my body. *This, this is what happiness is supposed to feel like.*

"Fine," I nod, "just forgot about brunch with my only remaining friend on campus so she probably thinks I'm being held hostage in one of the many creepy, abandoned buildings in town with a group of wanna-be Texas mobsters."

Tyson freezes against my back before spinning me towards him with his eyebrow arched high.

"Sounds like you have thought that scenario through a little more than a normal person would. Are you involved in some kind of drug smuggling, mafia crime that you're unable to tell me about? Blink once for yes, twice for no if you are wired and can't talk."

I shrug slyly, stifling the laughter in order to play along. I blink once, slowly. He gasps, dramatically covering his mouth, and sends me into a fit of laughter so hard that I start crying. As I wipe the tears from the corners of my eyes, he pulls me against his chiseled body and kisses my forehead.

"Honestly, Houston is just pretty lonely when Lucy isn't around and Parker had been busy quite often back in the day," I pause, gritting my teeth as I wince, realizing I said *his* name. When Tyson's face remains unbothered, I continue. "Wandering the streets early in the mornings or anywhere close to dark, they leave a person to wonder who or what might be out there. The usual string of serial killer documentaries flooding the screen of my dorm television over the years likely onset my paranoia early on after moving from a safe, small town in Washington."

"Do you need to let her know you're safe?" he asks. I shrug again.

"Honestly, I probably should tell her I'm fine so that she doesn't worry. On the other hand, telling her I'm fine will only lead to questions about where I am, who I'm with."

"Let her know you're safe, Lyla. A good friend is right to be worried."

"And if she asks questions?"

"We'll figure it out."

His body tenses as he presses another gentle kiss to my hairline and steps back, running a hand through his hair before turning to walk down the hall away from me. I choke back tears at the sight of watching him walk away from me, even if only for a minute. We've spent the perfect day together and the last thing I want is Lucy's overbearing mannerisms cause a rift in, well, whatever *this* is. My fingers glide across the keyboard, shooting off a lie to her for the first time.

ME: Shit, sorry Lil. I'm okay, just took the weekend to blow off some steam and went to the museum first thing this morning.

Going to the museum isn't out of the ordinary for me, she shouldn't think anything of it.

LUCY: You sure you're ok? I can come back if you need me, Lyla.

ME: No, it's fine. I'm sure you have plans for a Saturday night. I'm just going to catch a movie and call it an early night.

I toss my phone back into my bag before she has a chance to respond, then head down the hall in search of Tyson. Nearing the end of the hall, passing by silent rooms behind closed doors, I feel the floor vibrating beneath my feet. I grip the knob on the last of the doors, opening it to find a staircase to a basement he hadn't shown off on our mock tour after breakfast. Hearing the beat of heavy drum riffs coming from downstairs, I take each step carefully in the dim lighting. The music gets louder the further down the stairs I get and I reach the bottom before seeing a bright light emitting from another room around the corner.

"Tyson?" I call out, likely inaudible over the volume of the music. I round the corner and gasp, taken aback by the sight of Tyson running shirtless on a treadmill— sweat dripping down his ripped, muscular back. I lean against the doorframe, biting my lip as a throbbing begins to pulse between my legs watching his raw, carnal state. His arms move in a perfect tempo with his feet, pushing himself harder with each step— unbothered by the sweat drenching his body.

How much sex would be needed and in what positions to get him that sweaty? How vigorous of an exercise would it have to be? With those muscles, he could hold me in the air while licking my pussy until I finished... his wet tongue inside me and his teeth pulling at my clit....

My eyes widen at my dirty train of thoughts. I shake my head, hoping to push the thoughts away, and look up to see his rhythm slowing down as the treadmill slows with him. He turns the machine off, hops down, and rests his hands against his knees as he hunches over to catch his breath. I clap for his performance as I saunter towards him. His head snaps up and I watch his shoulders heave as his lungs slowly begin to refill with proper air.

"How long have you been standing there?" he asks.

"Long enough to sear this image into my mind forever," I wink, reaching to wipe a lone bead of sweat from trailing down the side of his face. "But would be happy to stick around for an encore."

He chuckles, regaining his posture and pushing his hair back. I push up to my tiptoes and forcefully press my lips to his, tasting the salty remnants of his workout on his mouth. He gasps into my mouth as his hands slide down my ribs, grasping my waist and pulling me up against him.

"Sort things out with your friend?" he questions between kisses.

"Mmmmhmm," I murmur, trailing my lips down the side of his neck now.

"Good," he whispers. "Let's take a shower."

He winks when he sees my eyes meet his and I nod.

Hurriedly, he slides his hands under my ass and lifts my legs around his waist, and carries me up both flights of stairs with ease, *putting those muscles to work,* as our lips mold together. When my feet hit the floor again, my hands find the waistband of his pants and shove them down so I can grasp his hardened member in my hand— a deep growl emitting from his throat in response. He yanks my shirt off over my head, pulling away from me only long enough to let it fall from my arms as he slides my underwear down before reaching to turn on the water. He pulls me inside as the water warms up, the immediate chill hardening my nipples on contact. We let the water drench us as our hands roam, I gasp as he gently nibbles my nipple in between his teeth. He spins me around so I'm flush with the cool wall, his hand trailing down my stomach until reaching my clit as he slides his finger against it gently.

"Oh god, Tyson, yes," I moan, arching my back towards him and feeling his length pressed against my ass. "I need you, please."

"Are you on the pill?" he asks, his finger quickening its pace against my swollen clit before sliding two inside of me.

"Yes, fuck," I gasp, "You're asking me this now? I need you inside me, please."

I don't have to ask again, he repositions himself and gently thrusts inwards as we both gasp in unison. Sex with a condom on Tyson all night had been magical, but sex with Tyson completely bare is a mind-blowing experience as his warm length slides in and out of

253

me. The feel of every inch of his soft skin atop his hard cock, the head pressing against my inner walls causes moans to escape my throat are loud, almost animal-like, echoing through the tiled bathroom as the water sloshes against our skin.

"Dammit, Lyla," he mumbles, "this feels so fucking good. I'm not going to last long."

I arch into him, squeezing my muscles together inside, another growl escapes his throat as his hand pushes on the small of my back to hold me steady. His pace quickens both inside me and on my clit, an eruption brewing inside of me. As he draws me closer to the edge I can feel him quivering inside me with each thrust.

"Oh fuck! Tyson!" I scream, riding my orgasm out as my knees shake.

He thrusts two more times before collapsing, sprawled against my back, yelling my name but sounding so far away as my orgasm still rings in my ears. We stand still, his arms wrapped around me as I keep my palms against the wall to steady us. His lips trail up my shoulder, my neck, and against my earlobe.

"What are you doing to me?" he asks, his heart rapidly beating against my back.

Still basking in ecstasy over spending the weekend with Lyla, the morning passes quickly as I count down the minutes until I see her for my afternoon class. The students know there's a quiz today, which should take them most of the class time— and what we'll be grading quickly this evening in my office. She'd asked me to drop her off at her apartment before heading for the faculty lot, not wanting to chance the possibility of anyone seeing us leave my car together. Just because there's a rule against dating a student, I've yet to find anything that says giving one a ride at a time of need is also against the rules and could easily have been justified. I stare at the clock at the back of the room, tapping my pen anxiously against the desk as the second hand slows down under my watchful eye.

I close my eyes, taking a deep breath, and loosen the tie around my neck— a tie that Lyla had picked out this morning. *It's a perfect blend of both of our eyes, I love it,* she had said, wrapping it around my neck and tying it like an expert. She isn't wrong, and I had kicked myself on the inside, never noticing for myself. This tie, with the swirls of teal and gold intertwining, is eerily similar to the colors of our eyes with the stitching looking like flecks within an iris itself.

"Where did you learn to tie a tie this well? I ask.

255

The smirk splayed across her lips as she shrugs her shoulders, continuing to twist the fabric together makes me want to throw her back into bed.

"I made my dad teach me when I was around seven or eight, I think. I thought that maybe if I could help him with his tie in the mornings, find a way to be useful, and insert myself into his life, he would want to spend more time with me," she says, biting her lip.

My throat tightens as I feel her sigh, then wrap my arms around her once she finishes tightening it. She looks up, resting her palms on my chest as she fights back with her quickly batting eyelashes and I place a finger under her chin. My thumb traces the dip in her chin as her hot breath glides over my fingertips, sending a chill down my spine.

"I'm sorry that you felt that was necessary in order to spend time with your father," I say. She shrugs, her eyes averting my gaze. "Anyone that doesn't make you feel that you are worth every second of their time is severely missing out."

"Earth to professor," Lyla's voice, she's somehow snuck up on me during my trance, snaps me out of the memory, her hand waving in front of my face. "The class thinks you're losing it."

I clear my throat, realizing the entire class has filed in and is waiting patiently for me to begin. Quickly, I stand up and grab the stack of quizzes in front of me to distribute. The few snickers from the students up front are silenced by my daggering stare as I count out the

256

sheets for each row, handing them to the front students and they pass them back. Once everyone has a quiz, I lean against the front of my desk and tap my watch.

"You all knew it was quiz day," I announce. "Take your time, hand it in before you leave. Good luck."

The sound of shuffling paper and scratches of pens fill the room as I return to my seat, feeling Lyla's eyes on me as I sit down. She discreetly slides her chair closer to me, her laptop resting on the side of my desk. She points her pen towards the screen, a note written on the open document.

You ok?

I nod, discreetly resting my hand on her thigh and squeezing gently before reaching for the laptop myself.

Fine, just a bit distracted. The weekend was filled with memories I can't seem to get out of my head.

Her cheeks turn pink as she bites her thumbnail to hide her smile, peeking over through the corner of her eye. She skips a line, then her fingers fly across the keyboard at lightning speed and I'm awestruck, unsure of how I never noticed how efficient she was up until now.

Sounds like how my morning classes went, as well.

I suck the inside of my cheek as I suppress the urge to smile like an idiot in front of the class, even if they are busy focusing on their quizzes. Lyla busies herself, looking through her desk quietly as I type back to her.

In order to allow you to focus on your studies, I believe you should refrain from any further weekend activities. Perhaps, you should even get a tutor.

Her hand covers her mouth, stifling her laughter as she reads my response. Her lips purse, eyes squinting as she fires back playfully.

That's a splendid suggestion, Professor. Would you happen to know of one I could ask to cram me fully, all night long?

"Fucking hell," I whisper under my breath as she giggles softly. My hands clench, knuckles turning white as I settle my natural reaction to her suggestive words. She slyly grabs the laptop back, a smirk spreading across her face as her fingers begin to fly again. When she pushes it back towards me, resting her head on her hand propped up by her elbow, she bats her eyelashes at me innocently.

258

What's wrong, Prof? You look uncomfortable. Anything
I can help with?

    I glance at the clock, ten more minutes left of class and no one
has handed in their quizzes yet. I announce how much time they have
left, reassuring them that anyone still working after I call time will get
an automatic zero. I pull the laptop towards me and type quickly.

As soon as the last student leaves this room I'm
going to get you back for that, Miss Fischer.

    I watch as she shifts in her seat, the sound of her gasp filling the
air between us. Students begin to file towards the front of the room,
cutting it close with only three minutes left, and she slams the screen
down and packs her belongings away hastily. I nod towards each
student while watching Lyla in my peripheral tap her foot in the air
with her one leg crossed over the other. She rubs her fingertips
together on one hand while the other drums against the desk, her eyes
never leaving the clock at the back of the room.

    When the last student leaves, she jumps out of her chair and
grabs her bag, swinging it over her shoulder and turning to leave—
but I grab her hand and pull her back to me. I wait for the door to slam
shut before pulling her down into my lap, catching her before she falls

259

backward, and cupping her face with one hand while holding her with the other arm.

"I believe I owe you," I whisper into her ear.

She squirms in my lap, letting her bag fall from her shoulder as her lips part, waiting impatiently. I trace my thumb across her pink, lower lip gently and feel the beat of her heart quicken through her chest. I breathe in, leaning close enough to barely let my lips brush hers as she starts to lean in eagerly. Intertwining my fingers in her hair, I gently pull on it to hold her still. As I swipe my tongue across her parted lips, she lets another whimper escape her throat and I smile against her lips. I tighten my hold on her, keeping her at bay while she's growing more impatient. I'm enjoying this moment of dishing out the same teasing that she gave me in a classroom full of students.

"Do you want me to kiss you now, Lyla?" I ask. She nods dramatically, reaching her hand to the back of my neck to try and pull me closer. "Ask me nicely, then."

"Please, Tyson," she whispers. "Kiss me."

I brush my lips against hers again softly, feeling her squirm again. When I can tell she can't take it any longer, I bring my lips back to her ear.

"Later."

She gasps, her eyes shooting open and her mouth dropping in surprise.

"This is an unlocked classroom, Miss Fischer, a student could waltz in at any time and see us in this compromising position with no way to explain ourselves."

"Wouldn't want that now would we."

Lyla rolls her eyes as her lips form a thin line, she pushes herself off my lap, grabbing her bag and heading for the door. As her hand begins to turn the handle, I take hastened strides towards her and turn her body, pressing her back against the door at the same time my lips crash against hers. Her mouth parts and I slip my tongue through, flicking against hers as she grabs fistfuls of my shirt to pull me closer. I grab her waist tightly, letting her feel the length of me pressed against her hip, rolling mine slightly, and she moans into my mouth. Her lips are urgent, moving quicker as we stand here just begging for someone to catch us at this moment. It would all be worth it in the end, losing my career and having to start over— as long as I could keep Lyla. I release my hold on her mouth as we gaze at each other and catch our breath.

"You didn't actually think I would leave you unsatisfied, did you?" I whisper, nuzzling my nose against hers. She shakes her head, rattled breaths shaking from her body. "So tell me, are you satisfied?"

"Exceeds expectations, Professor Moxley," she smirks with flushed cheeks. "But I'd like a chance to reevaluate, somewhere more private perhaps."

I press my lips to the tip of her nose before stepping back from her.

"See you at the office, Miss Fischer," I call out as she opens the door, offering a small wave goodbye.

The easiest way to tell that it's nearing the end of a semester and students have suddenly begun to care about their grades is when office hours are suddenly packed full until the end of the night. It's been three *very long, excruciating* nights in a row that Tyson has had a line of students waiting, asking for his help to better their grades until long after the end of his technically scheduled hours. Tonight, it's quarter 'til eight and there are still seven students waiting— *I'll probably send at least four home, telling them to come back tomorrow.*

One student leaves his office, another one jumps out of her seat and walks quickly inside before someone can cut in front of her. I groan, rubbing my forehead with the back of my hand, shifting the pile of papers into my drawer as I shake my head in dismay. The weekend together had been so perfect and then that kiss after class Monday has been the last real interaction we've had since. He'd sent me home before nine the last two nights, but tonight I'm determined to stick around— even if just to give him a quick kiss goodbye.

I need to feel his skin against mine, even if it's a short kiss or squeeze of his hand.

"Okay, guys, the four of you last in the line need to get out of here for the night. He's been swamped all week," I announce. They all groan, but no one protests as they stand and swing their bags over their shoulders. "If you want to put your name on this list on my desk, you'll have first priority if you come back tomorrow."

263

They shuffle towards my desk, each taking a few seconds to scribble their names down on the sign-in sheet I've laid out, hanging their heads as they walk out the door. My heart aches for them— just a little bit. If they'd been less careless throughout the semester they likely wouldn't be in this position, but I've seen the work Tyson hands out first hand and know the final exam will be harder than any of them are expecting. As I'm packing my bag up, taking my time to do so, another set of footsteps walks through the door.

"Office hours are over, you can sign in to put your name on the list for tomorrow," I say, rolling my eyes without picking my head up.

"I don't think I need an appointment to see my dad, lady," an icy voice shoots back at me.

My head snaps up and before me stands the long, blonde-haired teenage perfection that resembles Regina George in *Mean Girls*— in more ways than one. She's tall, lean, and her long legs look muscled against her tennis skirt. The scowl on her unblemished, makeup-free face pulls together her expertly crafted eyebrows. Her eyes are the spitting image of Tyson's, making it clear that she's not lying about who her father is. The resemblances between the two of them are uncanny, except even on Tyson's worst days the sight of him has never sent this kind of shiver down my spine.

"Oh, sorry, Ivy, right?" I ask, shaking my head as I swallow hard.

"Duh," she says, rolling her eyes. "So can I go talk to my dad now or do you have more stupid questions?"

Wow, I can definitely see how Tyson thinks she takes after her mom because damn. That was unnecessary.

I straighten my posture, refusing to let a teenager knock me down tonight, and give her a stern, professional look.

"Your father is with a student right now, but you're welcome to have a seat and you can go in when they're done. It's the week before finals, he's a little busy."

She scoffs, her jaw hanging open as if I've insulted her to her core and she wrinkles her nose as she looks around the room at the folding chairs set up throughout.

"I think I'll stand," she says, walking away from my desk and pulling her phone out of her black Louis Vuitton purse.

As she stands there, scowling as her fingers fly across the screen of her phone I wonder— *how did someone that has half of Tyson inside of them turn out like this?* Sloan has gotten under her skin, digging her claws inside of her daughter and turning every ounce of good in her rotten. As Tyson's office door opens, the student steps out with her head in her hands as she mumbles to herself about never finishing at this rate. Again, a small ounce of pity forms in my chest but I've grown numb to it as I've worked my ass off over the years.

"Ivy?" Tyson calls out.

She perks up, putting her phone back into her purse and plastering a smile across her face as she jogs into his arms.

"Daddy!" she yells, wrapping her arms around him before they walk inside his office, shutting the door.

Instead of sticking around like I had been hell-bent on doing, I opt to head out for the evening. My desire to kiss Tyson goodnight does not outweigh my desire to not come face to face with Ivy again anytime soon. The thought occurs to me that if Tyson and I are going to have anything that comes close to a relationship, my time with Ivy will increase— but for now, while we're still in a bit of a limbo, I don't need to add this strain to our current state. I walk slowly through the dim hallway, taking the stairs with ease before heading outside, inhaling the dewy scent of the winter air. It's getting colder by the day, finally signaling that Christmas is coming, and with each passing Christmas comes a New Year to follow. Next year, I will finally graduate, turn twenty-five and hopefully land a kick-ass job to begin my career. I would love to become a Principal Investigator, but know that starting I'm more likely to find work as a Museum Curator or Research Assistant.

I reach my apartment in a foggy state, thinking about the places I would want to apply to and what cities would be fun to live in. It makes me wonder, *is this thing with Tyson worth it in the grand scheme of things?* His life is here— his career, his daughter, his home. I'm just getting my foot in the door and have aspirations that don't involve falling into someone else's routine. Of course, he said he would love to travel again, but traveling doesn't mean uprooting his entire life for a relationship when you're a stable adult.

I sigh, tossing my bag onto the counter as I uncork a bottle of wine— filling the closest glass I can to almost full. Coincidentally, it's a coffee mug and not even a wine glass because that is parallel to how many shits I give at this point in my day. I kick off my shoes as I carry the mug to my bedroom, scrounging for a clean pair of sweatpants and a long sleeve shirt before settling on the couch to watch another episode of *The Office*. As the theme song plays, my phone beeps from inside my bag, and I slowly walk across the room and fish it out, my heart skipping a beat when I read the message.

> **T.M.:** This is a weird thing to say, but I miss you, are you still awake?
> **ME:** It's not weird. I miss you too, and yes.

I smile, clutching the phone to my chest. Even if there's a chance that this won't last forever, at least I can enjoy the moment while it's here. Being with Tyson is exhilarating, which could easily be the root fact that under no circumstances should we be together. He's older—much older—and he's a professor while I'm a student. Two wrongs may not make a right, but it does make for passionate love stories in the end.

> **T.M.:** Can I come over? I need to see you.
> **T.M.:** And kiss you.

I squeal, sounding exactly like the teenage girl I compared Ivy to less than an hour ago.

> **ME:** Hell yes.
> **ME:** Fair warning, I may not let you leave.
> **T.M.:** I have no intention of leaving tonight, Lyla.

Parking my car three blocks down from Lyla's apartment, keeping my head down as I briskly walk there reminds me tremendously of sneaking around back in high school—not something I had ever intended on needing to do in my late thirties. Luckily, the moment her door opens after I knock once and her lips meet mine, it's all worth the risk of being caught. Her lips on mine, her fingers in my hair as she pulls me closer, the taste of the wine on her tongue as she slips it into my mouth— it's the most euphoric feeling I've ever experienced.

"God I've missed this," I murmur between kisses. "I've missed you so much."

Her hands trail down my chest, but she doesn't attempt to remove my clothes. I'm fine with that tonight; the only thing on my mind on my drive over was wrapping her in my arms and drifting off to sleep.

"Sex is great and all, but there are far more romantic moments that happen with clothes on than off…. and I think I'd like to experience some of the ones with our clothes on, now."

My heart swells as I rest my chin atop her head, trailing my fingers through her smooth, black hair. Her heart beats again my chest, smooth rhythmic thumps as she rests her head on my shoulder.

"I'd planned on waiting for you until everyone left tonight," she whispers.

Her eyes don't meet mine when I look at her, she's nibbling her lower lip between her teeth as her finger twirls around one of my buttons.

"Why didn't you?" I ask, likely already knowing the answer.

Ivy.

She had been on a rampage after I closed the office door, dropping her honey-thick sweetness act, and if she was that angry with me, there's no way she let Lyla off the hook when she made her wait instead of letting her burst into my office. Something I need to thank her for because other TA's let it happen. The only time Ivy shows up there is when she needs something or is relaying a message from Sloan that can't wait.

"I didn't want to interrupt any of the time you get with Ivy. I know what you get isn't enough, or as much as you deserve."

My heart could burst as I'm flooded with warmth, watching the corner of her mouth turn upwards as she finally looks into my eyes. Her face is kind, her golden eyes soft and full of admiration.

"Thank you, Lyla," I say, tracing my thumb on her cheekbone as she leans into my touch. "I assume another thank you is in order for tolerating whatever she put you through by not letting her tornado through my door, as well."

She stifles a laugh by biting her lip again, shrugging.

"I couldn't just let the students assume that's the way to get to you after hours," she teases, poking a finger into my chest.

270

She wraps her arms around my waist, pressing the side of her face to my chest. I hold her tightly as she relaxes in my arms, pressing my lips to the top of her head and inhaling her perfume.

"As much as I really do want to rip your clothes off and take you into my room, despite what I said earlier, I also want to hand you a glass of wine and curl up on the couch in your arms."

"I guess that will depend on what kind of wine you have," I laugh.

She pulls away from me, walking carefully to the kitchen and opening a cabinet before gesturing to look inside.

"Take your pick," she says with a smirk.

I laugh, walking through the kitchen, and see a cabinet stocked full of bottles, more than the average college student would have on hand. Normal students buy cheap vodka or tequila, taking shots or mixing it with whatever they can find— but Lyla isn't a normal student, something she quite often reminds me of these days.

"These are all quite exquisite choices," I tell her, spinning the bottles in my hand as I read the labels. "Aren't women your age usually more into Moscato and fruity wines rather than a more sophisticated Cabernet?"

"I assume you're intelligent enough to notice that I'm not exactly like the other women my age," she retorts.

I place a bottle on the counter, tapping the top twice and replacing the rest in the cabinet as she opens a drawer, rummaging around before pulling out a corkscrew. I hold my hand out, insisting on opening the bottle myself and she reluctantly lets me, then hands me a wine glass. She walks to the other room and picks up a mug off the coffee table, draining the last of the contents and placing it on the counter next to the glass I'm filling for myself with a wink. My brow raises in confusion and her laughter fills the room.

"I was too lazy to do anything but grab the first cup I touched when I got home," she says. "So I'm drinking my wine from a mug tonight."

I pour her mug half full before holding my glass out. "Cheers, professor." She taps her mug against my glass, winking before taking my hand and leading me to the couch. After several minutes of staring at the television, with her curled up against me and my shoulder around her, she rests her head against my chest.

"What on earth are you watching?" I ask as the show switches between people talking to the cameramen in a room and shots of people working throughout an office place.

"Oh my god," she spins in her seat, her mouth hanging open as she gasps. "If you aren't a fan of *The Office*..... I'm just not sure I can be with you anymore!"

My eyes widen, unaware that a television show could hold so much power from our newfound companionship.

"What if I give it a chance?" I ask wearily. She nods, returning to her cuddled position against me until the episode ends.

"Do you want to talk about Ivy coming to see you tonight?" she asks. "It seemed to startle you, and since this is the first time she's come since I've started working for you, I'm assuming it's not a regular thing for her to show up there."

My throat clenches as my heart stutters, *of course, she's capable of noticing something like that.* I take a deep breath, compiling my words before I give her the best explanation that I can.

"Are you sure you want to hear about it?" I ask, hoping that the question will deter her.

"Tyson, if we're going to do this, I need you to be honest with me about all things," she says, reaching up to peck my cheek with her lips. "Honesty is the most important thing to me."

Pride, that's what I feel regarding Lyla right now. The ability to walk into this situation, an older man with a teenage daughter and an ex-wife from beyond the gates of hell, and want to immerse herself in all of it.

"Okay, then," I say, taking a deep breath and rotating myself to see her face better. She sits up straighter, making eye contact and waiting for me to continue, her hand resting in mine as her thumb gingerly strokes mine. "Ivy came to me because Sloan has been in a state of disarray all week. She's been lashing out and angrier than usual, spewing more venom to her about me than usual, and let Ivy know that it all comes down to being my fault she's so unhappy." I pause, letting her soak in what I've said. Once she nods in understanding, I continue.

"Lyla, when you told me to fight for us, for you, I chose to honor that, but in doing that I also refused to lead Sloan to believe that I was even remotely entertaining the idea of getting back together with her. I was right when I said there was only one correct choice in her ultimatum, and in her eyes I chose wrong. Ivy came today because she wanted to reiterate that Sloan is only asking for another chance and she doesn't understand why I can't give that to her, why I can't choose to forgive her for the sake of reuniting our family."

Lyla begins to chew on her bottom lip, darting her eyes around the room as the silence between us thickens in my pause. I stroke the side of her jaw gently, pushing the hair behind her ear. She's a strong, brilliant woman but even I could understand if this goes beyond her limit that she's willing to put up with. Everyone has a limit to what they can handle, whether they are consciously aware of it from the beginning or discover it after they're in too deep, unable to let themselves out.

"What did you tell her?" she whispers, refusing to look back into my eyes.

"I told her that the damage Sloan did to my heart is irreparable and I can't just move on from the deceit she has put me through for the last decade," I say. "Lyla, sweetheart, please, know that none of this situation is ideal and I promise, I would fully understand if you were

274

to choose to walk away from it— but I am trying. It has been a very, *very* long time since I've chosen to go against whatever Sloan has wanted out of me, it's usually in my best interest to take her side. But when it comes to you and the way I feel about you, even if it's new and we're still figuring out what this is, it's not something I am willing to walk away from, despite the consequences. And yes, I do believe Sloan will find a way for there to be consequences, but I will try my damndest to keep you out of the crossfire."

The vein in her neck bulges as she swallows, taking a deep breath, closing her eyes for a few seconds, and then leaning her head forward onto my chest. I bend down and kiss her hair, pressing a hand behind her head and holding her to me. Everything I've just said is true. I am not willing to walk away from this, from her. It might be selfish to put her through this agony, but I'm willing to take the chance on her choosing when she can't handle it anymore.

"Is Ivy angry with you for not choosing what Sloan wants from you?" she asks, muffled against my chest. "Is she upset that you won't get back with her mom? That you don't want to be a family again?"

"She is," I reply, a groan escaping her throat. I lean back, lifting her chin for her to look at me. "But what I can assure you of, is that she is quite honestly angry with me about ninety-five percent of the time, but ninety percent of those times are in direct correlation with something Sloan has said or used against me. Rarely is it ever my direct fault that she is angry with me."

"Ugggghhhhhh…..," she groans, dramatically throwing her head back. "Listen, I want to fight for this right along with you. I want it to all be worth it and I definitely don't want to give up these feelings I have for you. The risks and the consequences, we can cross those bridges when we come to them. If that Tyrannosaurus Bitch wants to come down on us like a fucking meteor, let her. I never knew that I could feel about someone the way I feel about you and giving up on us might sound like taking the easy way out, but I think it would break me."

"Tyrannosaurus bitch?" A deep laugh bellows from me, definitely not great timing but how could someone not laugh at that. She rolls her eyes at first, then gasps and covers her mouth as if she's surprised she said that.

"Oh shit, I'm sorry, she's your ex and I shouldn't say things like that about her but-" she rambles. I grab her face between my hands and kiss her deeply until she relaxes.

"You're the first person to ever come up with a proper name for what that woman is, Lyla," I say, then wrap her in my arms and kiss her again. "If you want to weather this storm with me, we'll do it hand in hand. We'll fight together, we can figure it out."

It is too early, before dawn, when Tyson attempts to slip out of my bed unnoticed. I roll over, grumbling and asking him to come back to bed — which he promptly does, wrapping me in his arms. His chest is still damp from the heat of our bodies intertwined like a pretzel throughout the night, my throat dry as the desert as I reach up to press my lips to his. Then, he explains that he should probably leave before anyone in the complex begins getting up to leave for classes, but I am welcome to come with him.

"Thanks, but I'd rather sleep until I absolutely have to get up for my afternoon class," I giggle, pushing him out of bed. "You're welcome to blow off your professor duties and stay curled up here with me, though."

"That sounds like a perfect way to spend the day," he laughs, "but I've canceled class a few too many times lately and I wouldn't want to draw attention to myself with the Dean."

"Mmmmm…. okay then…. suit yourself."

"I'll see you tonight, sweetheart."

He gathers his clothes, kisses me on the forehead, and leaves quietly.

Visions of us falling asleep entangled on the couch shortly after our conversation about Ivy and Sloan play behind my closed eyelids. This followed by him carrying me to bed, stripping off our clothes, and

277

molding our bodies together once more. Even without sex involved, the evening had turned itself around into a state of romantic bliss.

Instead of sleeping until class as I would prefer, I force myself up out of bed and busy myself by doing some much-needed laundry. While it's running, I resort to scrubbing the apartment. It was all long overdue and the fact Tyson had seen my overflowing laundry basket would have embarrassed me if we'd come in my room with the lights on. With hours still left before class, I sit down and study for next week's exams, knowing that my weekend will likely be filled with more time with Tyson— not studying as a good grad student would.

The walk to his office today is a somber moment as I realize in just a few short days, I'll be finished as his assistant—giving up my guaranteed hours almost every night with him. My schedule has already been changed for the next semester and if I were to ask for my TA position back, questions would be asked, suspicions drawn. Putting us into that position could only lead to something terrible. I pull my phone out of my pocket, quickly typing a text to Tyson.

> **ME:** I'm going to miss not seeing you every day next semester.

I could have waited until I got to his office for that, but knowing a line of students would likely be waiting before I ever get upstairs is putting me in a shitty mood already. With a buzz, my phone lights up to a new message from him.

T.M.: Just because you didn't want to work with me anymore doesn't mean you won't see me every day.
ME: Promise?

Damn, what am I? An insecure teenager?

Actually, yes, that's exactly what I feel like. An insecure, moody, hormonal teenager with the hots for her teacher. That would be a legitimate, logical explanation for my justification for my actions from the outside. Sure, I might be in my twenties but that doesn't make me feel any different right now. The only difference is that the teacher has the hots for me too— which feels empowering, for now.

T.M.: Pinky promise. Everything ok?

My cheeks heat quickly as I read his message, then turn through the door into his office where a line of students is, in fact, already waiting.

ME: Just realizing how short our time left together in this office is.

Tyson sounds frazzled as he's shaking his head at another student inside his office, shaking his hands around like he's losing his shit. A good girlfriend would go in and save him from this interaction, but a great assistant knows that he is perfectly capable of handling his shit. As the student leaves the room, frustrated and cursing under their breath, I hear his fist slam against his desk loud enough that even I jump in my seat. The next student looks at the door and shakes their head, turning to walk out and leave.

ME: Is everything ok with YOU?

The next student in line gulps loudly, closing their eyes, and walks slowly towards his door. I give a half-smile of encouragement and whisper "good luck," as they slide by me. Tyson hasn't left a pile of work for me tonight, so I take the opportunity to flip through my study guides and make notes to look over. After three more students leave in the same frustrated state, my phone buzzes on my desk.

T.M.: If one more of these shitheads asks me for extra credit when they have more than half of their assignments not turned in this semester I might actually lose my shit.

ME: Calm down, killer. Take a deep breath. You don't need them crying to the Dean.

T.M.: What I need is to kick them all out of this office and kiss you until our mouths physically can't take it any longer.

ME: Good, now think about that instead of ways to berate the students.

I send the next kid in, their eyes sunken with fear as they close the door behind them. I get through three more pages of my notes before the door opens again, surprisingly not followed by a slew of curses as they walk past me.

"Lyla," Tyson yells, apparently forgetting to call me Miss Fischer in the office. "Can you come in here for a moment?"

I hold my finger up to the last student waiting to see him, noticing there are now only thirty minutes left of his time in the office. When I walk inside, he motions to close the door and collapses with his face buried in his arms on his desk when it's shut. Having been inside the office the majority of the last few weeks, I know where a student can and can not see inside through the windows on the wall and walk around to him, rubbing his back gently.

"I hate all these fucking kids this year," he complains.

"There's only one more left out there for tonight," I reassure him. "I'll send anyone else that shows up away."

He reaches a hand out and gives my hand resting on his desk a squeeze before looking up at me, sadness filling his eyes.

"Thank you," he says. I nod, squeezing his hand back and going back towards the door. "Will you stay with me this weekend?"

I shrug back at him with a smile.

"Maybe, but I'm another one of those kids with exams next week, you know."

"Oh fuck," he groans. "You're right, I'm taking up all of your study time. I'm so sorry."

"I'm kidding," I squeeze his hand gently, "but you're welcome to show me how sorry you are." I wink, then leave his office and let the last student know he's ready to see them.

I tense as his voice rises, the poor girl is probably trembling in her chair as he's losing it. As I finish packing away my papers, the lights in the hall begin to shut off. I hear the janitor making their rounds. *They're earlier than usual tonight.* The girl leaves his office with her head held high, a smug smile on her lips as she tosses her bag over her shoulder and leaves— giving me a wink as she walks by, causing my heart to sink. Rage boils in my blood without warning as if my gut knows she's up to something deplorable. Once she's out the door and I hear her footsteps down the stairs, I stride into Tyson's office to find

282

him staring blankly at the wall in front of him. His eyes are wide, his jaw hanging open in shock.

"I'm going to assume that by the look on your face and the smug smile on hers, on top of the wink she gave me, that either she knows about us and is trying to use it against you or she offered sexual favors of her own for a better grade."

He nods, but he doesn't say which part is true. His eyes blink a few times as he regains his composure, then turns to look at me.

"I've been teaching for a decade and in all of those years, not once has a student had the audacity and nerve to offer to have sex with me to improve their grades," he mutters. "I'm not sure if I should file for sexual harassment or be impressed and give her a better grade just for having the fucking balls to do that."

"She's going to be a fantastic lawyer one day," I laugh. "But if she lays a hand on you, I'm the one that will require a lawyer."

He throws his head back laughing, then walks around the desk and wraps his arms around me before kissing my forehead.

"Someone sounds jealous," he whispers.

"Trust me, I'm not sure I've ever felt like punching someone in the face as much as I did the moment she winked at me and I could just tell what she was up to," I laugh. "I wasn't even aware that I was capable of being jealous before that moment."

"I like that you're jealous, Lyla," he says, pressing his lips to mine. "It means that you're as invested in this as I am unless you're forgetting about my interaction with Mr. Bennett."

"Absolutely haven't forgotten about that macho, alpha male witnessing experience," I say, wrapping my arms behind his head and pulling him to me. We become entangled into a web of lips and teeth, passion and desire.

This week has been taxing and my time at the office has been a complete shit show, to put it gently. I've become increasingly frustrated about getting minimal time with Lyla, the asshole side of Tyson Moxley becoming more frequently shown. Normally going through the motions of my usual routine would be fine, but now they're interrupted with thoughts of what Lyla is doing or what we could be doing together instead. At least when I was in my routine, set in stone on being an asshole to everyone around me, I enjoyed my career and enriched the minds of others. Now, all that these students have done lately is irritating me to the core and causing me to feel as though I'm going to self-combust, dreading each passing day in their presence. The only good parts of my day are the ones spent with Lyla.

Before the students begin to file in, I scribble a note for her to leave on her desk.

Dinner tonight, 7:00 p.m.? Please.
I need some alone time with you more than anything else.

I plan on canceling office hours for the evening. If they need my help at this point, there's very little chance that any advice I can give them will help them pass the final exam on Wednesday. I hear the staff door open and breathe a sigh of relief, relaxing at the sound of

285

her footsteps as she walks close behind me and leaves a trail of floral perfume. She arches an eyebrow when she sees the note and I begin to work on an email to send out to inform everyone of the canceled office hours for this evening. She begins to unpack, then picks up the note she purses her lips before staring at me. She taps her wrist two times and holds her hands up in confusion when I look back at her. I tap the key to hit send without looking back at my computer, then point to hers as the notification pops up that she's received a new email. She smiles, then nods— accepting my dinner proposal.

Now I just have to find somewhere far enough away from campus that no one will recognize us together.

I begin my study and review lesson for the class, going over half of the necessary information that will, unquestionably, be included on the exam and frown at the number of students not taking notes today. The ones that are, will potentially exceed my expectations of the group as far as the exam grades will go. I've been more lenient on this class than I have in previous years but for that, they should have an easier time with the test— *if they are smart enough to take some fucking notes.* I end up dismissing the class five minutes early, exhausted from the lack of participation and insufficient answers when letting Lyla call on any random student when none offered up an answer. As I fall into my chair at the desk, I can hear Lyla giggling in her seat.

"What the hell are you finding so amusing, Miss Fischer?" I growl.

"Damn, grumpy ass, chill," she grumbles.

I sigh, knowing inside that my mood is going to ruin our night if I don't let it go.

"I'm sorry, I didn't mean to snap at you."

She crosses her arms in front of her, pressing her lips together tightly.

"I'm literally giggling at Lucy's text reminding me about brunch tomorrow and asking if I plan to show up or disappear again." She leans against the side of my desk and whispers quietly.

"I assumed that since Ivy was not at your place last weekend, that she would be this weekend and we wouldn't be able to spend it together. I can cancel brunch if you want me to, though."

Fuck, she's right. Ivy is supposed to be at my house this weekend. Though there's a good chance that she won't show up after our argument the other night.

"No, go to brunch with your friend, Lyla," I tell her, shaking my head. "You're right, Ivy should be there and I did forget about that myself…. I just don't know that she'll show up…. or if I care anymore if she does."

"You don't mean that, Tyson," she says, giving my shoulder a quick squeeze. "She's your daughter and you love her, even if she's hurt and lashing out on you right now. It would. however, not be in our best interest to get caught by her when she's already angry with you."

I nod, again acknowledging that she's right and more capable of handling this situation maturely than I am right now.

"You're remarkable, you know that right?" I ask.

"I do know that," she says, smugly. "I'll see you at seven?"

"I'll be on time, I promise."

As she heads out the door, I pack my computer up and throw the papers into the desk before quickly leaving the room— almost sprinting across the campus towards my car. If we're only getting this one night together this weekend, I'm damn well going to make it the best date she's ever been on. I toss my bag into the backseat and peel out of the faculty lot, heading towards home as fast as the afternoon traffic will carry me— which isn't very fast, because it is Houston on a Friday evening, after all.

I don't bother with pulling in the garage, just less time I have to get things ready. I sprint inside and run towards my room, stripping my clothes off along the way— reminding me of last weekend when Lyla was here and we did the same thing. I lather myself in soap once I'm inside the shower, letting the hot water run down my back as I try to concentrate on anything besides the memory of Lyla's naked body pressed against the tiles. *The woman isn't even here and she's driving me crazy.*

"What the hell do I even wear on a date like this?"

I push clothes around, grumbling and shaking my head at every option. Too fancy, not nice enough, too ragged—nothing looks just right, nothing looks as perfect as Lyla surely will. Finally, I toss on a pair of dark jeans and a button-up maroon shirt, tousling my hair into the perfect combination of messy and put together. I'm out the door by six and let her know I'm on my way before pulling the Camaro back out of the driveway— antsy in my seat with anticipation and excitement. It's been years since I've taken a woman out on a date, even more since going on a first date.

I pull into her apartment lot and as I get out of the car, her door opens. Standing there with my hand clutching the door frame, the breath is knocked out of me at the sight of her. She looks up from slipping into her jacket, a smile spreads across her lips that are painted as red as the dress she's put on, and pulls her hair out from inside her coat. My mouth hangs open as she walks towards me in sky-high red heels and perfectly composed, while I'm unable to form a coherent sentence as my heart races. Her cheeks flush as she gets closer to me, never once letting her black-lined, golden eyes stray from my face. Suddenly, it hits me how out in the open we are and that I'm unable to pull her into me and kiss her right at this moment— so as my knees unbuckle I run around the side of the car, and open her door for her.

"You look unequivocally stunning tonight, Lyla," I whisper in her ear as her cheek brushes my jaw when she slides into the car. She smiles, her cheeks are now more flushed than they already were. As

289

she mouths, a quick "thank you," her eyes scan down the front of me hungrily. I get back into the driver's seat and start the car, whipping out of the parking lot in a hurry. I need to get to the restaurant as quickly as possible, but not for the food— I need to taste her lips on mine, to cherish every second of this night.

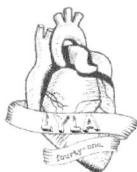

Instead of watching the city lights out the window, I rest my head on the seat in the direction of Tyson. Seeing the flashes of color as they bounce off his skin, his lips curled into a smirk, and seeing the glances he steals out of the corner of his eye at me— it all sends my heart over the edge and I feel as though I've suddenly jumped off a cliff with this man. Having sex, being together outside of work in our respective homes are nothing compared to the intimacy of risking being caught like going on an actual date in public together. The car darkens as the city lights fade behind us. I'm not sure where we're going but as long as I'm with him it doesn't matter.

"You're quiet tonight," he murmurs, reaching for my hand.

"Just enjoying the view," I tell him, smiling into the darkness.

As we continue driving, the illuminated sign for the Kemah Boardwalk comes into view, rows of palm trees line the area as we pull into the parking lot. He pulls into a spot under a streetlight, tapping his hand against the steering wheel as the song playing comes to an end with a dramatic drum solo. He shuts the car off, opening his door and signaling for me to wait as he walks around, then opens my door himself. I smile, the streetlight illuminating his face, and take his hand as he holds it out. He pulls me close and lightly kisses me, my hands grasping his biceps to pull him flush against my chest. As we break and he takes my hand to lead me away from the car, he freezes.

291

"You do like seafood, right?" he asks. "I think I just kind of assumed that everyone does these days but we can go somewhere else if you don't, there are plenty of places around or we can get back in the car and keep driving. It really doesn't matter, I just wanted to be able to take you out for once and be able to feel like we're in a normal situation. I don't want you to think that I want to hide you away because I don't. I promise I would love nothing more than to show you off to the world and kiss you all day, every day."

"Oh my goodness, Tyson," I laugh at his rambling. I spin towards him, pulling him to me and tenderly grasping his face in my hand. "You're as nervous as a wild turkey before Thanksgiving."

He snorts as he laughs, a smile spreading across his face as his face softens.

"I guess I am a little nervous," he admits, running a hand through his hair. "It's been a very, very long time since I've done anything like this."

"What do you mean?" I ask, puzzled. "Like, go on a date?"

He clasps his hand behind his neck nervously as he nods in response. Pressing his lips together and the corners turned down. This admission fills my chest with elation as I realize how true every word he's spoken about how I'm the one chipping away at his walls are. This gorgeous, intelligent man has been dormant in the woman department since losing his family all those years ago and he chose me— of all people, to allow himself to feel something again. Tears of

292

happiness well in my eyes as I bite them back, my throat tightening as my fingers slide down the side of his jawline. I pull him to me with a firm hand on his shoulder, desperately seeking his mouth and the taste of his tongue. He grabs my waist and holds me firmly in place until I break our kiss, my stomach rumbling against his hip.

"Hungry?" he asks with a chuckle.

"Very," I say, "and I do, in fact, love seafood."

His expression perks up as he takes my hand again and leads me through the boardwalk as I watch around us, awestruck by the bright and colorful lighting on the rides. There's a mixture of families with small children, older teenagers, and just old enough to date couples walking hand in hand— just like us. He leads me to a nicer building on the boardwalk, the sign above reading Landry's Seafood House, and opens the door before gesturing me inside. He gives the hostess his name, stating that he's called ahead for a reservation, and she leads us to a table against a window with a clear view of the Bay.

"I'd rather us be outside, but given the season I thought it would be best if we enjoyed the view from indoors tonight," he says, taking a seat across from me.

"It's beautiful either way," I promise him.

"Not as beautiful as you," he says, leaning forward on the table to take my hand. My cheeks flush at the compliment and I let my hair fall around my face. He reaches up to brush my hair behind my ear as his thumb traces my cheek. "You act as though you don't receive compliments very often."

"Probably because I don't," I admit, suddenly feeling the air leave the room as my lungs inhale only his cologne.

"I'll have to change that, then," he says with a disapproving frown.

A waitress comes and takes our drink order, two glasses of Raeburn Chardonnay, and we begin to look over our menus. I cross my legs beneath the table as my foot taps in the air— a nervous habit I've yet to outgrow. I see Tyson slide his menu away from him, focusing only on me as I continue to read diligently to decide the best item to eat that I can ensure I won't drop anything on my dress. Maturity with age and sophistication while eating did not come hand in hand with me, more likely than ever to miss my mouth while taking a bite. When the waitress returns and I've made a decision, Tyson orders first—stuffed flounder with rice and vegetables, plus an order of fried calamari for the table. I order the cedar-planked salmon, with the rice and vegetables as well. We sip our wine as we watch the waves crash under the winter moon, soft violin music filling the room with so few patrons this evening.

"What are your plans after finishing grad school, Lyla?" he asks, breaking the silence.

I gulp, not prepared for this conversation, though I knew it would have to come one of these days— preferably before we got too invested.

"I've begun to apply to a few different places to work as a Curator, but have a better chance of being pulled on as a research assistant in the beginning," I say.

"Where have you been applying?" he says, taking another sip of wine.

My shoulders drop as I look down at the table, fidgeting with my napkin while I chew on my lip. "Lyla, you've made it clear that Houston has never been your long-term home, and that's okay. I'd just like to know where your dreams are leading you. I'm curious about where you see yourself in the future, whether that's next year or ten years down the road."

"Tyson, you should know that I began these applications before any of this with you began," I start. He stifles a grin, waiting for me to continue. "So far I've sent my resumé to the Museum of Paleontology in Berkeley, the Virginia Museum of Natural History, the Museum of Comparative Zoology at Harvard, and the Yale Peabody Museum of Natural History."

"Every one of those museums would be lucky to have you, Lyla," he says, reaching for my hand again. "You've mentioned before that you have a brother in Connecticut, correct?"

I nod, surprised that he remembers that conversation.

"Yale would be my first choice, if given the chance," I admit.

"It has been a while since I've seen snow," he mutters.

What?

"Do you miss the snow, Tyson?" I inquire.

He smirks, his thumb stroking my hand as he gazes into my eyes.

"Not really," he says, a devious glint sparkling in his eyes. "But I would suffer through it if it meant I got to be with you, Lyla. If that's ever something that you would want."

And just like that, every string I was keeping my heart in my chest was snapped and my heart was handed to him. Tyson Moxley has become the sole keeper of my most valuable possession, free to handle it however he pleases. He could break it with the snap of his finger or he could lock it away and keep it forever. In my almost twenty-five years on this Earth, I've never felt a love like this from another person. Not my family, not my friends, not even Parker— only Tyson.

While this scares the hell out of me, I also feel at peace as I mentally surrender myself to him. If he's willing to move across the country to be with me, leaving everything he's ever known behind— I could walk through the gates of hell and fight whatever battles come our way.

A better date couldn't have happened if I'd wished on every shooting star in every night sky I'd ever seen. Something changed in Lyla after I mentioned that I would brave the snow if it meant getting to be with her.

That was something I hadn't known myself until I said it out loud. Ivy is likely off to college next semester, a year and a half earlier than I had anticipated, and once she is living her own life there will be no ties holding me to Houston. With my inheritance of this house came a handwritten letter, one stating that when the time came that I was ready to live for myself, to stop letting everyone else dictate my life, to sell the house and run. I never wanted to sell this piece of my family's history when it was left to me, always thinking the letter had been written when my great-grandfather was at his most senile. In retrospect, he had been the only one to see Sloan and the rest of my family for what they were— backstabbing, lying, money-hungry pains in everyone's asses.

Ivy, unsurprisingly, had never shown up last night and now that it's almost two in the afternoon, I don't expect her to be by today either. The love I feel for Ivy will always be there, she's my daughter after all, but times like this make me wish she could see Sloan with clear eyes. Maybe she could even learn to see that most great things that have come of her life have been in thanks to me. While Sloan may get most of the credit, it is my alimony and child support checks sustaining their ludicrous and extravagant lifestyle, though I am sure

297

my parents have treated Ivy as one of their own— even after cutting me out of their life completely.

With the afternoon sun high in the sky, still lying in my bed in nothing but a pair of boxers and sweatpants, I give in and send a message to Lyla. I'd honored her desire to attend brunch with her friend this morning and held back from inserting myself into her friend's time with her. *Brunches are usually over by one, right?* Of course, they are, even if there are bottomless mimosas involved.

> **ME:** Did you have a good time at brunch, sweetheart?

The typing bubble appeared quickly, showcasing that Lyla had maybe been waiting to hear from me as well.

> **LYLA:** It was delicious, full of Lucy's usual flirtatious banter with the waiters and plenty of mimosas….
> **LYLA:** But it was no pancakes in your kitchen in our underwear.

I giggle, sounding like a fucking lovesick school girl, as I read her text and remember the morning spent together. It kills me that she isn't here every night, her warm body flush against me as we sleep, and the sight of her sleeping after I wake up is a peaceful way to start

298

my day. I've grown to yearn for her throughout the day, craving her touch and missing the sound of her voice.

> **LYLA:** What about your morning? Did Ivy show up?

I groan, knowing that she will likely regret sending me home last night after our date— promising that the next time we're together will be worth the wait.

> **ME:** Nope. At this point, I don't see her showing up tonight either.
> **LYLA:** Sounds like you might be lonely.
> **ME:** You have no idea how much I wish you were here with me.

She starts to type again, but her bubbles soon disappear and I toss the phone onto the cold pillow next to me. *I guess I should get my ass out of bed now.* I take a scalding hot shower, the burn of the water hurts less than the heartache I feel towards Ivy. Knowing that while I'm excited she'll be away from the claws that Sloan sinks so deeply into her every day, also leaves me with the dread that comes along with not being naive enough to believe she'll make the time for me after that. Slipping into yet another pair of sweatpants and a t-shirt, I go down and rummage through the kitchen— settling on leftover pizza from two days ago for a late brunch, *is it just lunch at this point?* The best part of winter is neverending college football on Saturdays so I settle in on the couch with the first game I find. By the end of the first half, I've stuffed myself full of pizza and two beers— surprised when there's a knock at my door.

When I pull the door open, a wave of black hair blows in the wind and knocks my breath from my lungs as I watch Lyla's face turn upwards. I reach for her without hesitation, pulling her as close to me as possible so our lips can meet, and walk her inside without letting go. With her back against the wall, she drops her bag to the floor and reaches her hands behind my neck— her fingers stroking my hair.

"It sounded like you needed me," she whispers between kisses. I bury my face in her neck and nod vigorously, a lump forming in my throat. She leans in, whispering into my ear as her hot breath trickles down my neck. "Don't worry, I need you, too."

Hungrily, I capture her lips with mine again and pull her up in my arms before running up the stairs as hastily as I can without tripping over my own feet. Her moans into my mouth as she pulls her shirt over her head let me know that we're on the same page. Her hands meet the hem of my shirt as I lay her onto my bed, yanking it over my head with one quick movement. She dressed for just this, wearing only leggings and nothing underneath them— a close match to myself, forgoing the boxers after my shower. She pushes my sweatpants down as I reach behind her arched back to unsnap her bra, sucking her peaked nipples as I free each breast, slowly. Her hand is grasped around my member as I quiver at her touch groan against her breast. Though her strokes are gentle, every movement mixed with the warmth from her skin sends fireworks through my veins. We pause only to reach for a condom out of the drawer, rolling it on before teasing her clit with my finger. She grows wetter by the second until I finally give in to her pleads, her hands lining me up with her dripping wet opening and I slowly push inside. She gasps, her nails dragging their way down my back in such a way that should hurt but the only thing I feel is pleasure.

"Fuck…. Yes….," she moans, "faster, Tyson. Please."

"Dammit, Lyla," I growl, moving my hips faster as she holds me against her.

Her heels push against my ass, pushing me further inside her each time I try to ease up on her— knowing I want to do this all night long, trying to make this first round last a little longer. I reach a hand behind her head, tugging her hair slightly, and suck my way down her neck. Her arched back presses her breasts against my chest as she writhes in pleasure beneath me.

"Oh god," she gasps, "I'm going to cum."

I slow my pace and smirk, pressing my lips against her and nibbling her lip gently.

"Are you sure you want to do that already?" I whisper, pulling my cock almost completely out of her so only the tip is left inside. She wiggles beneath me, trying to push me back inside.

"Tyson, I fucking swear….,"

"What do you swear, Lyla?" I tease, stroking her clit with my thumb as she gasps.

"I swear I'll never show you how far I can take you down my throat if you keep teasing me like this."

Fucking hell, Lyla.

"Such a dirty mouth for such a sweet girl."

"You have no idea just how dirty I can be," she giggles.

I lean down, pressing my lips to hers as I slam back inside her, my cock filling her tightness.

"Cum for me, sweetheart," I whisper, quickening my pace.

The next few thrusts are filled with her screaming my name as she finishes before I follow suit. My legs buckling at the knees, collapsing my body against her chest as we kiss gently and catch our breath. Her hand strokes my cheek as I roll off her and onto the bed next to her. She repositions, resting her head against my chest where my heart must be hammering so hard that it's pounding against her skull.

"I'm glad I made the impulsive decision to show up here," she says.

"Me too, baby," I tell her, "me fucking too."

Bottomless mimosas at brunch and a lot of guts were what it had taken for me to show up at Tyson's house yesterday without being asked to come over. It was impulsive and I spent the entire drive over reassuring myself that he was going to love the surprise— which he did, showing me just how much many, *many* times since. Here it is, after eight in the morning and he's still soundly sleeping next to me—completely exhausted from the various forms of exercise throughout the night. I swipe my finger across my lips, rubbing my tongue against the roof of my mouth as I remember living up to my promise to show him just how dirty my mouth can be.

Not once has he flinched in the last forty-five minutes that I've been laying next to him watching him sleep, even when I moved out from under his arm to enjoy this moment of tranquility. The evenly spread rise and fall of his chest, his tousled hair brushing over his forehead, and the way his mouth is just barely parted as he breathes. It's all so surreal to remember that at one time, not really that long ago, I hated this man with a fiery passion— a passion that is now fueled by love instead.

Swiftly and quietly, I slide off the bed and toss on one of his t-shirts before tiptoeing out of the room and down the stairs. It's clear that Tyson has always been the one to cook for anyone in his life, so I'd like to return the favor this morning— maybe even get him to eat something other than pancakes for breakfast. It feels invasive as I rummage through his cabinets, but the result will be worth it and I don't foresee my scrounging causing an issue. I find an assortment of vegetables, shredded cheeses, and plenty of eggs in the fridge, setting them on the counter before moving on to find a cutting board. It only takes opening three more cabinets, but I miraculously find a knife on the first try at least. I turn my favorite upbeat pop playlist on as I get to work chopping vegetables to make the best omelets this man will taste in his life.

Our entire relationship has been mostly surrounded by food and sex.

I chuckle as I sort the vegetables into four even piles, ready to make extra in case he's as famished as I am when he wakes up. I hum along with Selena Gomez as I beat the eggs, happy that the man keeps a skillet on top of the stove and I don't have to look for one. I add the first pile of vegetables, sprinkle some cheese, fold the egg and count to thirty— quickly tossing it on a plate when I know it's cooked to perfection. I repeat the process two more times, getting more comfortable as the music switches from Selena Gomez to Lizzo and swaying my hips along with the sassy lyrics, lip-syncing into the spatula. As I flip the last omelet onto the plate, an icy voice from behind me shakes me to my core— causing me to drop the skillet onto the floor.

"Well fuck, isn't this what every daughter wants to find in her father's kitchen on a Sunday morning," she says. "A whore cooking breakfast in nothing but a t-shirt."

304

I can't speak, my lungs emptied of all air as I watch Ivy's smirk spread across her face, letting her words bury themself under my skin. The deafening silence in the room is enough to allow the sound of Tyson's footsteps running down the stairs to be heard.

"Lyla!" he yells, I want to tell him to turn around and not come in here, but the damage is done. "Lyla, are you okay?"

He skids into the room, somehow, luckily, managing to throw on a pair of boxers before running to my supposed rescue, but freezes in the doorway as he looks between myself and Ivy. He gulps, his eyes widening as I stay frozen in place. I should run, get the hell out of this kitchen, and to my car as quickly as possible, but my feet just won't move. As Ivy continues to stare at me, her eyes widen and she covers her now gaping mouth with her hand as a laugh comes from deep in her throat.

"Oh shit, daddy, I guess I know why you're so hell-bent on not getting back together with mom," she laughs, reaching for the edge of the counter as she doubles over. "You're too busy fucking your assistant instead! I thought I recognized you. I will say, you look much prettier at *work* than you do in my daddy's kitchen."

The color drains from my face and from the sight of it, Tyson's too. We've been caught, by none other than his daughter— we don't have to ask to know that she's going to run straight to Sloan. There's nothing we can say or do that will convince her to keep this to herself, but nevertheless, Tyson tries.

"Ivy, honey," he starts, holding his hands up in surrender. "Please, hear me out."

"Why the fuck would I want to hear anything you have to say?"

"Because somewhere inside of you, you love me and want me to be happy," he says, calmly. "Yes, Lyla is my assistant but has already resigned. Effective at the end of the week."

"So? She's still a student, daddy. There has got to be something in the ethics portion of the employee handbook about sleeping with students," she snaps. She flicks her fingers together in the air, a wide grin spreading across her face. "I have an idea! I'll ask mom to let me read through her handbook since she signed her contract yesterday and all."

She winks in my direction, but I still can't react. This is going from bad to worse quickly.

"That won't be necessary, Ivy, seriously," Tyson begins to plead. "Please, just leave your mother out of this."

"Why the hell should I do that? At least when she is dating someone she has the decency to introduce them to me before I find them what might as well be naked in the kitchen!" She shoots daggers at me, suddenly I regain my composure and put the plate on the counter. I look to Tyson, begging to be let out of this situation. He nods in understanding, then jerks his head to the staircase— but Ivy isn't having it.

"Don't even fucking think about leaving the room, *Lyla*," she sneers as she says my name. "I came over here to enjoy a morning coffee with my dad and tell him all about my official early acceptance, to celebrate getting the hell out of this town in a few weeks, but instead I found *you* in here and the least you can do is enlighten me as to how long this has been going on and when you plan to break his heart. You don't honestly see yourself having a future with him right? You're just enthralled by the idea of this forbidden romance and you'll be over it just as soon as you've convinced him you really love him so much and he's ruined his life, his career, all for your worthless ass. For fucks sake, he's at least a decade older than you. Did you even consider how uncomfortable it would be to be closer to my age than his?"

"DAMMIT IVY THAT IS ENOUGH!" Tyson shouts, Ivy and I both flinch as his voice echoes through the room. He walks across the room, wrapping an arm around my waist and pressing his lips to my hair, whispering an apology into my ear. I stand, glued to his side, as he continues to berate Ivy. "This is my house, Ivy, and you will not speak to Lyla that way. She is not the reason I have no interest in restarting a relationship with your mother, as appealing as the idea of our family reuniting might be to you, you were too young to understand the toxicity she spewed and the pain she left me with when she took you away from me. I love you, Ivy. I always have, and I always will, but under no circumstance will you treat Lyla with anything but respect."

Her face falls as she sinks herself into one of the barstools, biting her lip as a lone tear falls from the corner of her eye. I wonder if this is staged, a mere thought-out plan of action she's used many times before when he's lost his temper— because something in my gut tells me she's acted out like this on more than just this occasion.

"I'm sorry, daddy," she murmurs.

"You should be apologizing to Lyla," he states, squeezing me tighter to him.

"Sorry," she says, rolling her eyes as she looks away from him.

"It's f-fine," I stutter, "I know this situation isn't ideal, and I apologize for you having to find out this way. For what it's worth, I don't plan on breaking your father's heart, Ivy."

She shrugs, dismissing my acceptance and I push a plate towards her with an omelet.

"These smell delicious," Tyson whispers into my ear. "Thank you."

We sit and eat as my mind fogs over, barely able to pay attention as the two of them talk. Tyson asks Ivy about when she will get to start school and what her plans are for the summer. I think she mentions California, something about learning how to surf and he tells her to find a female instructor—not a male to take advantage of her. The tension in the room lifts but I can't help the sinking feeling in my gut, reminding me that this is likely all a game to her. When we're finished eating, she excuses herself and lets him know that she's already made plans with her friends to go shopping this afternoon. As he hugs her goodbye he places a hand on either of her shoulders and looks into her eyes sternly.

"I expect you to leave your mother out of my personal relationships, Ivy," he says.

She nods, but the smirk on her face sends a sinking feeling through my gut.

Ivy caught us and that just started the countdown until the inevitable shitstorm that Tyson warned me about, leaving our days together to be numbered and waiting for the consequences.

ME: Lyla, are you sure that you're okay? I know Ivy seeing us together didn't go over well but I do think that she won't cause a problem for us.

LYLA: I'm fine, Tyson. I just needed to finish studying. My exam starts in ten minutes, I'll see you this afternoon. Ok?

ME: Ok. You're going to do great, sweetheart.

LYLA: Thanks :)

Lyla's lack of contact since rushing out of my house within thirty minutes of Ivy leaving yesterday morning has stirred up some uneasy feelings in my gut: insecurity, anxiety, and being on edge. I'm doing my best to suppress them as I finish the prep work for my class review session today. Sloan hasn't had any contact with me yet, which allows me to believe that though Ivy was upset, she hasn't gone running to tell her mother what she walked in on. There are a million ways that I could have introduced Ivy to Lyla and better prepared them both for it to go well, but she had to walk in at the worst time and in the worst situation.

When I'd rushed downstairs, I'd just thought Lyla had hurt herself in the kitchen and was not prepared for that conversation with my daughter. Ivy could have also handled herself better in my eyes, but she's a teenage girl that caught her dad with his first girlfriend since her mom. I can only hope that the initial hurt and betrayal she

felt by the situation will subside and she will honor my request—
Sloan never finding out about Lyla, at least not until after graduation.

I take a break from the review notes to grab some coffee from
the lounge a few doors down, somewhere I usually avoid at all costs
but I just don't feel like going to the nearest coffee shop right now.
There's only one other professor in here, I think he teaches something
involving liberal arts, but he nods towards me and I give him a
friendly smile back— causing his eyes to widen and quickly bury
himself back into his book.

What's that about?

"Everything going well with exams in your classes?" I ask him.

His brow pinches together as he watches me, I lean against the
counter after filling one of the styrofoam cups with black coffee and
taking a sip of the bitter, burnt drink.

"Um, yeah, I guess so," he says, confused. "What about yours?"

"Finishing up the last of the review today," I shrug. "Hardly
anyone took notes on Friday, so maybe they'll have more initiative
today if they care about their grade at all."

"I've heard you run a tight ship over there in Environmental
Law," he smiles, raising his cup of coffee towards me in salute. "One
of these days I'd like that kind of control over my students, but all
these dreaming classic lit lovers just keep their heads in the clouds."

I scrunch my nose, knowing that I can't blame his students one bit for daydreaming during what sounds like a dreadfully tedious class.

"Don't worry, I'm sure those students respect the hell out of you," I say, surprising myself with my compliment. "I'm going to get back to finishing up my notes. Have a great break, Professor."

"You too, Professor Moxley," he says, returning to his book as I head out of the room.

Perhaps this job wouldn't be as dreadful to show up to every day if I managed to make some friends.

I could do that, I could befriend some of the other professors. Maybe we could even start a Tight Ship Asshole kind of club or something along those lines to pass the time. I try to think of other colleagues I would want to invite to join such an elite opportunity but fall short, truth be told, I couldn't tell you which professors are still around from last year or who are retired or moved on from the school. University staff mixers and holiday parties have never been on my agenda, but maybe I'll test the waters and attend the next one over break.

As amused as I am, nothing prepares me for when I walk back into my office to find the shadow of someone inside my smaller, usually locked office. I walk slowly, prepared to catch and discipline whichever student has chosen today to break in and get a look at the exam— something that has happened to other professors before from what I've gathered from emails the Dean sends out. My steps are slow, quiet and deliberate, as I inch my way closer to the door only to breathe a sigh of relief when I'm hit with the floral scent of Lyla's perfume as she spins around, her black hair pulled up into a ponytail cascading over her shoulder. Her eyes are sparkling with excitement, a wide pink smile across her lips. The air is knocked out of my lungs as I stand at the edge of the doorway, taking in her effortless outfit of a pair of leggings and an oversized sweatshirt— a sweatshirt that looks vaguely familiar.

"Hi," she smiles wider.

"Hi, yourself," I say, my eyes still stuck on her sweatshirt. "Is that….?"

"Yours?" she responds with a shrug, smiling slyly. "Sorry, I didn't think you'd notice if I took it."

Now I'm the one donning a cheesy smile as I shut the door to the office, putting my coffee on the desk before pulling her to my chest.

"I can't tell you the last time I wore that sweatshirt, but it looks better on you," I press my lips to hers, wrapping my arms around her waist.

"It smelled like you, too," she explains. "I thought it would keep me focused on my exam this morning if I knew that when I was finished, I could sneak up here and catch a few moments with you."

Her hands snake their way up my spine, twisting her fingers into my hair as she pulls my mouth back to hers while I'm still smiling. I should be concerned that someone could recognize the sweatshirt from a time that I, maybe, wore it around campus, but the thought appears for a second and disappears as her tongue swipes across my lip and I open my mouth to her. Kissing her like this, in my office in the middle of the day, is another thing I should be worried about. But right now, all that matters is that Lyla hasn't been scared off by Ivy— not yet, at least. I want to soak in this moment forever, but she breaks our kiss long before I'm ready.

"I have another exam in ten minutes," she says, pouting, "but I needed to see you before that. I felt really bad about leaving right after Ivy did, and I know that probably looked really bad and like I was running away from you and all of this, but I'm not. I promise, I'm not. Maybe at the time, I was startled and a little scared, but I did have to finish studying since I left so abruptly and on a whim the day before to see you and I did need to do my laundry before I leave for Connecticut."

I press my lips to her forehead, thrilled that she's reiterated that she isn't running away from us. She asked me to fight for us and she's still willing to do the same. She'll never know how much that means to me.

"Plus I kind of just assumed that you might need some time to process what just happened and could come up with one of your

314

infamous flawless game plans for moving forward because I just....,"
she trails off, biting her lip now. "I just don't want to be the reason
there are more issues between you and Ivy. You deserve better than
that, Tyson."

I cup her face in my hands and kiss her gently, resting my
forehead against hers.

"You are not going to be the cause of any more issues between
my daughter and myself, Lyla," I reassure her. "She's leaving for
UCSD at the start of the new year and will be starting her own life. I
have high hopes that the time away from Sloan will only improve our
relationship, and perhaps she'll have a change of heart when it comes
to how she treats others."

She nods, wrapping her arms around me tightly as her head
rests on my chest.

"Thank you for not running away from us, Lyla," I whisper.

"I asked you to fight for me, Tyson," she whispers, "it's only
right that I fight for you, too."

"LAST DAY OF FINALS, BITCH!" Lucy exclaims, busting through my apartment door with the energy of a toddler that kept their parents up all night. "How are we celebrating tonight? Clubbing? Drinking? Both?"

She grabs a mug from my cabinet, helping herself to the pot of coffee that just finished brewing, and waits for my response. In all honesty, I hadn't planned on celebrating with Lucy tonight— but instead with Tyson, naked. However, I have spent the majority of the last few weeks blowing her off to spend more time with him and did miss that brunch that one week. I probably should just give her tonight, *one night won't be the end of the world— right?*

"Ugh, you choose Lucy," I groan. It's way too early to think about drinking and dancing when I've barely made a dent in my first mug of coffee. "You know all the good places and the ones I choose usually end up sucking."

She laughs, trying to not offend me, but we both know I'm right. She taps her finger against her chin, pondering as if she hasn't had somewhere picked out this entire time.

"We're going to Numbers!" she squeals. I groan internally, having feared this would likely be her top choice. It shouldn't be horribly busy on a Tuesday night, at least, and I can try to get back home at a reasonable hour without a huge hangover. Most clubs aren't even open on Tuesdays so I'm sure she had researched which ones we

316

would even be able to get into tonight and not end up scrounging around downtown for drinks.

"Fine, but I have office hours until eight so why don't you just meet me here when I get home and we can take a cab or something together?"

She nods vigorously.

"I'd fully expected you to fight me on this," she admits. "You've been so M.I.A lately that I just assumed we weren't friends anymore or something!"

She fakes a pout, but winks.

"Luc, you know that isn't true! I've just been busy with classes and applying for different positions so that I'm not floundering when graduation time comes."

I shake my head and wander into my bedroom as she trails behind me. I have two more exams today and then I'm finished for the semester. Tyson had promised to have dinner for us in his office tonight, so at least that is something to look forward to.

Tyson.

How is he going to react to his much younger girlfriend going out with her friends to a sweaty nightclub where other guys will almost definitely hit on her? Not that I'm being conceited at all, but isn't that the only point in a man going to one of those places? To hit on any and all clearly not taken women? I groan, shoving clothes aside in my closet and trying to find something comfortable to wear. Tyson's sweatshirt a second day in a row is a no-go, especially with Lucy sitting on the edge of my bed jabbering away at what she wants to wear tonight.

"And we are absolutely finding you some hot as all hell man to bone and get Parker completely out of your system," she says, having not heard the first half of her rambling.

Don't worry about that, Lucy. Parker has long been boned out of my system by someone much more worthy than any man inside the nightclub ever could be.

I grab a pair of skinny jeans and a long sleeve t-shirt, throwing it on and slipping into my Uggs.

"We should wear red tonight!" she squeals. "It looks great on both of us and we'll be able to find each other easier that way if we get separated."

I nod in agreement, knowing there's a red bodycon dress in my closet I've been dying to wear out anyways. She squeals again, taking my hands into hers and bouncing up and down. I can't help but laugh at her, wishing I had the energy that she does most days.

"I need to get to my exam, Lucy," I tell her, "but meet me back here tonight and we'll go out. I promise."

"Okay! Good luck, Lyla!" She hugs me tightly, blows a kiss, and leaves out the door.

I toss our mugs in the dishwasher and pull my phone out to give Tyson a heads up of tonight's plans— because that's what I should be doing, right?

> **ME:** Lucy wants to go out tonight for dancing and drinks to celebrate finishing up our exams today. I told her I still have office hours, but can't blow her off again. I'm sorry.

Why am I apologizing?

I grab my bag, checking the apartment quickly before leaving and strolling through campus immersed in conversation with Tyson.

> **T.M.:** Why are you sorry, Lyla? Do you think that I'll protest you spending time with your friends instead of me?
> **ME:** I don't know, maybe? I think you're a little too old to think that going to a nightclub sounds like fun. I don't know if I even find it appealing, but it'll make Lucy happy.
> **T.M.:** As long as I don't have to be worried about someone else touching what's mine, I don't mind you going out at all. Where will you be going?
> **ME:** Numbers. *groan*

T.M.: Hah, while that doesn't seem like
your scene at all, I do hope you have fun
tonight. You deserve to let loose, Lyla.
You've been thrown an extraordinary
amount of excess stress lately.
ME: God, why are you the perfect
boyfriend?
ME: Oh, shit. We never established that.
Sorry. Fuck.

My phone rings in my hand, his initials appearing on the caller
ID. I gulp before I answer, holding the phone tightly to the side of my
face as others are rushing past me.

"Listen, I'm really sorry. I know we haven't talked about it and
I didn't mean to say boyfriend! I take it back, we don't have to put a
label on anything!" I exclaim.

"Hello, Lyla," he says, cheerfully.

"You sound pretty chipper this morning," I retort, biting my lip
as I wait for him to call me out on the *boyfriend* word.

"Why wouldn't I be?" he asks. "I have one day left before break
begins, I'm drinking a fantastic caramel drizzle coffee with just a
splash of toffee nut while eating my favorite raspberry crumble muffin
and this mesmerizing woman just called me her boyfriend."

My cheeks begin to stiffen and hurt, I realize that I've begun
smiling while listening to him ramble on.

320

"A mesmerizing woman, huh? Sounds like I should give you back your sweatshirt. She might want claims of it in the future," I laugh.

"On the contrary, *girlfriend* Lyla," he emphasizes, "I think you should keep it, accept the compliment and absolutely, most definitely agree to be my girlfriend and not take back calling me your boyfriend because I quite like the sound of that."

"Your *secret* girlfriend, though," I say, the word leaving a nasty taste on my tongue. It's not like I didn't know this was how it had to be, just hearing it out loud made it all that more real. It makes it sound as if what we feel for each other doesn't deserve to be shouted from the fucking rooftops of the Houston skyline.

"Only for now, sweetheart," he assures me. "I promise, after graduation, the world will know how I feel about you— if you'll wait it out with me. I would understand if that's too much to ask, but I'm asking, anyways."

Tears well in my eyes, because how could this man want to risk everything just to wait out time with me? He deserves to be someone older, more accomplished, and capable of being shown off on his arm on every street in town.

But deep inside, I know that isn't what he's looking for. He wants me, only me.

"I would be happy to be your secret girlfriend for as long as you'll have me, Tyson," I tell him. "As long as you're willing to be my very exclusive, secret boyfriend."

"Nothing would make me happier than an agreement on our exclusivity," he says.

There's a silence, a void that neither of us is sure how to fill. Several seconds pass as I bite my lip, unsure of how to respond. I stop at the door leading into the lecture hall, suddenly unprepared to take this exam as my brain has turned to mush.

"This is the part where I would kiss you if I was right there."

Well, that's one way to end the silence.

"I would do a lot more than kiss you if I wasn't walking into my exam room," I laugh.

"Good luck, sweetheart. I'll see you this evening," he whispers. "Lyla?"

"I'm still here."

"Lyla, I….," he pauses, I can hear the tapping of a pen against a hard surface in the background. My heart pounds, a ringing sounds in my ears as my breaths become shallow. *Say it, Tyson. Please.* "Lyla, I think you're going to do great. Don't panic, just think of me when you get stuck on a question."

My heart drops to my gut, glass shattering from within.

"I will, Tyson. Thank you."

I hang up, turn my phone off and shove it into my bag as I take a deep breath and walk inside. I feel fearless, on top of the world and ready to fight through hellfire— Tyson Moxley is my boyfriend, and he might even be falling in love with me. Even if he can't bring himself to say the words just yet.

This realization makes my heart soar. I feel warm, safer than I've ever been all because of him. Something hits me as I sit down with the exam in front of me— I've already fallen in love with him.

The sensation of Lyla's lips on mine lasts longer than my drive home, away from the office where we spent the last two hours sipping sparkling water and eating her favorite tacos. She was bubbly and personable tonight, chatting freely like we were two friends catching up rather than a professor and his assistant.

"Promise me that you'll be careful tonight, please," I whisper, pulling Lyla against my chest. She hums against me, pressing her lips softly against my neck.

"You mean don't let anyone drug my drink or take advantage of me in the club, right?" She laughs, her fingers tracing the buttons down the front of my shirt. "It's not like this is my twenty-first birthday and I plan to get black-out drunk and lose control, Tyson."

I swear I can hear her eyes roll as she talks, chastising me for worrying.

"It's not your actions I'm worried about, sweetheart. Not that I was ever as despicable as some of the men in the world today, but I was once a man that operated with only the use of one head— not usually the one atop my shoulders."

She snorts, gripping the back of my neck and pulling my lips to hers.

"Let me assure you, then, that your other head is the only one I want near my body."

"Promise?"

324

"Geez, are you really that insecure and worried?"

I've struck a nerve, crossed an invisible line. Her face hardens as she watches my reaction. On one hand, she's not incorrect—I am that insecure. A decade of celibacy and loneliness will do that to a person. But on the other, I'm not worried that she's only telling me what she thinks I want to hear. I do trust Lyla, as crazy as it sounds. Hell, I'd almost told her that I loved her on the phone just this morning if only I hadn't chickened out at the last second.

"I'm sorry, sweetheart. I'm not worried, I'm just figuring out how to do this boyfriend thing again." I press my lips to her forehead, inhaling the scent of her perfume and letting it singe my nostrils, imprinting it into my mind to remember when I'm alone at home tonight. "Go have fun with Lucy, just let me know when you're home safely. Okay?"

"You got it, boyfriend," she winks, pulling me in for another deep, passionate kiss before strutting out of the room, swaying her hips as she tosses her hair over her shoulder.

It felt relaxed, easy enough to forget that we are still not in the clear when it comes to our relationship. Ivy had left, seemingly content with the instruction to leave Sloan out of my business, but knowing the Tyrannosaurus Bitch could resurface at any time has left me with an unsettling pit in my stomach.

The too-large house is void of all sounds when I step inside. For the first time since moving in, it's almost eerie to be in the house alone— though I have been alone for the last decade. The house feels cold and lifeless without Lyla's laughter echoing through the halls, without her warm body pressed against mine. I squeeze my eyes shut, refraining from becoming the obsessive *boyfriend* that texts her while she's out with her friends. I'd meant it when I'd told her to go out with Lucy. It hasn't slipped my notice that I tend to be the only person she sees outside of classes, which is unfortunate for a woman like herself. I had pegged her for a sorority outcast, party girl when she first started working for me— but like most other parts of my life, she's found a way to prove my assumptions inaccurate. When my phone buzzes in my pocket, I eagerly yank it out in hopes that she's the one who has reached out first— maybe even on her way over. But my heart drops when I see that it's not her, but instead the she-devil herself.

SLOAN: We need to talk about Ivy leaving
in a few weeks.

"Fuck you, Sloan," I grumble.

In reality, there is nothing we need to discuss pertaining to our daughter's college. It's a full ride, an early acceptance scholarship, and they're including room and board. The only thing we need to do is sign the forms allowing her to graduate high school early and attend the university— neither requires us to see each other or speak to each other.

326

ME: What do you want, Sloan?

Perhaps I can hasten this conversation, getting her to cut to the chase is the best-case scenario right now. Nothing good ever comes from a conversation with Sloan these days. After she's finished pissing me off for the night I can retreat to my personal gym and run the anger out of my system until I'm weak enough to barely crawl into my bed before passing out.

SLOAN: I don't think it's safe for her to be such a young girl, that far away from her parents and everyone that loves her.

My eyes roll so hard I swear they scrape against my skull on their way around. Of course, Sloan doesn't want her to go because then she can't hold Ivy over my head. Without Ivy, there is no reason for us to have any contact at all— not that I would complain about that for one second.

ME: You can't seriously be considering the idea of taking such an honorable and prestigious opportunity away from our daughter.

I grab the bottle of Macallan 18 Year scotch and pour myself a double into one of my great-grandfather's crystal glasses. I swirl the amber liquid in the glass lightly before raising it to my lips as my phone goes off again.

> **SLOAN:** I think you should tell her she
> can't go, that way only one of us has to
> look bad.

"What the fuck, Sloan?" I yell, slamming my glass onto the countertop. I flinch when I hear the crystal shattering from the impact and a trickle of blood runs down my palm. Running to the kitchen, I grab a washcloth from the sink and run cool water over the cut. The pain from the cut doesn't dim the anger welling up as I clean up the mess, dumping shards of crystal into the trash can. My face is burning, likely completely red if I looked in a mirror right now, and I swear I can feel the anger melting my phone as I speed-type a response.

> **ME:** Sloan, you have completely lost your
> fucking mind if you think I would ever
> take the fall for you wanting to keep her
> at home, under your control, and letting
> you sink your claws any further into our
> innocent young girl. You are delirious
> for thinking you'll be able to turn her

```
against me forever and your reign of
terror is coming to an end. I can not
fucking wait for her to see you for the
person you really are.
```

I press send, the anger overpowers the regret as I watch her name indicate that she's replying slowly. She's crossed the final line tonight, and I'll be damned if I'm going to let her use me to ruin our daughter's life and the last shred of love she has for me.

```
SLOAN: Do you feel better now, Tyson? I
hope you don't lose your temper like that
with your little girlfriend. The
assistant, correct? What a shame that
would be.
```

My phone slips out of my hands, clattering against the hardwood as it lands. Ivy told Sloan about Lyla. She went behind my back and did something I directly asked her not to do—even if it's a secret that no father should ever ask their daughter to hold. Now it's going to come back and bite us, mostly me, in the ass the minute I don't succumb to Sloan's demands. She didn't get her way once and now she has the ammunition to turn our worlds upside down, ruining every shred of happiness I've found. I can try to deny her claims, but it will look like a sad attempt to save us from a fate we both knew was

329

bound to come. Striking a deal with Sloan is a more possible scenario if I can find something that she wants more than my head on a stake— or in more proper context, smeared all over the headlines, again.

> **ME:** Come to my office at 2:45 tomorrow
> afternoon. Let's talk like reasonable
> adults and come to an agreement on how we
> can all get what we want, Sloan.
> **SLOAN:** But what if what I want isn't
> what you want?
> **ME:** Have your demands ready, Sloan. Just
> for the love of God, leave the girls out
> of our fight.
> **SLOAN:** I'll see you tomorrow. Goodnight.
> ;-)

Instead of going downstairs to run as I planned, I drag myself up to bed with legs that feel like Jell-O, but heavier. Hours ago I was happy, blissfully ignorant of the world outside of my relationship with Lyla. Now, as she's dancing her night away without a worry in the world, our world is beginning to burn, closing in on us. The dreaded fight is knocking on our door, but the least I can try to do is save her from the crossfire. She'll understand that whatever I have to do tomorrow, I will only be doing to save us. I'm fighting for her, for us, with every drop of blood in my body and I will let Sloan spill it all in battle— as long as not so much as a hair on Lyla's head is harmed.

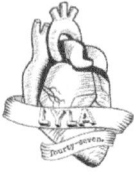

As if Tyson had known that we were bound to get carried away last night in our celebrations, or rather just heeded my text at close to three in the morning as such; he let me know it was fine for me to miss a class— nothing for me to do with exams and such. At first, I had been sad about not seeing him, but that's while I was still drunk. Now that I'm awake, head throbbing and nauseous, I'm mentally thanking him as I down some Tylenol and chug water from the faucet. Never, in all of my years, have I let myself drink so much in one night. Lucy had been in her element, dancing with every slightly attractive man and getting us free drinks. Meanwhile, I had hung back and made friends with whoever wasn't trying to get our clothes off at the end of the night— an unexpectedly easy option.

Flopping on the couch, I yank my phone off the table and decide that Tyson might want to know that I'm alive and well—*if that's really what I can call this.*

ME: I'm sorry I drank so much, but I'm glad you were gracious enough to give me a chance to recover.
T.M.: You had a late night, I'd like for you to be well-rested for our celebrations tonight :)
ME: Mmmmm…. Wonder what that will entail ;)

```
T.M.: I need to catch up on a few things
in my office after the exam, meet me at
my house around 6? There are a few things
I'd like to discuss with you.
ME: Is that code for "we need to talk"?
Because that's never ended well for
anyone in the history of the universe.
T.M.: No, not exactly. Just something
that has come up that I'd rather talk
about in person.
ME: Okay, see you then. *kisses*
```

Tyson hadn't mentioned yesterday that he would need to work in the office today or needing me to come in to help with anything. *And what the hell do we need to talk about? Maybe he is mad about me going out with Lucy and he just wants to have that discussion in person.* Ugh. Shit. I hate when I have to spend a day obsessing over something like that. I look down at my disheveled pajamas, feeling the weight of last night's makeup still on my face and hairspray holding my hair in place— I need a shower before I go anywhere. Reluctantly, the Tylenol has kicked in and I suffer through the steps and let the steaming water run down my skin as I scrub every inch of my body, shaving in all the right places.

If he's going to get some work done in his office, I could surprise him there and perhaps make whatever menial tasks he has left to do a little more exciting. Hours are technically closed for the semester, no one will be around to interrupt us or catch us together. Maybe we could get whatever he needs to talk about off his chest early enough that it doesn't end up taking up whatever time we have together tonight.

The thought of surprising Tyson perks me up, images of hiding underneath his desk with my head between his legs cause the mound between my legs to begin to throb. Thoughts of sneaky, mind-blowing sex with Tyson wake me up better than any coffee ever has in my life. Drying off quickly, I sort through my drawers to find a matching set of sheer blue undergarments to wear underneath my favorite tight, black pixie pants and a deep v-cut emerald green sweater. I falter momentarily, deciding between a pair of sexy, spiked black heels and a pair of short, velvet green booties— ultimately deciding on comfort over style. *Though I'll keep those heels in mind for our next date.* After applying some lipstick and curling my hair loosely, I trek outside in the cool, afternoon air towards the building.

Jitters flutter about my stomach. Eagerness, nerves, and enthusiasm build in my chest the closer I get to his building, all the faces of surprise he could make racing through my mind. My heart beating quickly, a smile spreading across my face— I've never felt this kind of euphoria towards just seeing a man before. It's just after three as I walk up the stairs to his office, quiet voices drift through the halls but I dismiss them as others inside their offices finishing up before heading home for the holidays.

As I round the corner into Tyson's office, all of the happiness leaves from every pore in my body. Frozen, I watch in horror as he wraps his arms around another woman and pulls her lips to his. It feels like an eternity that I stand there, feeling like I'm being held down by a boulder repeatedly falling on my chest as my heart shatters like a stained glass window being hit with a hammer. Except it doesn't just shatter once, it breaks into smaller and smaller pieces as my jaw hangs open and I watch as she twists her fingers into his hair— just like I do.

He was going to end things with me. What other explanation for any of this could there be?

The air in my lungs disappears as I choke back the vomit swirling up from my stomach. I try to breathe, try to run— anything just to get as far away from this spot as I can. She opens her eye mid-kiss and sees me out of the corner of her eyes, with a wink and a smirk she kisses him deeper. It strikes me like a thousand cuts against my skin, *it's Sloan.* It feels like another boulder comes crashing down on top of the first one. She expertly spins him around, her hand trailing down his chest and resting against the front of his pants. As soon as she pulls away from him, he opens his eyes and I am the first thing he sees.

The shocked look forming across his face as his eyes flit between Sloan and me is all I need to regain the strength in my legs, turning so quickly and running down the stairs. *Don't come after me, do*

335

not chase me, I do not want to hear your voice right now. I need to get as far away from Tyson, and Sloan, as I can— as quickly as my legs can carry me. I hear his heavy footsteps coming after me, but they freeze as Sloan speaks just loud enough for me to hear her over the ringing in my ears.

"Tyson, don't forget about our deal," she demands, her icy voice shaking me to my core.

I push through the doors and the cold air brings the hot tears streaming down my face to my attention for the first time as they burn against the wind. I mentally praise myself for my choice of shoes as I wind through the grounds, the sides of my stomach in excruciating pain from the hasty pace I've kept. A million thoughts racing through my mind, how I'm not tripping over my own feet I'm unsure.

Why Sloan? Why insist on us being an official couple and then get back together with her? Why would he allow her in his office? Have I just been an inside joke between all of them? Did Ivy tell her about us? Did she threaten him? Me? Is she going to tell the Dean? Does he still love her? Did he ever feel anything for me other than just lust? Was I just a hot, young piece of ass for him?

I bolt through my front door, locking both deadbolts inside and crashing to the floor in the entryway as I sob into my knees, hunched over on the floor. My breaths are short and scarce, my lungs flaming in my chest with each heaving attempt for air. My fists slam against the hard tiles, repeatedly, as if the change of pain could alleviate it from

336

my breaking heart. I'd been stupid, foolish, and lovesick— I'd let myself fall in love with him. All of our sneaking around, all of the secrets are now coming back to bite me in the ass. I'd fallen for his good looks and his charming words at a time when I was vulnerable, only to be knocked right back down. Maybe I always knew Parker hadn't been the one, but the way Tyson talked about a future and creating a life together had been enough to make me believe him.

He said he was going to fight for us, then he let Sloan win.

He said he wanted to be with me, then he kissed her.

He made me fall for him while he was falling for her, again.

As my sadness begins to fade and fury starts to take over, the vibrations of fists pounding against my door shudder down my back as the shouting ensues.

"Lyla!" Tyson's voice echoes through the cracks around the door. "Lyla, please! Let me explain!"

"GO AWAY!" Lyla screeches, slamming her fist against the door back at me. I deserve her rage, her anger— I deserve every last shred of the hatred she is feeling right now but I can't accept it. I can't just leave, not like this— not after what she saw.

"Lyla, please!" I beg, my legs aching from chasing after her. I ran after her as soon as I told Sloan to get out of my office, never to speak to me again. "Just let me in, let me explain!"

"NO!" she yells. "FUCK OFF, TYSON."

I shudder, the venom spewing from her words could melt the door between us with their poison.

"Please, it wasn't what it looked like!" I beg, again.

I rest my head against the door, withholding the rippling tears that are forcing their way through my body. Seeing Lyla's face after pushing Sloan off of me, pleased with myself for fulfilling my debt to her, and knowing it was finally over between us, was the worst surprise of my life. My heart felt as though it had cracked every rib in my chest as it broke, seeing her standing there with tears streaming down her face— unable to look away from the trainwreck that she had walked in on. Of all the days she could have shown up unannounced, it had to be today, at that exact moment. Five minutes before and she would have heard it all, she would have understood what was happening and why I was so willing to give in to Sloan's demands.

338

The door flies open and I stumble, catching myself on the frame to keep from falling.

"Get the fuck inside before someone sees your pathetic ass screaming at a student outside their apartment and calls the fucking Dean," she seethes.

My head hangs low, my chin pressing to my chest, as she slams the door behind me standing on the tiled entryway, the vibrations jerking through my body. I tremble in place, seeing her bags packed on her couch through my eyelashes. *She's leaving. She's going to Connecticut and this could be it, I could never see her again.*

"Are you going to stand here and insult my intelligence as you try to tell me that I didn't just see you kissing your ex-wife? That getting back together with her isn't what you wanted to talk to me about tonight?" she spews.

I don't move, still unable to look at her face.

She thought I was going to leave her… for Sloan.

"So that wasn't what it looked like or it was? Because I don't know what else that could fucking look like, Tyson. It looked a lot like you doing the exact fucking thing you made me promise you that I wouldn't let happen when I went out with my *only friend* to celebrate last night. I never even got to tell you that she took the blunt force of every man in the club wanting to size us up and she enjoyed every second of the attention while I sat in our booth sipping free drinks, without letting a single person lay a hand on me or even dance with someone the entire night that wasn't Lucy."

I bite down hard on my lip, forcing the sobs threatening my chest to stay inside. I pick my head up, knowing she'll never believe a word I say until she calms down— but seeing her face streaked with mascara, her eyes burning red and her lips pressed into a fine line, it unravels me. She isn't even trying to wipe away the tears streaming down her face and my hand aches to reach up and wipe them away. I want to pull her close to me, apologize with every fiber of my being, and swear to her that what she saw was merely the end of what could have been an ugly fight—a fight that I saved us from, saved her from being thrown in the middle of. When I can't find the words to say, she continues yelling— and I let her.

"I trusted you, Tyson. I came to surprise you, thankful for your understanding behavior about letting me skip out on class today and trusting that you had only good intentions. That's the problem though, I fucking trusted you, and instead, you scheduled a rendezvous with the Tyrannosaurus Bitch herself. I have believed every fucking word you ever said to me about how what we had was mutual, that you felt the same way that I did. I thought that you were different from Parker," her eyes narrow, "I let myself fall in love with you, I trusted you with my still healing heart, and you completely shattered me in that second."

She fell in love with me, too.

340

A moment that should have been celebrated, now debilitated me to the marrow in my bones— making me wish that I had let Sloan have her way in the argument. It would have been uglier, I probably would have lost my job in the long run but at least Lyla wouldn't have seen anything but an argument. We would be spending the night celebrating and I would have told her I loved her before she left for Connecticut tomorrow. Now, she'll only be leaving with hate in her broken heart, a heart that I was lucky to have received a shred of in the first place.

"Lyla, I'm sorry," I whisper, the words catching in my throat. "It wasn't like that, you weren't supposed to be there, you weren't supposed to-"

"To what? Find out? Know about it? Well, guess what, I did."

Her hand flies to her mouth, stifling a sob from so deep inside her that she hunches over as though it's causing her physical pain. My heart wants me to run to her, to hold her and let us cry together— but I don't. My body freezes, forcing me to stand here as though my feet have filled with concrete too heavy to lift and wait as she cries with my head hung low. My hands clasp together at the back of my neck, letting my tears fall as I listen to her break. Each time she gasps for air, a knife shoves its way through my heart.

"Lyla, I don't love her," I murmur through broken weeping.

"Well you sure as fuck don't love me either, Tyson," she snarls.

"Sweetheart, please'-" I start.

"Don't you even think about calling me sweetheart, ever, EVER again."

"I'm sorry, I just, I don't know what to say to explain."

"That's the thing, Tyson," she says, straightening her back as she narrows her eyes at me again. Her fluctuation between heartbreaking sadness and red-hot fury is a force to be reckoned with, her fury once being the part of her that I loved the most. "We shouldn't be having this conversation. We should be curled up on your bed, naked and drinking champagne. Discussing holiday plans, sorting out how to spend time together when school resumes in January. We should be celebrating and overflowing with happiness, but instead, you fucked up and kissed your ex-wife, breaking my heart and every shred of desire I have to ever see your face again."

Lyla could have slapped me across the face with her hand wrapped in barbed wire and nails between her fingers and it would have still hurt less than hearing her say that she never wants to see me again. I'd been hurt when Sloan cheated on me a decade ago, but the only real heartbreak that time had been watching her take Ivy away from me. Being in love with Sloan all those years doesn't come close to what I've felt for Lyla in such a short amount of time. Yet, somehow, Sloan is again the reason for someone I love being ripped away from my grasp.

Feeling my soul crushing inside of me as I wrap my arms around my chest, hearing the shattering of my heart in my ears. I

342

could have survived anything that life threw my way— except this. I can't handle losing Lyla, especially not like this. I force a deep breath into my lungs and lift my foot to step forward, only making it one step closer as she quickly takes a step back. She holds her hand up, warning me to stop.

"Do not come near me," she shrieks.

"Lyla," I whimper, falling to my knees as I succumb to the pain. "I need you, I love you."

Seconds pass that feel like hours, and then she takes three steps towards me and leans down to me. She puts a hand under my chin, lifting my face to look at her twisted expression with anger still flaming in her eyes. Her pursed lips are swollen from wiping her face with her sweater sleeve and grinding her teeth across them.

"You know what I've always said, Tyson," she whispers. "Actions speak louder than words, and your actions tell a much different story."

I gulp, exhaling as a sob rips through my chest and I wail on her floor. I crumble as her perfume lingers in my nose and fogs my mind. The heat of her finger under my chin lingers as she presses upwards harder so I'm looking more directly at her.

"Please, please don't let this be it," I grovel, wanting to reach out and wrap my arms around her legs and pull her down to me.

"You made your choice, Tyson," she seethes. "Now get the fuck out of my apartment."

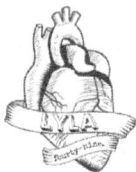

As Tyson sits there crumbling on my floor, my heart aches to soothe him. I want to throw myself on the floor into his lap, hold him against me as our tears flow together, and cry until we can work through this. He'd admitted that he did love me too, but how could his words mean anything when he did choose Sloan— even if only for a minute. He hadn't fought for us, he'd stopped fighting at that moment. Maybe he can't see that now, but he did. The moment he gave in to what Sloan wanted, he chose her over me and I can't live with that. The pounding fury in my head is still pressing against my skull, making it impossible to think rationally. I loved him so much, but as I watch him sob on my floor, I hate him. I'd once assumed my hate for him had been fueled only by the unexplained, lurking passion beneath the surface but no— Tyson Moxley deserves to be hated.

"I need you to leave, Tyson," I growl, the sound of my voice so low it sounds inhuman.

He looks up at me with pleading eyes, tears streaming down his cheeks as my face hardens. I've been naive long enough, I let myself fall for someone whose heart had been so closed off and broken that he did nothing but extend that pain unto others. His face is streaked with water stains as his shoulders move up and down in rapid movements, trying to catch his breath. Even his biceps bulging against the clean-cut of his dress shirt, the muscles I'd spent hours tracing with my fingertips and admiring, are doing nothing for my

344

onset rage. As his eyes flutter close, he stands slowly and holds his hands in front of him in defeat.

"I know you're angry with me now, you have every right to be, but one day I hope you'll let me explain," he turns to leave, pausing only for a second before spinning around and looking into my eyes. I feel the weight of my emotions crushing me into place as he stalks towards me, pressing his lips to my forehead. The tenderness of his lips, the warmth of his hot breath against my clammy skin— I want to grab him by his shirt and hold him to me, but I can't move. I just stand there, as frozen in time as the dinosaur bones in the museum. His cologne drifts inside my nostrils begging me to let him in again as my hands ball into fists at my side. He leans in, moving his lips closer to my ear as I'm still unable to bring myself to protest. "I love you, Lyla. I mean it. Words alone will never be adequate in expressing how truly sorry I am for letting you be caught in the middle of my problems, Lyla. One day, I truly hope you let me explain, maybe even make it up to you."

"Get out," my arm raises, a finger pointing towards the door with venom strung through my voice.

He nods, turning around and walking through the door without another word, no glances back at me over his shoulder. As the apartment walls close in around me, I exhale a deep, raspy breath as I crumble to the floor. My head is thrown back as I wail, giving zero shits if my neighbors hear at this point. Our fight hadn't been quiet, anyone listening close enough could already know who had been in my apartment. A much lesser person than I could be going to the Dean right now to expose our illicit relationship, though Sloan is likely taking care of that herself. My palms smack the floor as I grasp for every breath through the sobs choking my throat. The pain of a thousand flesh wounds couldn't compare to the heart-wrenching aches in my chest and I would do anything to never feel like this again.

"How do you know when what you've found is true love, Lucy?" I ask.

"You know it's true when it hurts when it feels like your soul is connected to theirs in ways you can't understand. Being unable to fathom a life without them in it, even if they hurt you, that's how you'll know it's real," she says, sipping her mimosa slowly, with her eyebrow raised. "Do you think that you love this secret man, Lyla?"

My cheeks burn as I avert her gaze, trying to hide the truth sprawled across my face.

"I think it's too soon to really tell," I shrug, poking aimlessly at my food.

"Oh my god!" she shrieks, grabbing my hand from across the table. "Lyla! Holy shit you ARE in love!"

I giggle, now hiding behind the hair falling in front of my face. I try to shake my head to disagree but Lucy's mouth is gaping and the sparkle in her eyes clues me in that she knows anything I say in protest is a lie.

346

"I don't know, Lucy," I say, feigning disinterest. "It's so soon, too early on, and I'm not sure that he even feels the same way."

She squeezes my hand harder with a wide grin. I can hear her feet tapping in excitement against the tile floor beneath us as she squeals, too loudly for a morning brunch crew.

"It doesn't matter if it's been one day or ten years with someone, Lyla," she insists. "When you love someone, time doesn't matter. Time means nothing to the heart, it's a made-up concept that humans created as a tracking device because we're too inadequate to function without the false security of time and being able to track every second of our lives. Hearts run on emotion, passion, understanding, and connection. I know the logical side of you wants to believe that you can control when and if you'll fall in love someday, but that's the thing about love — it isn't logical. It makes the smartest people do the stupidest things sometimes. You can't control your heart in the way you can convince your mind to believe something. Your heart will know before you know yourself, and then you can only hope that his heart feels the same."

I swallow hard, as I process the speech she's just given. For an art major, Lucy has been more insightful in the last few minutes than I've heard her be in all our years together.

"The way your eyes light up every time you check your phone, the flush of your cheeks every time you get lost in a daydream... it all says that you're already there, Ly. You may not be ready to believe it yet, but that's just your too intelligent for your own damn good brain arguing against what your heart already knows. A piece of you already knows that, but the logic that has

been instilled for so long wants to fight it. Stop fighting it, start fighting for it instead. Lean into those feelings and trust them. Love isn't easy, whether you're fifteen or eighty, in any circumstance, and you're going to have obstacles that get in your way. You're going to have the kind of fights that feel as though the world is crashing down around you, so many tears that you'll think they will drown you and outweigh the happiness but if he's the one, if he's your soulmate, it will all be worth it."

In the replay of our last brunch flashing through my mind, all of Lucy's words echo in my head. Lucy had warned me there would be fights and tears, that I would feel as if it would never get better but that it would if he was my soulmate. I don't believe in soulmates though, nor do I believe that Tyson Moxley can be my 'one and only' when he's so willing to break me like glass, throw what we have away like an old toy he's gotten bored with. He played with my heart, he used my body, and he made his own choice. He had made a conscious choice to kiss Sloan even though it was wrong. The logical part of my mind takes over. It tells me to run, to leave now, and get an earlier flight, to put as much distance between myself and Tyson Moxley as possible, as quickly as I can.

I push myself up from the ground, wiping the tears away once more, and letting the regained strength lift me as I grab my bags from the couch. If there is one thing that I have learned from my parents over the years, it's that you should never rely on someone else in your time of need— but right now I need my brother. I need to be somewhere that I can't be found, if only for a little while. I can't look around my apartment and not see the sparse remains of our relationship threatening to suffocate me at every turn, so I leave. I put my bags in the car and drive away, my heart aching in one direction as my mind turns the car in another.

"Goodbye, Tyson," I whisper. "I loved you, too."

Every passing minute of every hour, every day seems to drag by at minuscule speed. The first day I had run until my legs had given out, only to get back up and switch to weights until my arms did the same. I laid there on the gym floor for hours, exactly how many I still don't know. My phone never rang. No one came to check on me because no one knew the extent of the pain I was in, not that there was anyone to care. The second day I sat at the kitchen counter, writing letter after letter trying to work out the words to explain myself—my actions—to Lyla. I wrote until the calluses on my hands began to burn, break open, and bleed. Nothing I wrote sounded correct, none of it felt worthy of her forgiveness. On the third day, I opened the first bottle of scotch. I started a new cycle of drinking until I passed out just to collect the slightest amount of sleep without dreaming of her shattered face.

Once I woke up, I'd start the drinking again and repeated my wasted efforts. No matter where I went in my house, it all reminded me of her— the one person that was truly able to break down my walls, to love me, and I ruined her. When I watched the pain and heartbreak first hand after Mr.Bennett cheated on her, I couldn't fathom the idea of someone else getting the chance to hurt her like that. But then I did it myself. I broke her heart. I have officially been written off, tossed aside as worthless trash because I did exactly what she said would be unforgivable.

350

Christmas is only a few days away but given the story Sloan, that evil fucking Tyrannosaurus Bitch, went home to tell our daughter, I expect I'll be spending it alone. New Year's as well, and if I'm being honest, I think I'm okay with that. I didn't bother with the tree, the decorations, or the lights this year. Anything that might give the illusion of happiness or that I'm not a dishonest, arrogant, foolish asshole doesn't deserve to be present, not this year.

I swirl the amber liquid around the glass as I stumble in an attempt to stand from the couch in the dark room, the sun setting beyond the horizon through the glass windows. I once found beauty in the sunsets, sunrises, and Houston's skyline in the distance. Now, the only beauty I know is the beauty of Lyla's face when she blushes, the amber of her eyes, and the way her creamy skin looks against her favorite emerald green tones. A vivid memory of Lyla dropping her dress that first night in my office, taking control over her desires and what she wanted from me, plays in my head. I groan as I swallow down the rest of the liquid in the glass before stumbling towards the nearest bathroom.

The disheveled reflection in the mirror gawks back at me through sunken, hollowed eyes. Skin so ghastly it seemed to be translucent, a scraggly beard resting upon my once defined jawline, and who the hell knows when I last showered. The t-shirt I was wearing looked crumbled over my flaccid skin, I splash water across my face, dragging my hands down the sides in dismay.

"What the fuck am I doing?" I ask, rhetorically. "Lyla would never want this version of the man I've turned into."

I strip the clothes from my body, noticing the sheen of dirt and sweat in my pores, and turn the water on in the shower— as hot as it can go. As it runs down and over my body, the numbness begins to subside as my skin turns red from the heat of the water. I scrub every inch of my body, shaving the parts of me that haven't been kept up in over a week, and lather my hair thrice to ensure it's clean to the roots. As I step out into a fog of steam, I wrap myself in the only available towel and step out of the bathroom to hear a pounding on the front door.

"Who the hell could that be?" I sigh, quickly making my way upstairs and throwing on a clean pair of sweatpants and a long sleeve t-shirt before making my way to the door. I don't bother checking to see who it is, I'm not expecting anyone as it is and I'll likely tell whoever is there to fuck off which seems more satisfying to say to their face.

Except it's Ivy, and I stand there in shock as I take in her tear-stricken face and the suitcases next to her. She's rubbing one hand up and down her other arm, fidgeting in place as her eyes shift to stare at the ground.

"Ivy?" I ask, surprised.

"Hi dad," she says, refusing to look up.

"Are you….," I pause, stepping aside to motion her inside. She takes a deep breath, picking up a suitcase in each hand, and walks through the door. She wraps her arms around her chest, biting her lip as she waits for me to talk. "Are you okay?"

"Daddy, I'm so sorry," she whimpers, sobbing as her hands fly up over her face. I move quickly, wrapping my arms around her and pulling her close. She stands as still as a statue in my embrace, except for the shudder of her shoulders as she cries against my chest.

"Ivy, honey, whatever it is, it's okay, I promise," I assure her, stroking my hand through her hair. It's been years since she's come to me when she's upset, the only way I know to comfort her now is to resort to how I did when she was younger. "Do you want some hot chocolate?"

She peeks out through her fingers, nodding her head carefully. I keep an arm around her shoulder as we walk to the kitchen, her sniffling fading as she sits on the barstool as I busy myself making the hot chocolate from scratch— with peppermint extract and white chocolate, just the way she likes it. I work in silence, seeing her twist the hem of her sweater in between her fingers as she quickly wipes lone tears from her eyes in my peripheral. I fill two mugs, placing one in front of her, and sit down next to her. She takes a few sips, moaning at the delightful taste as it touches her tongue, and then takes a deep breath before turning to face me.

"I'm sorry that I told mom about Lyla, daddy," she says. My body goes rigid at the mention of her name, "I didn't think she would blackmail you. I didn't actually think she would hurt you, or Lyla for that matter. I know what she did was wrong and I can't believe I played a part in letting your life get fucked over again and again. Has she always been this mean, daddy? Why does she do this to people?"

She starts sobbing again, burying her head in her arms on the counter. I rub her back gently. I should be elated that she's finally seen Sloan for who she is, but what has happened between her mother and myself is not her burden to bear.

"What happened, Ivy?" I ask, not sure I want to know the answer.

She lifts her head, taking another long sip from her mug as she settles herself.

"I overheard mom talking to Mrs. Kellan next door about how she had you wrapped around her finger, how your new girlfriend put you in a vulnerable position, and how she could use that against you in order to keep me from going to college early," she grits her teeth, her eyes narrowing to slits. "She said she didn't think I was capable of going out on my own, not mature enough to handle being away from her yet, and someone needed to be the bad guy to not sign the papers so she knew just how to get you to do it. I never thought she would do it until she showed up yesterday as I was packing and told me that you had refused to sign the papers for me to finish school here early.

She handed me the papers and I just completely lost it on her. I told her I knew what she had done, how I couldn't believe that she would orchestrate this shit storm of drama and ruin an innocent girl's life just to mess with you."

My eyes widened as her words got angrier. By the end of her rant, she was red in the face and fuming.

"Ivy, this isn't your fight and I have already made sure that you are registered for classes and your paperwork here is all in order. Your mother might have had one copy of the papers, but I had another set. I copied them when she got to my office, keeping the original for myself and she was too smug to realize I'd only given her a copy," I tell her. Her eyes brighten with my words, the corners of her mouth pulling upwards. "I would never let the bullshit between us affect your future, darling."

"Oh my god," she whispers, smiling so wide that I have to wonder if I've ever seen her this happy with me before. "Thank you, daddy!"

"I would do anything for you, Ivy. Please, remember that while you're forging a path of your own in California."

She squeals, wrapping her arms around me tightly. I press my lips to the top of her head, knowing now that even if I've lost Lyla in this mess, at least I've regained my daughter.

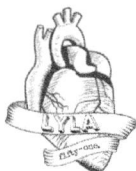

"What the fuck is going on with you, sis?"

Tyler's voice startles me from the trance I'd been in, staring out his kitchen window as the snow falls peacefully on their backyard. *Tyson would love to see this.* I drop the glass of juice I'm holding, luckily into the sink and without shattering the glass, and look up at him. My face scrunches together as I try to pull myself together.

"What are you talking about, Ty?" I roll my eyes, picking the glass up from the sink and rinsing out the juice.

"Do you think that none of us have noticed the moping, Debbie-downer you've been since you got here?" he asks, crossing his arms as he leans against the counter.

I groan internally, knowing that if anyone could have picked up on me being a sourpuss on the inside it would have been him. We've always told each other everything, so of course, he's probably feeling hurt and left out now that he can tell something has happened that I haven't talked to him about— not that there's any reason to tell him anything. The memory of Tyson telling me how he would brave the snow for me had been a flitting moment of weakness as I saw the snow outside. I'd held myself together during the day, making sure to only break down silently in the shower each night.

"I don't want to talk about it, Ty," I grumble. "It's Christmas, I don't want to spoil anyone's day."

356

He moves closer to me, wrapping an arm around my shoulder as he follows my gaze out the window.

"We're your family, Lyla," he reminds me, "if something is upsetting you that's what we're supposed to do, help you through it. I know our parents really sucked when it came to doing that for us while we were growing up, but we're not them. So just talk to me, please, before Cassie kicks my ass for not being more invasive in your personal life because I don't know what, or who, you're so torn up about."

I laugh, knowing that's exactly something his wife would do. She has always been protective of me, ever since their first date. I think she cared for me more than she had him in the first few years, always making sure I wasn't spending too much time alone and insisting I join them when they go out. Tyler had hated it when he was hoping for alone time with her in the early, but every time she had insisted I come along it had always been because she could sense something was upsetting me that day— she was always right.

"Tyler, I love you, but there are some things that I promise you don't want your sister to share with you," I assure him.

Senselessly fucking a professor, falling in love with him, and then getting my heart ripped out are all definitely on the do not discuss with your brother list.

"CASSIE!" he shouts, huffing as he stalks out of the kitchen. "You're up! I think it's about a boy!"

Great, now I'll get to explain myself to her instead.

I grip the counter tightly as I hear their muffled voices, her light footsteps quickly turning the corner to the kitchen and closing the door behind her. She opens a cabinet and pulls out a bottle of champagne with a smile and points towards the fridge.

"Will you grab the orange juice?" she asks, winking before digging for flutes to drink from.

My heart warms with her expertly thought-out plan, grabbing the juice from in the fridge and filling each glass half full. She tops them both off with the bubbles and hands me a glass, nodding her head towards the table as she sits. I fall into a chair, taking a long swig of the mimosa, and watch as she leans forward with her elbows on the table.

"Who is he, Lyla?" she asks, her intuition not failing her once again.

I groan, my head falling into my head as I shake it violently in defeat.

"Promise me that you won't be judgemental, Cass?"

She nods, holding her hands up in agreement and I start.

"Long story short, I fucked a professor, we fell in love, and then he cheated on me. The end."

She cackles, her head thrown back as her red hair blows around her face with her movements.

"Geez, Cassie, I didn't know my heartbreak was that funny," I say, my eyes narrowing as she regains her composure.

"I'm not laughing at your heartbreak, Lyla," she says, warmly. "I'm laughing because that's only a small fraction of the story and you can't possibly think I'm going to buy that version. So either give me the full version, or I'll rescind your mimosa privileges and drink it for myself."

I smile a real smile for the first time since that day and take a deep breath as I rub my fingers against my temples and start again.

"Professor Moxley is an asshole to everyone he meets, I was his TA this past semester and the only one he's ever had made it more than six weeks. When Parker cheated on me, damn him to hell, he comforted me and he opened up as we shared bourbon instead of working. I stupidly kissed him that night, right before Thanksgiving, and regretted it until he kissed me at the museum a few days later. He said he didn't regret it, but it wasn't right either. I got defensive and we fought more than usual, but we were always bickering with a borderline of passion," I pause, she nods in acknowledgment as she processes the information. "After that, it was a disarray of arguing to the point of him driving me insane. Parker showed up drunk one night, he lost his shit on Parker, and then tried to tell me he didn't want anyone touching me but him— except he hadn't touched me in forever! I got so angry that I stripped my clothes off right there in his office and that was the first night we had sex. Then, things got complicated."

"Complicated how?" she asks. "I mean, other than the whole professor and student relationship being unethical and clearly a big age difference. I should probably have more to say about that, but I'll see if it's warranted at the end of the story."

I laugh, appreciating in a new light the woman my brother has chosen to spend his life with.

"His ex-wife is a she-devil in human form and his teenage daughter does not fall far from her mother's tree. The ex has had him wrapped around her finger, toying around and fucking with his life for years. I told him to fight for us when she tried to split us up, so he did, at least he told me he did. We were happy for a while, blissfully unaware of the consequences of our actions, and ready to take on whatever came next," I take a deep breath, biting my lip as the tears begin to form in my eyes again. Reliving our time together was breaking my heart all over again, but I had to move on. "I was willing to fight for and with him, for us, to be with him and even he made it sound like he saw a future with me. While sneaking around was hot, nothing compared to the quiet nights in one of our homes, talking and just being together."

"So, what went wrong?" she says, curiously.

"I went to surprise him at his office last Wednesday. I walked in on him kissing his ex-wife."

360

Cassie's jaw drops, her eyes wide with remorse and sorrow as she reaches across the table for my hand.

"Have you spoken to him since?"

"He came to my apartment very quickly after I got back there myself after running out of his office. He must have followed me but all I did was yell at him. I was so hurt, upset, and broken. He cried, I cried. It was a shitshow, Cass."

"Lyla," her voice is soft as she squeezes my hand. I let the tears fall as I watch her turn on her mother-like charm. "Do you love him?"

I nod, I shrug— tears pouring from my eyes. My chest hurts as I try to fill my lungs with desperately needed air, not realizing I'd been holding my breath most of this time.

"Does it matter, Cassie?" I retort. "He cheated on me, he did exactly what he watched someone else do to me. It doesn't matter if I love him or not, because I'll never be able to forgive him or trust him after that."

"Did you let him tell you his side of what happened in that office?" I shake my head no. "Then how do you know it was his fault?"

I gulp, realizing that wasn't a factor I had considered. Sloan was an evil, conniving, traitorous bitch that could easily orchestrate that kiss. But she didn't, because I know what I saw.

"I watched as he wrapped his arm around her, pulling her to him, and he kissed her."

She smiles slyly at me, refilling our glasses with only champagne this time, and takes a long sip before setting hers down.

"Now, I need you to listen to me for a second. You might not want to hear it, but did you know that once upon a time, Tyler cheated on me, too?" she asks.

"What the fuck!" I shriek, pushing my chair backward as I see red, ready to walk into the other room and punch my brother in his face. She laughs, motioning for me to sit back down.

"Lyla, sit down," she laughs. "I'm only telling you that to show you that just because someone has a moment of weakness doesn't mean that they don't love you. Sometimes people do bad things and hurt the people they love, but that doesn't mean that they deserve to be written off forever," she cocks her head to the side. "If you love him, Lyla, you'll give him a chance to tell you what happened. If you don't, then it's on you to find a way to move on and let him go. But from what I hear, it sounds like you should hear him out. Now, let's talk about something other than how he hurt you. Like the fact that he's your professor, clearly older than you. Am I to assume he's balding and gross or are you going to paint a better picture for me?"

ME: Happy New Year, Lyla.

I press send, knowing that it will go just as unanswered as the "Merry Christmas" message I sent. If I can just show her that I'm still here—still waiting for her to come back to me—maybe one day she'll decide that's enough to give me one more chance. Maybe she'll show up next week, maybe in a year, but either way I would still be in love with her. Time can change the way you feel about someone—good and bad. What I spent years of my youth thinking was love that I felt for Sloan, I can now understand was a mere fraction of lust and attraction mixed with the thrill of a new life. Lyla, she's different—she makes me want to be different, better even. The drastic changes in how I've begun to treat other people prove that. For so long I felt numb, like darkness had taken over my body and I was merely struggling to survive. Even after losing Lyla, there is still a glimmer of light, hope, inside of me that burns on.

Ivy being around for the holidays has been surprisingly pleasant, given the circumstances. We'd gotten out the decorations and spent the entire first few days decking every room in my house out with all of the garland and lights that I owned as far as Christmas and we had promptly gone to buy different lights, stringing up the new blue and white strands for New Year's. We'd had a blast shopping together, picking out pieces for her dorm, and readying her belongings for her trip across the country. I'd offered to drive her myself, flying back as soon as she was settled but she wouldn't have it.

"I'm going to college, becoming an adult, and setting off on my own, daddy. Mom or you have done everything for me in life, I've never had to lift a finger or figure anything out on my own. I need to do this for myself," she had said while we sipped more hot chocolate last night, waiting for the ball to drop. She was right, we had always done our best to take care of her and keep her focused solely on her school work—paving the way for a bright future. I'd agreed, convincing her to turn the location tracker on her phone and sharing her location with me, just for her drive there so I could know she was safe—in true overbearing father fashion.

"Still nothing from Lyla?" Ivy asks, her brow cocked up as she points to my phone still resting in my hand. I shake my head, placing it back in my pocket, and flip the pancakes on the griddle. "She'll come back, daddy. She loved you."

My throat swells as I choke back tears, I won't cry in front of Ivy. The days have been easier with her but the nights haven't been any less lonely as I lay alone in my empty bed. I'd lost hope after Christmas that she would make a grand gesture in coming back right away, begging for me to explain everything to her. I could handle if she chose to leave me after that, but she needs to know the truth about why she saw what she did. She needs to know that I lied to save her, to fight for us— just like she'd wanted me to.

"We'll see," I tell her, sliding pancakes onto the plate she's placed on the counter next to me. I've spent the days teaching Ivy how to make all of her favorite meals, how to grocery shop, and even check her oil. All of the things her mother neglected to teach her, I've spent every waking moment ensuring she knows before letting her go so far from us. On one hand, I'm thrilled that she's getting this experience. On the other, my baby girl is leaving and I feel as if all the time in the world we had to spend together is being ripped away. "What are your plans for today?"

She shrugs, picking at her breakfast and popping a blueberry into her mouth.

"I need to grab a few more things from mom's, hopefully, while she's at the spa or club, and I need to say goodbye to a few friends before I leave tomorrow."

"Will you be back tonight?" I ask. She nods, smiling at me. Being on the receiving end of Ivy's smiles lately has brought some of the joy back into my heart, knowing that she was on my side for the first time in years. "Pizza or Chinese?"

"Pizza, dad," she laughs. "Always pizza. But I swear if you put pineapple on it I'll never forgive you"

I nod with a smile on my face as I begin shoveling my food into my mouth.

"I need to go by the office, anyways," I tell her. She freezes, giving me a puzzled look. "Just some last-minute things to finish up."

"Whatever you say, dad," she shrugs, putting her plate in the dishwasher, and heads to her room to get ready for the day. I clean up the kitchen and tell her goodbye as she runs out the front door a little while later.

I've been putting off going back to that building since I ran out, but Dean Marco has been emailing me incessantly since I handed in my resignation minutes before Sloan came to my office. I need to get my shit from the office before it gets thrown out, but I've wanted to make sure when I get there that there is no chance of being seen by another student. After sliding into a comfortable pair of jeans and my leather jacket, pick the keys out of the bowl by the door, and get in the Camaro, I manage to relax as I sink into the soft leather seat and let the engine rumble shake through my skin.

The city streets are peculiarly quiet as I drive swiftly through, finding a parking spot close to the building— knowing security enforcements are off duty today. I use my key to enter the building, my heart pounding in my chest as I ascend the stairs. Images of Sloan screaming at me, Lyla's face stricken with tears, and the sound of slamming doors prominent in my mind as I make my way up. The office is cold, empty, and dark when I step inside, a pile of empty boxes tucked under my arm. Packing flies by quickly, most of my belongings fit into one of the boxes since I'm taking only what I deem worthwhile to keep. The pictures of Ivy, the framed copy of my degree, and a few other knick-knacks being the most important. When

366

my stuff is packed, I sit the box down on the floor outside the office and return to what was one Lyla's desk. Sitting down in her chair, the scent of her perfume still drifts through the air as it has spent hours soaking into the fabric. A new student will be taking her place at this desk under the supervision of a new professor, perhaps one better-liked than myself in the long run.

It feels like an invasion of privacy as I take down her pictures, packing her notes and files away into a box. Another drag of her perfume stings my nostrils, sending sharp pains through my heart, as I open the drawers and the scent drifts out. So many hours spent in this room, wasted time fighting with her over the menial bullshit tasks and rules, the time I could have spent loving her. Another crack splits through my chest as I twirl her favorite pen between my fingertips, and I succumb to the pain. I let myself wallow in misery as I rest my head against the corner of her desk.

Lyla may never come back to me, she may never let me explain, but there's a good chance that she will come back for her things when the semester begins.

I can write her a letter. She might not forgive me, but I can be sure she knows the truth this way.

Grabbing one of her notebooks from the box, I uncap her purple pen and begin scribbling the truth—the words flowing from my brain, through my hand, and onto the paper at lightning speed. I read the letter over and over, double-checking that I've done my best

367

to enlighten her to the situation, the outcome, and what I had to do to get us to the point of safety. I find an envelope crumbled in a corner of my desk drawer and seal the letter inside. Carefully, I write her name in elegant calligraphy on the outside before placing it inside the box, leaving the tidily packed box sitting on her desk. Maybe she'll never allow me to speak to her again, and maybe she'll never forgive me for what I've done— but this woman will forever be responsible for bringing love back into my life, making me believe that happiness is out there again.

I tap the box twice with the palm of my hand, pocketing her purple pen for myself as a reminder of love found—and lost— before picking my box off the floor. Standing in the threshold, I take a moment to glance around the room that has become almost like a second home to me for the last ten years. Sighing deeply, I shut off the lights, close the door behind me, and walk away— closing that chapter of my life forever.

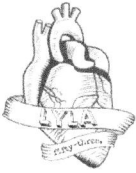

"Home sweet home," I mutter to the empty apartment, taking my bags directly to the laundry room. The closer they are to the washer and dryer, the more likely I might get around to emptying them in the next couple of days.

ME: Made it home, checking everything out now. Thanks for putting up with my moping ass for break. Love you guys. <3

Walking through the apartment, I go through the mental checklist for when I return.

No water laying around, no mouse shit, nothing's frozen or broken. No signs that anyone was here while I was gone. Everything is still working, appliances still running.

Living alone had never been a problem for me, even moving out and across the country as soon as I turned eighteen. Tyler had been able to come out for a while and was smart enough to teach me how to handle basic aspects of fixing plumbing and electrical problems over the years. I've only come home to a leak once, but that one time was enough to remind me to check the place upon returning. I turn some coffee on and flip through the options on the TV, not in the mood for *The Office*. As I fill my mug up, a knock at the door startles me.

Is he stalking me already? Fuck.

Another knock.

"Go away, Tyson," I yell, not bothering to check. Lucy won't be back for another three days and there's no one else that would be here.

Two more rasps on the door make my skin crawl. I groan and stalk towards the door, yanking on the handle and letting it fly open as I start yelling with my eyes squeezed shut. If I can't see his face, it'll be easier to stay angry. Cassie's story about my brother cheating on her had done a number on me when we talked at Christmas. My heart and my brain have been at war ever since, unsure of what I want anymore.

I love him, he loves me. It should be simple but it's not—and is it worth it? Is he worth it?

"I have been back all of five seconds and you're already somehow aware that I'm home and banging on my fucking door? How dare you," I rattle off, but stop when he doesn't interrupt me, I open my eyes enough to see, it isn't Tyson standing at my door. "Ivy?"

The corner of her mouth turns upwards slightly as she stands in my doorway. She looks less like Regina George incarnated today, her usual smug look across her face wiped clean and a sadness filling her eyes. *Perhaps she does have a single shred of decency in her bones.* My body stiffens at the sight of her, my breaths becoming short and raspy as I tense in preparation for whatever she's here to spew this time. She's biting her lip nervously, wringing her hands together in front of her.

"Can I come in?" she asks, her voice timid and soft. "I'd really like a chance to talk to you, girl to girl."

I nod apprehensively, but my feet move quickly as I step aside and watch her slowly come in. She looks like a normal teenager today with her hair in a ponytail and dressing in a pair of plain black leggings with Ugg boots— nothing like the girl hurling insults at me in her father's kitchen not that long ago.

Shouldn't she be in California soon? What is she doing here talking to me instead of partying her remaining time away with her friends?

"Thank you," she says, licking her lips as she takes a deep breath. "I know I'm likely the last person you'd want to find standing on your doorstep, Lyla, well, except for apparently, maybe my dad... but I'm here because I owe you an apology."

"Did you tell her, Ivy? After he specifically asked you not to?" I butt in, malice riddles my voice as my eyes narrow into slits. "You are his biggest joy, favorite person, and the only person he's spent the last ten years loving." She nods, biting her lip. "You deceived him and stabbed him in the fucking back. You hurt not only him, but me— a woman that you wrote off the second you met me. I agree that you owe me an apology, but I can assure you that forgiveness isn't going to be found here today."

My arms are crossed in front of my chest as my fingers dig into the skin on them, my nails pushing in deeper with pent-up anger. The hammering of my heart drums in my ears and makes the room look

371

hazy through my eyes. I swear that Ivy might be crying, but not a bone in my body feels a twinge of remorse.

"I don't deserve you, or anyone else's, forgiveness for the things that I have done over the years. I-I... understand that." Her voice cracks as she wipes away a lone tear from her cheek. "It took me a long time to see what kind of woman my mother has turned into, what she is willing to do to other people to get what she wants. I want no part of that anymore. I spent years believing that everything she did, she did out of love, but I was wrong," her face pops up as she stares into my eyes. "That's not the kind of person my mother is, not at all. But, that is my father. He is a genuinely kind-hearted, loving, and generous person... and he deserves to be happy."

My brow furrows. *Who even is this woman?* This isn't the same Ivy that I've met before or heard stories about even. It's like in the short period that I've been away she's done a complete one-eighty and turned her life around— but this kind of work happens over time, not overnight. It doesn't matter how expensive or great your life coach or therapist is, they still can't work miracles like this.

"Lyla, yes, I went to my mother after acquiring the information that you were a student and dating my father. She'd already had her assumptions that he was seeing someone and it became my job to get him to open up about who. She'd promised to ensure that I continue my luxurious lifestyle, opening up another line of endless credit when I moved to California if I did this for her. Being the gullible, self-centered, egotistical teenager that I have been, I accepted it without question," she admits, shaking her head in defeat. "Walking in on you guys together, it made my life easier because I didn't have to try and sneak around and get information from him. I love my dad, despite everything we have been through, and I hated the idea of doing that."

"So then why not just tell her to go fuck herself?" I ask, still seething.

"You've never been alone in a room with my mother, have you?" she laughs.

"I don't think I need to be to know what kind of person she is. She's been perfectly capable of ruining my life from afar," I retort.

"You should understand that her repercussions don't just extend outside of the family, Lyla," she says. "Being her daughter would not warrant my own personal safety from her wrath if she's challenged. She'd never physically harm me, but the emotional and mental torment would be astronomical." Ivy takes a deep breath, bringing her eyes to meet mine. "It doesn't matter much now, though, because I'll be in California by tomorrow and away from her altogether— which is why I came here before I left."

"Does Tyson know that you're here?" I ask.

"No," she smiles. "He thinks I left for college when I left his house a little while ago. I parked my car a few streets down at a gas station and left my phone there since my over-protective dad came out of hiding and insisted I share my location with him at all times. After walking the few blocks, I was thrilled that I even remembered your car from that morning and that you were actually home when I got here."

"How did you know where to find me?" I question, realizing that up until now I had just assumed Tyson had given her that information.

"Daddy leaves his computer unlocked and unsurprisingly, all of his student files are easy enough to access. Your address is on your forms and I wrote it down while he was out yesterday. Again, I don't like sneaking around behind my dad's back or going through his stuff, but I knew that I needed to talk to you myself if I ever wanted to find a way to help him."

"Ivy, I appreciate you coming here and your apology," I tell her, gently, "but what he did to me was unforgivable. I can't just allow him back into my life, not knowing if that will ever happen again or always having to be on edge worrying about what plan of attack your mother is coming up with next. I love him. I love him so much that it hurts. I've never loved anyone in the way that I've loved him, but if that were to ever happen again— it would destroy me."

She reaches a hand out and grasps my arm, tears spilling from her eyes.

"Lyla, he might have loved my mom at one time but you are the only reason he gets out of bed these days. I've been at his house since before Christmas and he walks around in a trance. Sometimes he'll sigh and shake his head when he looks into a room or at a certain piece of furniture. He hasn't slept in his own bed since I've been there. Usually, he winds up on the couch or in another guest room if I've been out late. He works out at all ungodly hours of the day, pushing himself harder every time as if he's trying to ease the pain of his broken heart. He hardly eats, he looks sad all the fucking time. He pulls his phone out with a sense of excitement every time it goes off only to sink back into himself when it isn't you. I don't know what happened in full detail, I know the parts of it that involved me and that my mother is a raging bitch, but I also believe that everyone deserves to have their side of a story told."

I gasp, soaking in every word she says.

Tyson is a wreck without me.

Ivy walked away from her mom and has been with Tyson this entire time.

I've been ignoring him, while he's been waiting around for any word from me.

He does love me.

"He told me that you once asked him to fight for you. You may not see it right now but that's exactly what he was doing," her voice is stern now, defensive in honor of her father. "Maybe it wasn't the kind of fight that you had expected, but forgive me for being so blunt, but you owe him the chance to explain. He gave up everything for you,

Lyla. Even if you don't see it. Even if he hurt you in the process, he gave it all up. For you."

I gulp, holding my breath as the idea of seeing him again makes my chest ache.

"Thank you, Ivy," I say, wrapping my arms around her without another thought. "I think you told me exactly what I needed to hear."

Ivy is gone.

She'll be in California tomorrow, starting a new life in a new town with new people.

With Ivy gone, the house became dark and quiet again. I spent the first part of the morning at the police station to file a restraining order against Sloan. I'll rest easier now that I've ensured that she can't come anywhere near me. Ivy changed all of her emergency contact information solely to my name before leaving for school this morning. We'd loaded her Jeep full of her suitcases, dorm decor, and snacks for her drive. Perhaps it was foolish of me to send her on her own, but if she can handle Sloan's wrath for all these years, I think she can handle the drive as well. She's changed in the past few weeks, opening up and becoming a better, well-rounded version of herself.

Lyla is gone.

She's still here, but she's not with me.

I tried my best to shield Ivy from the pain wreaking havoc on my heart, to not let her see how crumbled up inside I am. I retreated to the gym when the barren house became too much to handle, the only place where one pain can outweigh another in a short amount of time. I turn up the speed of the treadmill, pushing through the aching, burning muscles in my legs. Running used to be a happier form of an escape, now it's my last chance at attempting to keep my sanity intact.

I'll run until I can't run anymore, but there's nothing that can keep Lyla from forcing her way into my mind.

Lyla... Her silky, black hair sprawled across my chest as the morning sun shines across her face.

Lyla... The way her hips sway as she walks when she's feeling an extra burst of confidence.

Lyla... Her perfectly pink, velvet-soft lips wrapped around the tip of my cock as she peers up at me through her lashes.

My feet press harder against the mat, the sound of the footsteps echoes through the room as I try to force down the memories.

Lyla... What I would do to hear her laughter ringing through the walls of this house, even just one more time.

Please come back to me.

My breaths are sharp, painful in my chest as I try to suppress the tears.

I need you, God baby, I need you so much.

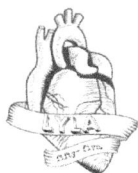

The night was long as Ivy's words rattled in my brain. I tossed, turned, and cried throughout the night. I argued in my head and out loud over what to do, how to feel. I've never been the kind of person to give someone a second chance, not after such a blatant betrayal— but I also realized that I've never been in love like this before. I've never given someone a second thought after cutting them off because there had never been a person worthy of the chance to break my heart again.

Some love is worth fighting for if you're strong enough to endure the battle.

I'd asked Tyson to fight for us again and again— he had. Me, though? I ran away, trembling, the minute the battlefield came into view and we needed to fight together. I'd run out that door with no second thoughts, away from him, and as far from Sloan as I could get. I didn't give him a chance to talk, to explain. He said he was fighting for us, but had he won the game? Or had Sloan?

As the sun breaks the sky, I throw the covers off the bed and get dressed in a hurry. It's close enough to the beginning of the term that the professors would be back in their offices to prepare lesson plans. I throw on a pair of leggings and tennis shoes, slip a hoodie over my head and run out the door. If Tyson will give me the time of day, I am going to let him explain. Then, after I've heard his story, I'll profusely grovel and tell him how sorry I am that I stopped fighting. I dismissed our chance at love before we ever got the chance to try.

The cold, winter air rips at my face as my ponytail flips around my head—smacking my wind-bitten cheeks. The campus is serene this morning, the sunlight peeking through the corners of the buildings. The slick grass beneath my feet almost takes me down a few times, my sides aching from the lack of exercise lately— but I push on. I know Tyson has always had a routine, it's late enough that he'll be in his office by now with a scowl on his face as he drinks his coffee. Black, no sugar, and absolutely no cream— dark and bitter, just like his soul used to be.

Before I came along, that is.

My lungs feel flickers of flames reaching through them as I near the building, yanking the door open with all of my strength and taking the stairs two at a time. I'm drenched in a cold sweat, surprised and thankful that I remembered to put on deodorant in my rush out the door. I reach his floor, slowing my run to a speed walk as the nerves settle in my gut, and take a few deep breaths before nearing his door. I stop, taking a few deep breaths as I shake my head, forcing away the memory from the last time I showed up unexpectedly. He and Sloan, lips pressed together, her hand stroking his crotch, and the sight of her smirking at me. Anger boils my blood as I stand around the corner of the threshold, swimming in my veins as I try to force the image out of my mind.

I can do this, I can hear him out.

I can move past this.

We can get through this.

After another deep breath, I step around the corner and open my eyes.

"Office hours have not resumed yet," a shrill, female voice says from inside his office.

I continue forward, pacing my steps evenly as a plump, tanned woman with dark hair turns to face me— her hands on her hips and lips pressed tightly together. I freeze, cocking my head to the side in confusion. She raises an eyebrow at me, waiting for me to say something as I stand here with my jaw agape.

"I'm sorry, I was just looking for Professor Moxley," I start, quickly realizing that it sounds as though I am supposed to be meeting him outside of an appointment. "I was his TA last semester and left my things here before the end of term. I was just hoping to clear them out before his new assistant starts."

I gulp, watching as her lips press down at the corners.

"You aren't yet aware of Professor Moxley's resignation?" she asks.

I shake my head, my eyes growing wide as my heart pounds in my chest.

He resigned.

He quit his job.

Ivy was right, he did give up everything for me.

I blink quickly, trying to even my breathing as she takes a few steps towards me. She points a finger towards my desk with a shrug.

"He quit on the last day of term, handed in his letter after his last class," she says. "Is your name... Lyla?" I nod, my mouth too dry to form words. "There's a letter on top here for you, so these must be your belongings already packed up for you. Go ahead and take them with you, I'll be around the corner if you need anything."

I barely whisper "thanks" as she turns her back to me and I focus solely on placing one foot in front of the other, little steps towards my desk. I peer inside the box on top, making note of all of my knick knacks packed away neatly, some wrapped in paper that were more fragile. On top of my possessions does, indeed, sit a letter written in his clear, unmistakable handwriting.

Lyla Fischer

He used my purple pen.

I hold the letter tightly between my hands, glancing over my shoulder as I open the corners carefully— ensuring that she—whoever that woman is inside the office—is unable to sneak a peek at the contents. I fall into the seat as I begin to read his words, so eloquently written that it feels as though he's standing next to me, whispering them into my ear.

My Dearest Lyla,

      In another world, we would be sipping fine wine and toasting to a life together, ringing in the new year... but instead, I'm writing this letter with only hope in my heart that you will find it within yours to read it all the way through. I don't blame you for leaving. After the small part of that day you saw with your own eyes, you had every right to assume the absolute worst and refuse to listen to anyone— any words I could have formed at the time would only have made things worse. I was distraught that you had walked in at the worst moment and couldn't focus on anything but watching the pain as your heart broke—because of me. I'll get to what happened that day, but before I do that, in case you rip this letter to shreds before the end— I want to thank you.

      I have spent the past decade of my life slowly rotting away from the inside out, dying, and my heart becoming a fossil inside of my chest. (I know you once loved that reference, so it feels worthy to use a second time)You swept into my life by a fated chance and with your exquisite, battle-ready demeanor, and empathy— you found a way to chisel away at the stone encompassing my heart to bring me back to life. You were the shining light to my heart of darkness, and dare I say you even managed to cause the darkness inside of me to become extinct.

383

You are a force to be reckoned with on a calm day, but when your fires are raging in the veins that bind you together— you are one of such beautiful, admirable vehemence that can make the world tremble with one look. When Mr. Bennett broke your heart, I felt mine break as you cried. At that moment, I wanted to vow to you that I would never let that kind of pain be inflicted upon you again— but the next person to break your heart was none other than myself. I have been honored to have been able to love you for this short period and would be honored to love you for the rest of eternity if you would give me the chance.

It was, of course, my naivety that allowed me to believe that Ivy would not betray us and inform Sloan of our relationship. Sloan wished for me to drive a further rift between Ivy and myself, blackmailing me with our relationship. She said that if I did not hand over the forms, without signing them first, that she would go straight to the Dean and blacklist us both. Knowing that Sloan could be persuaded, I invited her to my office that day— but made sure to hand in my resignation after leaving class so that she would have no leverage at that point. I purposefully gave you the afternoon off to shield you from the events I knew would transpire in my office when Sloan didn't get her way, again. She was clueless when I made a copy of the form, giving her the fake and keeping the original for

384

myself— ensuring my daughter's education. Even after handing over the forms, she still wanted more. I had expected that from her, so I offered her one last goodbye kiss. Sloan agreed, one last kiss and that I would never tell Ivy that she asked me to refuse her early acceptance. Never, not in a million years, did I expect you to show up at that moment. Of course, I never should have offered, to begin with, it was wrong on so many levels that I can not begin to explain my regret.

I should have informed you of what I had planned— if anything just to keep you away that day, but I could not bear the thought of burdening you with such information. This was never a battle you should have been pulled into, even if you wanted for us to fight it together. I don't hold it against you that in the end, the fight was too much of a burden. We barely had any time, any chance to be happy, before Sloan dug her claws into us, threatening to rip us to shreds.

You are the reason I was finally able to stand up to her, to take my life into my own hands again. You taught me that love is out there again, but I don't want it if it's not with you. I don't expect anything from you, Lyla. You deserve to move on with your life and forget about us if that's what you wish to do— I will never hold it against you. But, if there is a part of your heart that wants to give this a real chance, come to me— my sweetheart. You are the extinction of darkness in my life, and without you, I don't want the light.

With all of my love,

Tyson

As I clutch the note to my chest, cradling the box with one arm, my feet carry me across the grounds as tears stream down my face. Tears of love, sadness, and hope as the flames once again ignite in my heart, pushing me onward to do what needs to be done.

The sounds of knuckles rasping loudly against my front door pull me from the melatonin-induced slumber I finally succumbed to. I groan, pulling a pillow over my face as I wait for the noise to subside.

No one should be at my house, not ever. Ivy is halfway to California and Sloan, well she has hopefully been out finding someone else's life to ruin for a while. As the knocking continues, more desperately with each hit, I slide out of bed and slip into a pair of sweats. Shirts are for expected guests, whoever shows up without warning can see my bare, chiseled abs for all I care these days.

"Dammit, I'm coming!" I yell, the banging continuing as I half jog down the stairs. "Whoever the hell you are, you better have one damn fucking good explanation for waking my-," I stop bitching the moment I pull the door open. Lyla's tear-stricken face on the other side, clutching the letter I wrote to her chest. Her cheeks are flushed pink, her eyes swollen and dark circles encompass them. She doesn't bother to wipe the tears away as we stand there in silence. My throat tightens as I watch her weight shift between her feet, the cold air whipping around us. "Did-did you read it?"

She sucks her lips between her teeth as she nods, more tears spilling from her eyes.

"Did you... did you come to say goodbye?" I ask, my heart hammering against my chest. My lungs work rapidly to keep up enough air flowing through my body to keep me standing. With buckled knees, I wait. She lets her eyes graze downward, soaking in the sight of my naked chest before slowly bringing them back up to my face. I can feel my hair matted on one side, the remains of crusted drool along the side of my chin. I look like a fucking mess, but that's a clear representation of what I've been without her. She looks thinner, more tired, and worn down—just like if her body and mind have been put through absolute hell, and at war with her heart.

"I wasn't sure what I was going to say or do before I got here," she whispers. "I read the letter and I knew that I had to at least see you. I couldn't read those words, everything you said, and not. I assumed I would figure the rest out on the way." Her tongue peeks out between her lips, wetting them carefully as she holds her shoulders back. Her breaths are deep and noticeable as she mentally decides why she's here.

"But, are you sure now?" My heart flutters then stops. I ball my hands into fists as I hold myself back from yanking her inside this house, begging her to forgive me, and take her to bed. My hands are shaking as my side as my own eyes begin to water at the sight of her tears— tears I would desperately like to kiss away right now. "Do you know what you want to say now that you've seen me?"

"Tyson, you left me in the dark while plotting the fight we should have been battling together. In your own way, you were trying to be chivalrous and once again, you were trying to be the knight that saves the princess. By doing that you ripped my heart out and

388

shattered it into so many pieces that I don't know if it'll ever be able to be put back together in the way that it was" she says, pressing her lips together sternly. I nod, opening my mouth to speak but she holds a finger up to stop me. I nod again, gesturing for her to continue. "I've never been broken like that before, and it's not something I would ever like to experience again. You were an Argentinosaurus-sized asshole in that sense, but, if you can promise me that from this point forward, there are no more secrets or hidden agendas,-"

Without letting her finish, I grab her by the waist and pull her lips to mine. I press against her so quickly that her knees give out and I hold her tighter. She freezes against me, her arms pinned between our chests as I hold her. Her mouth opens slightly and I let my tongue sweep inside, dusting the tip of hers and she lets out a gentle moan. With my heart racing, I step backward and pull her inside— out of the cold wind and back her up against the wall. My arms fall from her waist to unpin her arms, pressing now against the wall on either side of her.

"I promise," I whisper between kisses. "No more secrets and never again will I treat you like the princess that needs to be saved. I will only ever treat you like the queen you are."

With this promise, the letter drops from her hands. She clasps her hands around the back of my neck and pulls my lips back to hers, urgently and hungrily. Our bodies ignite between us, our lips moving as our hands roam across every inch of skin. I gently remove her sweatshirt, pulling it over her head between kisses, and growl as I see she's in nothing but a thin, sheer bra beneath. She chuckles into my mouth, letting her fingers trace down my chest and outlining every muscle. I suck in a deep breath as she lets her fingertips brush the edge of my sweats. My hands slide down her sides, over her perfect, hourglass hips, and down her ass before I grasp her thighs and hoist her up. Her finger comes between our lips, pressing me away gently with fire blazing in her eyes.

"Do not ever break my heart again," she demands.

I trail soft kisses from her earlobe, down her neck, and to her shoulder blade— letting the gentle heat simmer on her skin. Her heart pounds against my lips as I kiss her collarbone, smiling as I rest my forehead against her chest. With her legs wrapped around me and one arm still around my neck, I use the weight of the wall to hold her up as I cup her face in one hand and hold her eyes to mine.

"Lyla, sweetheart, my fucking queen. I have never loved anyone in the way that I love you. Even if it takes a lifetime to rebuild the trust and deserve any ounce of love you will give me, I will fight for us every day of forever. I will travel the world with you, aid you in your studies, be your biggest cheerleader, or just the man you need to fuck to relieve yourself of stress at the end of the day. I will be any and everything that you need or want me to be, as long as I get to be with you. If you choose to walk away in the end, it will be your choice because I will never hurt you again. I could not stand to look at myself

390

in the mirror without hating the reflection of the man that caused you such pain, so soon after vowing to shield you from that. You have never needed or wanted anyone to save you, but you saved me, Lyla. You deserve to be loved, cherished, and adored, Lyla— please, for fuck's sake, let me be the man that does that."

Tears are once again falling down her face and I quickly brush my lips against them, wiping them away as I stroke her cheek with my thumb. Her mouth begins to turn upwards into a smile as I press my lips gently to her nose, her cheeks, and back to her lips.

"I love you, Tyson Moxley," she whispers, her breath hot against my ear as she leans in. "I loved you through every fight and I'll continue to love you through every fight to come because we both know there will be more. That's who we are and I wouldn't trade it for anything easier because you, Tyson Moxley, are the only thing in my life worth fighting for."

My heart explodes as tears stream down my face. I'm floating on a cloud, letting her words sink into my soul as she presses her lips to mine. I breathe in her perfume, letting the heat from her body overwhelm me. Her fingers run through my hair and down my cheeks as my eyes close in relief.

"I love you more, Lyla Fischer," I whisper, pressing my face into the crook of her neck. "I will spend the rest of my life proving that to you and being worthy of your love."

"Then take me upstairs and prove it," she demands, nipping at my earlobe and sending a feral growl up from my throat as I whisk us up the stairs, leaving a trail of clothes behind and nothing but love between us.

My feet glide across the stage as Dean Marco calls out my name, a smile spreads across my face even though I'm melting in the hot, Texas summer sun. I've worked my ass off for six years to deserve this piece of paper signaling that I achieved my Master's in Anthropology. The Dean shakes my hand with a wide smile as I, perhaps too enthusiastically, shake his back and cheer as I hold up my degree while walking off stage. As I walk down the stairs, I'm blissfully aware that Tyson is in the crowd cheering me on— along with my brother and his wife Cassie. My parents couldn't be bothered to even ask what day I was graduating, so I took it upon myself not to invite them at all. I return to my seat, unable to focus on the rest of the names being called out until they get to Lucy. I cheer and clap, watching her take a bow as she quickly flits off stage. When the tassels are turned, hats tossed, and we are processed out of the area, Lucy tackles me with a hug so tight I can feel my ribs beginning to crack as I remove my cap.

"WE DID IT, LYLA!" she yells, bouncing up and down.

"We're finally DONE!" I yell back, returning her enthusiasm.

We stand there embracing each other, despite the heat beating down on us as other students meander about looking for their families. Tears run down my cheeks, relief flooding every part of my body as I acknowledge the fact I never have to take another class in this university again. Through all the pain and tears this place has put me

393

through, it taught me so much about myself as well. I learned that I am cunning, strong, and intelligent— along with fulfilled, loved, and happy.

"Lyla," his deep voice booms from behind me. My heart flutters as Lucy releases me from her death grip, her face shocked to see the man behind me. I turn, smirking and wiping the tears from my cheeks.

"Professor Moxley," I retort. "How nice of you to take the time out of your day to applaud the graduating class."

"Not professor anymore," he winks.
Before my cheeks get the chance to turn pink, he grabs my waist and pulls me to him for such a passionate kiss that my legs turn to jelly. As his lips press against mine, the crowd of people—students and faculty combined—disappear from my mind as I wrap my arms around his neck.

"What the FUCK is happening?" Lucy bellows.

Tyson releases me, both of us falling into a fit of laughter at her surprise.

We'd chosen to keep our relationship under wraps after the semester began, just to avoid any rumors of us having been together while he was still a professor. Sloan had never managed to get to the Dean, thank the Lord.

He wraps his arm around my waist, holding me close to his body as Lucy crosses her arms and taps her foot. I rest my head against his shoulder and he presses his lips to the top of my hair.

"Oh my god, it's him, isn't it?" she asks. I smile, knowing that she's referring to our conversation at brunch so long ago. "He's the one you were so smitten with! I can't believe that you've been hiding this scandal from me all this time!"

I shrug, smirking and reaching up on my toes to kiss his cheek.

"Don't worry Luc, she's been keeping him from us too," Tyler's voice scoffs over the sound of the crowd. He clasps a hand on Tyson's shoulder, his eyes going wide as I feel the deep breath he inhales in preparation for whatever Tyler has coming his way. Tyler looks him up and down, putting his hand on his hip, and narrows his eyes at Tyson. "You gonna break my sister's heart again?"

"You have my sincerest word, that will never happen again," Tyson says, extending a hand to Tyler. "I take full responsibility for my wrongdoings in December and will grovel at her feet every day that she allows me to be in her life again. It's nice to meet you, Tyler."

Tyler nods, shaking Tyson's hand, and then beckoning Cassie over with a nod of his head. She comes shrieking, embracing us both as she hugs us at once before introducing herself.

"I would really like to be filled in on what the fuck you're all talking about," Lucy says, sternly.

"That's a story for another time," I laugh, wrapping my arms around Tyson tightly. "And a lot of wine."

His arm squeezes me flush against him, ready to never let me go. I take in this moment, soaking it up for the years after this that drags on and I wonder why I stuck it out at all. In one circle stands my best friend, my sister-in-law, my brother, and my professor turned the love of my life— against all odds. Everything I have gone through has all led me to them and these are my people. These are the only ones that matter now, until maybe one day, Tyson and I start a family of our own.

"Come on guys," I say, letting the happiness fill my chest. "Let's get brunch and I'll maybe spill some of these scandalous secrets after some champagne."

They nod in agreement, Tyler and Cassie taking the lead while Lucy tags along at Cassie's side in a deep conversation. I hold Tyson back, gliding my fingertips up his spine. He cups the side of my face, stroking my jaw with his fingertips and smiling down at me. I gaze into those beautiful cerulean eyes, now filled with love and warmth — instead of icy lifelessness—as the sun highlights the flecks of gold in his hair. His cologne is so potent, so familiar at this point that I could pick him out of a crowd with a blindfold on. I pull him down, crushing my lips against his as we bask in the freedom of this moment.

"I love you," I tell him.

With his lips on mine, his arm wraps around my waist as he pulls me closer. He gives even fewer shits about who sees us and what anyone thinks in the crowd around us, caring only about us— only has eyes for me.

"Thank you," he whispers, "for not giving up on us."

The sea of people disappears again as we rest our foreheads together, letting the sun beat down on us. We survived the wrath of Sloan, mended our relationship with Ivy, and even visited her for Spring Break. We spend every night together, I wake up to his arms holding me tightly every morning. We talk, we laugh, we live a life that is so full— even while keeping our relationship a secret. We are two perfect pieces of a puzzle, balance, and equality that go hand in hand. We can walk through hellfire and survive— next time, we'll do it together. We turn away from the grounds, one last look at what we're leaving behind over our shoulders, and step forward to begin forging a new life—together.

ACKNOWLEDGEMENTS

◎   To my family who has supported and encouraged my writing from a very young age, always pushing me to read more books and immerse myself into new worlds— I thank you.

◎   To Dale and Tiffany, for reading every chapter as I write it and offering your personal feedback. For supporting my visions, encouraging my obscure ideas, and being my biggest cheerleaders and critics at the same time.

◎   To Z & J, your continued, unmatched motivation has inspired my work in more ways than I will ever be able to thank you for.

◎   To the city of Houston, for having such memorable locations that even years after I've spent time there, I am still able to see it clearly and focus a story around the town. I can't wait to visit again.

◎   To the singers, songwriters, and bands mentioned in the story— you are responsible for an exuberant amount of the underlying characteristics and traits for these characters and found a way through your music to help bring them to life.

◎   Grammarly, Canva, and 123rf— for design, editing, general help, and photos used throughout this book.

◎   Last but not least, I want to thank the wineries that created all the wines I drank while writing the intimate scenes in this book that managed to make the process a little less intrusive and awkward.

Made in the USA
Monee, IL
25 October 2021